Reinhold Pauli

Simon de Montfort

Earl of Leicester, the Creator of the House of Commons

Reinhold Pauli

Simon de Montfort
Earl of Leicester, the Creator of the House of Commons

ISBN/EAN: 9783337267490

Printed in Europe, USA, Canada, Australia, Japan

Cover: Foto ©Raphael Reischuk / pixelio.de

More available books at **www.hansebooks.com**

SIMON DE MONTFORT,

EARL OF LEICESTER,

THE CREATOR OF THE HOUSE OF COMMONS.

BY

REINHOLD PAULI.

TRANSLATED BY UNA M. GOODWIN.

WITH INTRODUCTION BY HARRIET MARTINEAU.

LONDON:

TRÜBNER & CO., LUDGATE HILL.

1876.

INTRODUCTION

BY

HARRIET MARTINEAU.

—◆—

Dr. Pauli's observation at the opening of the Preface of his work,—that every great movement in human Society is embodied and illustrated in the character of one pre-eminent man,—will hardly be objected to by any order of readers ; but it probably approves itself most warmly to those who are the oldest, as well as the most worthy. The relish of the study of History follows the same law in the case, in regard to age, of a people and an individual. In the youthful days of a nation the Historical interest is implicated in the suspense and romance of war and conquest, in the poetry of adventure, and the triumph or grief of mighty revolutions of fortune. As a community grows older in experience, the character of its interest in History changes essentially. Institutions and Laws become more attractive than invasions and battles ; a stage in civilisation is seen to be more valuable than an extension of territory ; and the general mind opens to a sense of the qualities necessary to the acquisition of the higher good. Just in the same way does the interest in the study of History change its ground with lapse of time. The child asks only for fairy tales; the school-boy devours narratives of adventure and conquest; and his attraction to any consideration of character lies in its daring first,—then in its magnanimity,—and, when the conceptions coalesce,—its heroism.

These conceptions, however, are exhaustible; and a whole realm of wisdom lies ready to be entered upon when the community on the one hand, and the individual student on the other, becomes qualified by experience and contemplation to appreciate acquisitions from the richer field. The conception and growth of good institutions and laws become interesting to Society; and in due time Society inquires, first as a matter of course, and at last with more or less eagerness, about the origin of political amelioration, and the head, heart, and hands by which it was wrought.

At the corresponding age attained by the individual student, he finds his best road to a knowledge of History in Biography, if it be but attainable. It is not merely that human character is always and everywhere supremely interesting to meditative men: it is that in a man's life we see his mind; and that the more we see of his life the better we understand his mind, and can interpret his ideas, designs, and acts. Thus we see the grey-haired student lay eager hands on the smallest fragment of newly-discovered records which can disclose any feature in the character or conduct of political philosopher or statesman who may have lent a hand to the formation or working of the constitution of his own or another country.

It is easily said that Political Biography naturally combines two different orders of interest,—that of narrative—the unfolding of a story ;—and that of individual experience and portraiture of character: this is true enough ; but the point before us regards the interest and efficacy of the study of History itself, by the road of Biography. If evidence of this fact had been necessary of late years it would have been found in the gratitude with which our own country and people, and some abroad, have received the inestimable gift conferred by the Master of the Rolls in rendering accessible to us documents illustrative in all manner of ways of the reigns of our sovereigns for successive centuries.

Amidst the wealth of that disclosure, one of the most prominent gifts is that which Dr. Pauli avows to have been his immediate stimulus to the production of his Life of Simon de Montfort. So noble a boon is fittingly acknowledged by the frank gratitude of the biographer ; but we, his readers, owe a double debt. The new materials are one boon ; but many of us would have known little of them if the Historian had not presented to us the great period following the event of Runnymede as the influences of that period were reflected in the life of its most remarkable man.

Till this late extension of our knowledge we were misled, or uninformed, on many points of story and

of individual and social character. We can now rest
in a cheering certainty of the most essential facts that
can concern a community. It is no small matter that
one of the greatest characters in our history is at length
canonized by the authority of History,—that he is
known now as no self-seeking rebel, no revolutionary
mischief-maker,—that he had clear aims and steadfast
purposes,—that, while of foreign birth and connection,
he was so thoroughly English by all the highest sorts
of qualification, that England will remember while the
world lasts that to him she owes her first place in the
history of nations as governed by true Representation
in Parliament. As a statesman he distinguished himself by the two conceptions on which his political
action was based,—the extension of political function
to the Commons, and the principle of Representation.,
Instead of mere assemblage of summoned classes on
the one hand, and the democratic method of delegation
on the other, he proposed and instituted REPRESENTA-
TION,—as it must in due time be exemplified wherever
Liberty is understood and enjoyed. In that institution
of his lies the proof of his appreciation of the people ;
and in their adoration of him lies the evidence of his
exemption from all those taints of foreign breeding
which made his French countrymen so odious to men
of all orders who had seen the strange spectacle of that
day and generation. They had seen confirmations of
MAGNA CHARTA succeed each other after ever-renewed
breaches of faith on the part of the King and his
foreign and courtly factions, and amidst the distrust,

the wrath, the turmoil under which society was heaving to and fro, one element of opinion and will remained stable,—the popular trust in the adviser of self-government,—" St. Simon the Righteous."

The people appreciated him as far as their qualifications enabled them, in this direction or in that. There were some, however few, who saw in him scholarship as distinctive as his active capacities,—statesmanship as thoroughly characteristic as his military eminence,—domestic affections as genial as his devotedness to the welfare of his country and his kind. Yet his great name was subject to eclipse, like that of many another leader of men. He was represented to successive generations as of the vulgar order of revolutionary agitator and ambitious rebel.

It seems to have been by the sort of anticipation which prepares Society for some new burst of historical light that since the beginning of our century a growing interest in Simon de Montfort has been observable, and a more lively curiosity in regard to his character and his story.

Now, at last, his position in History is so ascertained and established as to secure his name and fame from neglect or perversion. The records of his story are given into the hands of the public: Dr. Pauli has derived from them a thoroughly acceptable portrait of the man and his time : and those who do not read German may now by this translation study the institution of Representative Government in England in the interesting form of Political Biography.

Under the remarkable development of Historical study at present, as the education of both sexes receives extension, this work will surely be welcomed for any one of its several bearings ; and among them all there will scarcely be room left for any generation henceforth to ask, as our grandfathers too often did—" *Was* Simon de Montfort a great and good man ? "

H. M.

May, 1876.

[The original of Simon de Montfort was published nearly ten years ago, and, through the kindness of Dr. Pauli, the translation may be looked upon as a new edition. He has himself revised it throughout, introducing occasional changes in the text, and adding fresh references, chiefly to the works of Prof. Stubbs and new editions of the Chronicles.—*Translator.*]

CONTENTS.

— ◆ —

CONTENTS.

PREFACE.

In connection with the force of ideas and the energy of new political principles, there has been need in all ages for the one prominent individual in whom they may be personified, and who may break open a path for them where he himself essays to advance. And in the days of a great revolution some master spirit seldom fails to arise, a man who, being himself the product of great general excitement, concentrates in his own person the aspiration which gives it birth, and, venturing upon an enterprise resembling a riddle or a game of hazard, is proclaimed either conqueror or martyr by the result. His claim to notice is stronger in proportion as the principle of preservation of all that is fully tested and established is combined in him with the principle of innovation, and in proportion as the popular term of liberal or conservative is inapplicable to him.

It has never been questioned that Simon de Montfort, Earl of Leicester, gave a decisive direction to the early development of parliamentary government in England,

when, in venturing for the first time to summon the
Commons, he added the idea of representation to the
previously existing custom of severally convoking the
members of certain classes. Yet, mainly because of
his personal fate, he, centuries later, was universally
regarded, like Oliver Cromwell, as a revolutionist whose
influence had been evil, despite its undeniable results.

It is remarkable that though the defenders of parliamentary rights in the seventeenth century were zealous
in bringing to light documents and records relating to
earlier epochs in their country's history, they concerned
themselves but little about his life and achievements.*
The first to deal with the subject were men of opposite
politics, who wrote the history of England in a connected form, after the personal monarchy of the Stuarts
had been re-established and a second time destroyed.
Thomas Carte, the Jacobite, in his book treats of
Montfort as of a base and ungrateful rebel, and for a
whole century Tory historians have echoed his sentiments, notably Hume, who, though he cannot altogether
resist the impression of great qualities, finds much
more of hypocrisy and ambition, who condemns him as
" a bold and artful conspirator," and calls the House of

---

* Sir Roger Twysden stands almost alone. Certaine Considera-
tions upon the Government of England, ed. J. M. Kemble
(Camden Society, 1849), p. 97: And it is cleere the people of
England were so far from accounting them who dyed in armes
against their prince to have beene guilty of sinn for it, as they
have been hardly restrained from honouringe them as saints,
thinking them to dye " pro justitia ecclesiæ et regni."

Commons "a plant set up by an inauspicious hand."* Only in later days the Whigs have naturally adopted him as the unconscious champion of the freedom of after generations.†

Very recently an article in the Quarterly Review has attempted a much wider, higher, and more impartial estimate of his character, founded upon the best materials, which have now become unusually abundant; and from the same quarter a more extensive treatise upon Simon de Montfort is in prospect.‡ The author of the present work confesses that he has been stimulated thereby to take the subject in hand again, though scarcely treating it exhaustively. The inducements were, partly the fulness of the documents and annals made accessible during recent years in the collection issued under the superintendence of the Master of the Rolls, partly the wish to revise carefully by their help those episodes, at least, that relate to them in a section of the English History written fourteen years ago, when it was still necessary to collect laboriously the most im-

---

* History of England, ed. Basel, ii. 466, 487, 493.

† Sir James Mackintosh, History of England, 1830, i. 238. Macaulay passes him by altogether. Hallam, View of the State of Europe During the Middle Ages, ed. 1855, iii. 27. still speaks of the innovation of a usurper.

‡ Quarterly Review, vol. cxix. 26, from the pen of Dr. Shirley, the late lamented Professor of Ecclesiastical History at Oxford, who died in the prime of life in 1866. According to Shirley, Royal and other Historical Letters illustrative of the reign of Henry III., vol. ii. 434, Mr. Cobbe was engaged upon a life of Leicester.

portant materials from among the archives of the
Tower. The biographical form naturally suggested
itself for the monograph.

Its dedication to the revered and distinguished
teacher and master will be deemed fitting by all who
have perused Ranke's last great work, where, in a few
incomparable lines, he has indicated the place due
to the great creator of the Lower House.

SIMON DE MONTFORT.

INTRODUCTION.

THE NORMAN MONARCHY — JOHN LACKLAND — MAGNA CHARTA—THE COMPROMISE AFTER THE CIVIL WAR— FAVOURABLE AND ADVERSE TENDENCIES UNDER HENRY III.

THE strong monarchic power of the Norman kings in England, unique as it was in character at a time when self-governing feudal States everywhere else circumscribed the throne, had yet difficulty, after a few generations were passed, in preserving its foundations unshaken without disturbing the outlines once sketched by the Conqueror.

A contest for the throne, substituting for awhile the reign of violence for public tranquillity, the struggle between Church and State under the first Plantagenet, the crusade that caused his son and heir to forget the duties of sovereignty, each in turn had aided the

B

development of forces that had always existed immediately beneath the throne, and awakened claims
which were in part older than its supremacy. An
admirable administrative system by means of sheriffs
and judicial commissions united all authority, whether
civil, military, judicial, or financial, in the person of
the monarch. But, though this organization was still
maintained in tolerable efficiency, Henry II. had been
compelled gradually to expand the ancient royal courts
of his ancestors into a kind of national assembly, and
to summon at least the higher nobility to his assistance
against the haughty priest through whom the Church,
even in the little island kingdom, laid claim to all
those spiritual and temporal prerogatives won by the
mightiest Popes from Salic and Hohenstaufen monarchs.
The old Teutonic institutions, the legal customs of the
Anglo-Saxons, had never been forgotten : with each
new reign the foreign master had solemnly confirmed
them to the conquered people, and it was to them that
appeal was made against Thomas Becket and the
Canon Law. But, though very welcome to the monarchy for the purpose of sheltering the State against
the feudal supremacy of Rome, they became no less
dangerous to it when the tenants-in-chief learnt how
to make use of them for the purpose of attaining to
greater political consequence. In the circle of the
great Norman vassals the memory survived of the
vastly more important privileges exercised by their
predecessors, the Anglo-Saxon Witan. The lesser
Barons, attracted rather by the public life of the

county than by that of the kingdom, began to draw
near to the numerous Anglo-Saxon freeholders, and to
take part in their communal life, which had never been
interrupted. At least one town, the greatest in the
country, elected its own magistrates, farming the taxes
due to the Lord of the Manor and receiving in return
recognition of its corporate rights by royal charter.
And, lastly, the sentiment of nationality could never
be wholly stifled in the Church, either by the catholicity
of her aims or by William I.'s incorporation of the
Norman clergy in the ranks of his socially splendid,
but politically dependent, feudal organization. Thus,
in a narrow and isolated territory, many influences
combined to soften with the lapse of time the violent
enmity of race, to level by slow degrees the antagonism between victors and vanquished, and to open
the way for the reconciliation of Norman genius for
government with Saxon traditions of immemorial
personal and communal liberty. Moreover, the first
blending of two different nationalities in itself involved
a danger to the absolute monarchy, which in this form
had only become possible through the sharp antagonism
of race. The danger increased immeasurably when
Normandy was lost, the original continental heritage
of the rulers, and the fortunes of their dynasty became
bound up with those of the island more closely than
before.

King John, who had once treacherously helped to
overthrow the regency established by his crusading
brother, had at Richard's death set aside his nephew,

the lawful heir, and, in order to force his way to the
throne, had probably murdered him with his own hand.
He suffered the punishment of such misdeeds when
his liege lord, Philip Augustus of France, ignominiously
deprived him of the land of his fathers, both on the
field of battle and in the court of his peers.   His own
vassals, of whom he had sought to assure himself in
earlier enterprises, now regarded with abhorrence and
indignation   a prince whose wickedness threatened
them all alike, their property and estates, their power
and honour.   Even whilst in possession of the still
almost unshaken powers of sovereign authority, his
government was a system of licentious misrule.   Their
own safety required that the barons of Norman descent
should combine to resist the tyrant with their English-
speaking tenants and the independent freeholders of
the same race.

John   soon   afterwards   brought   upon   himself   the
censures of Rome also, for after a disputed election
to the archiepiscopal see of Canterbury he refused to
grant admission into the kingdom to the papal nominee,
Stephen   Langton,   an   Englishman   who   had   been   a
personal friend of Pope Innocent III. ever since their
student days in Paris.   Further, he joined with his
nephew, the banished Guelph Emperor Otto IV., in that
widely extended league which ventured to oppose the
policy of the allied Capets and Hohenstaufen in the
border States of France and Germany, assisting heresy
in Languedoc against the orthodox authority of the
Church, and the numerous chieftains on the slopes of

the Pyrenees against the progress of French centralization. There was a moment when the English Barons,
who had risen, as they solemnly declared, to defend
the rights of the Church as well as their own fiefs, appeared as the Pope's allies, and Philip Augustus himself prepared an expedition against England. John
must have been ruined if he had not seized this moment, before any decisive military catastrophe ensued
on the continent, to make terms with his most formidable antagonist. He was guarding the coast at
Dover with his foreign mercenaries, and there, on the
15th of May, 1213, as Innocent III. required, he took
at the hands of Pandulph, the Papal Legate, the oath
of fealty for England and Ireland which his ancestors
had constantly and resolutely refused. At the same
time he was compelled to sanction the return, not
only of Stephen Langton, but also of certain of the lay
nobility whom he had banished.

The antagonistic forces now changed their direction
in a manner surprising to all parties. The Barons, who
had aimed at privileges of security and independence,
were henceforth unable to look upon the Pope as an
ally : the Pope was rudely undeceived with regard to
his scholarly friend, and the King failed in his attempt
to wreak unchecked vengeance upon his enemies, because the same Archbishop Stephen did not withdraw
the sentence of excommunication until the ancient laws
of Edward the Confessor had been afresh confirmed
by oath. When the King, nevertheless, persisted in
his violence, the learned lawyer and patriot drew the

attention of his countrymen to earlier franchises, especially to the coronation charter of Henry I., whereby
in former times the first bounds had already been set
to the military supremacy of the feudal sovereigns.
Through him, clergy and aristocracy were inspired
with a new sentiment of nationality, which could no
longer be called Romance in character. The servant
of the Church not only left the confederate peers
unrestrained, he even aided them with his counsel
when, openly revolting against the sovereign, they
entered at the same time into a contest with the Pope,
whose paramount authority they had once well-nigh
desired, but now disowned as unworthy. Prudently
assuring themselves of the capital and the wealthy
citizen class which was supreme there, they scorned
both outlawry and interdict, and, as if inspired by a
holy cause, defied the King and presented themselves
to the country as an " army of the Lord." No one
came to John's help, for the Pope could not stretch his
arm across the channel without aid from Philip
Augustus, the victor of Bouvines, who would consent
to no terms with the English King. Beset on all sides ·
by clergy and laity, by his own subjects, the vassals
and their tenants without distinction of race, the King
came down from his castle of Windsor to the meadow
of Runemede on the 15th of June, 1215, and affixed
his seal to the Magna Charta, as drawn up in accordance with the articles presented to him by the Barons
with swords in their hands.

It may be that in the constitutional history of other

nations, one or another statute points to a similar political origin, but nothing can be found comparable to this pillar of the English constitution. When the monarchy was shaken by the consequences of irresponsible tyranny and arbitrary violence, it was owing to Magna Charta that a firm basis was regained in the old German birthright of personal liberty, and the first effort made to attain to constitutional government by means of the principle of representation.

With the closest possible adaptation to the feudal circumstances of the age, sixty-three clauses were drawn up to define the lawful limits of the liege lord's supremacy, military, civil, judicial, and financial, and to secure these limitations more firmly than by the charters that had been customary hitherto. For the latter purpose a solemn oath was to be sworn be the two contending parties, and a committee appointed of twenty-five Barons, who, as guardians of the agreement, were to be invested with power of making armed resistance and of distraining in case the King disregarded his engagement. (61.) John was obliged further to concede that when other feudal contributions were required by the crown than three ancient prescriptive dues, especially when scutage was demanded instead of personal military service, the great council of the realm should be called together; the great Barons individually by royal writ, the smaller nobility holding fiefs immediately of the crown, collectively through the sheriffs. (Art. 12, 14.) Without further interference in executive functions, the confederates hoped to obtain the best guarantee against their arbitrary exercise through this right of assent accorded to all concerned. A similar provision restrained the tyranny of penal jurisdiction in the famous clause that henceforth no free man should be imprisoned, disinherited, banished, or otherwise injured in life or limb, except by the verdict of his peers; that is, the judgment of his legal equals, and the law of the land. (Art. 39.)

But some general ideas impressed upon Magna Charta its peculiar and imperishable character. The people of Saxon and Norman descent, all ranks and all orders, had revolted against the same evils, and the great act not only marked an important step in the progress of national reconciliation, but also dis-covered the essential idea upon which a constitutional State is grounded, the common interest of all free classes of the population. Here we do not see a single vassal, or a single noble caste, insisting upon a new and exclusive privilege, as often happened upon the continent, but the legal protection of all was kept in view, with a clear and admirable recognition of the immutable supremacy of the commonwealth. There-fore the Norman undertook to observe towards the English freeholder, the noble toward his lower vassals, each in his degree, the same feudal engagements as those claimed by themselves from the crown. There-fore burghers and yeomen were not excluded, and a special mention distinguished the powerful city of London in the article ranking extraordinary aids con-

ditional upon the privileges of the estates. Therefore
the Prince of Wales and the King of Scotland, so far
as they had suffered from John's violence, and, above
all, the Church, despite her peculiar canonical privileges, all appeared closely interwoven in the secular
and national State, as allies of the Barons who won
the charter of legitimate freedom.

Nevertheless, there existed in the connection with
the clergy, although their privileges were guaranteed
in the first article, a seed of immediate danger to the
common work. No one was subsequently more
faithful to it than Archbishop Stephen, who had been
in a measure the spiritual father of the movement, but
a higher than royal absolutism, that of the Pope
to whom John had yielded his kingdom in fee, proved
at the time more powerful. A general promise to
seek no repeal of the concessions from the Roman
See was obtained for insertion in the charter, but no
personal pledge from Master Pandulph who was
present.

To this King John trusted. At the moment of
taking the oath, although fully determined not to
observe it, he offered no opposition to the formal
execution of the instrument, and suffered copies of it
to be deposited in the cathedral churches of the realm ;
but it was omitted in the Patent and Charter Rolls of
the year, an evident proof of the King's intention that
it should never become a law of the realm. On the
24th of August the bull of dispensation appeared,
as had been apprehended. Innocent III. there

described the Magna Charta as a " base, abominable, shameful, and unrighteous compact," and declared its authors to be worse than the Saracens. The Barons and the citizens of London were excommunicated, Stephen Langton was suspended, and the King himself solemnly forbidden to observe the agreement that had been forced upon him.

None could fail to perceive that the charter would have temporarily, perhaps permanently, restrained the free exercise of the royal authority, and it was equally undeniable that the measures adopted in order to bring about this result were revolutionary in character, however medieval views upon the vassals' right of coercion might differ from the views of to-day. King John saw in each limitation a derogation from his personal rule, but in his inmost soul he revolted most of all against the twenty-five guardians appointed to keep watch over him and the newly constituted public law, subjects who virtually presumed to suspend the action of the crown. He had no thought of dismissing his foreign troops, or depriving the foreign captains of the bailiwicks conferred upon them in England, as he had been compelled to swear. (Art. 50.) As soon as he was able, he disengaged himself from those who held him in restraint, and lurked about the southern coast until the arrival of the papal censures. Then, in possession of his foreign forces, the castles, and the treasury, he was well prepared to assume the offensive. At the commencement of the first civil war that blazed around Magna Charta, the bloody

prelude to a constitutional struggle of several generations, the vicious and despotic sovereign stood in the
more advantageous position, protected as he was by
the Pope and supported by the still almost unshaken
State machinery of the Norman monarchy. His
opponents, however just their cause might be, appeared
even morally as the weaker party, for, when their
twenty-five agents, a sort of committee of the estates,
failed to command either consideration or respect
among their fellow-countrymen, the Barons in their
despair applied for foreign help, and Louis, the heir to
the French throne, landed with an armed force in the
spring of 1216, doubtless with designs of personal
advantage. In the course of the following campaign,
when reduced to the last extremity, John suddenly
died on the 19th of October. The great Pope had
preceded him by several months, but not until he had
caused all such as had compromised themselves to feel
his vengeance, and provided for the future by de-
spatching a cardinal legate to England to quell the revolt and maintain the supremacy of the Holy Father.

It was perhaps well for the claims of monarchy
themselves that they passed to Henry III., a child
of nine years, and were represented by a sagacious
protector, William, Earl of Pembroke. Moreover,
the general course of affairs naturally tended towards
a peaceful compromise after the death of the two
most prominent actors on the scene. Some at least
of the nobility, offended as Englishmen by the bearing
of the French, and discouraged as a class by the

failure of their attempt to establish their own permanent authority side by side with that of the King,
met in conference at Bristol on the 11th of November,
with the representative of the Sovereign and the
representative of a Pope in whom the fierce and
noble characteristics of his great predecessor were
equally lacking. In order to escape the horrors of
excommunication and civil war, the three estates
united in an agreement based upon the confirmation
of Magna Charta, with omission of those premature
constitutional demands, the committee claiming a sort
of collateral government (Art. 61), and the right
of taxation demanded by the assembly of the estates
in certain extraordinary cases. The article concerning
personal liberty remained intact, likewise the provision that penal jurisdiction over the Barons should
rest with their peers, but the latter was so interpreted
that the legal privilege could only avail before the
King's supreme court. The same omissions occur in a
subsequent confirmation of November, 1217, soon
after the French had been obliged to withdraw upon
moderate terms, and the princes of Scotland and
Wales had been conciliated likewise. The influences
of foreign countries upon the development of the
national constitution were thus repelled on all sides,
but not without sacrificing meanwhile the most important principles upon which it was based. The
great Barons and vassals were themselves perplexed
and irresolute in their attempts to protect law and
justice. The crown could not regard either the

committee, with their power to distrain and appeal to
arms, or the privilege of the estates to grant taxes,
and necessarily also to refuse them, as compatible
with its authority. After these disputed points, therefore, had been postponed till more propitious times,
the expurgated draught of the 11th of February, 1224,
with the added forest charter, remained thenceforth the
official form of a compact which during following centuries was alternately broken and confirmed, and did not
preserve even its mutilated shape unchanged. Without
it the monarchy would scarcely have obtained even the
outward submission of the vassals. But how could
the Barons forget that which they had but now
struggled to attain, which had received only very
defective legal sanction, and which King and Pope
could vie with one another in revoking and anathe-
matizing? During the insecurity of Henry III.'s long
reign the political conflict continually threatened to
break out afresh, until it led at last to progress
whereby the constitution was essentially transformed.

The men of the reconciliation soon left the scene;
the old Earl of Pembroke was dead, and Cardinal
Guala returned to Italy when he believed that he
had provided for the foreign and domestic peace of the
kingdom. He was succeeded by the grasping
Pandulph, at whose side Pierre des Roches, the
imperious Poitevin Bishop of Winchester, sought to
govern the country at his pleasure. Other sentiments,
loyal and peaceful, but at the same time patriotic,
inspired the men who gathered round the great

justiciary Hubert de Burgh, Archbishop Stephen, the
sons of the late hereditary Earl Marshal Pembroke,
and other chiefs of the aristocracy. In these circles
the object kept in view was to save the realm during
the minority from the evils of faction, and especially
to purge it from a number of foreign adventurers who
had maintained themselves ever since King John's
days in isolated royal fortresses.

Henry III. took the government formally into his ✓
own hands at Oxford in 1227. The confirmation ✓
of the charters was omitted on this occasion, although
it had been universally expected. It soon became
evident that the wearer of the crown was a prince
without force of will, vacillating and dependent upon
others, one who would weakly submit to the supremacy of Rome, and prefer incompetent favourites to
any constitutional council of the tenants-in-chief The
latter, great and small, were still entirely without
experience and so far unqualified for organizing a
permanent political corporation, so that the financial,
military, and penal authority of the crown would have
remained practically as unlimited as before, if growing
pecuniary embarrassments had not made it necessary,
at nearly regular intervals, to call together the
Prelates and Barons, with whom it constantly became
more difficult to deal. Popular aspirations and the
individual goodwill of noble and discerning men, were
wholly insufficient to establish the firm political conviction by force of which alone constitutional struggles
achieve a salutary result. But the time of testing

and purifying had come, and some notable fruit
ripened in the course of one remarkable generation.

The quarrel between the crown and the estates was ✓
kept alive mainly through the King's anti-national
views, whilst the more worthy among the nobility
relied upon patriotic feeling for support. Not only
the clerical and financially disastrous rule of Papal
Legates was directed against the strengthening of
a distinct English nationality, but also the most
positive preference on the part of the King, whose
mother had contracted a second marriage with a
Poitevin nobleman, and whose eldest sister was
married to King Alexander II. of Scotland. In
his early years he himself attempted to resume the
war with France, in order to win back the numerous
continental possessions of his house; through all
his embarrassments he kept up his foreign relations, to
the permanent injury of his domestic power. Avail-
ing himself of these propensities, Bishop Peter of
Winchester in 1232 succeeded in making the Great
Justiciary, Hubert de Burgh, the victim of base
ingratitude and unworthy persecution : the noblemen of rank thereupon refused to contribute subsidies and gathered round the hereditary Earl Marshal, Richard of Pembroke, whom the Bishop then
contrived to remove by murder. It was not till a
conference at Westminster in the spring of 1234,
after the Barons had again appeared armed in
the field, and the Primate, the afterwards sainted
Edmund of Canterbury, had threatened the

King with excommunication, that the foreign
prelate, who had obtained for the King from
Gregory IX. another dispensation from the oath
upon Magna Charta, was dismissed from office with
other hated counsellors. In the struggle for the
right of appointing the royal council, which at
brief intervals continually broke out afresh, the crown
had been compelled to yield once more to the will
of the nation.

Nevertheless, with the internal difficulties of his
kingdom always in view, King Henry paused not
a moment in his efforts to form widely extended
connections with the greatest European powers.
Contrary to the Guelph traditions of the Plantagenets,
he at one time desired himself to espouse a Hohenstaufen princess, doubtless with the design of obtaining effectual assistance against France, and the
project of a matrimonial alliance succeeded at least so
far that his sister Isabella was married to the
Emperor Frederick II. in 1235. He hoped to obtain
patronage from Pope and Emperor at the same time,
and in the following year St. Louis also became his
brother-in-law through his own marriage with
Eleanor of Provence. The results were alliances and
treaties of most diverse character, and through them
monstrous demands upon his own kingdom and
subjects. When Pope Innocent IV. soon afterwards
undertook the great war of annihilation against
Frederick II., he treated the King of England already
as his most obsequious vassal, his country as part of

the papal domain. One cardinal as Nuncio of the Curia no longer sufficed ; in all dioceses of the British Isles permanent agents of the papal chamber collected the clerical revenues for their supreme master, and with his approval contrived to place the most lucrative English benefices in their own or their countrymen's hands. Soon the uncles of the new Queen found their way to court also, attracted by English wealth, which now first acquired European fame ; one of them, Boniface of Savoy, even took possession of the archbishopric of Canterbury at the death of the pious Edmund. The King's step-brothers and sisters followed as soon as they ceased to be children. It seemed as if England had become, through the weakness and knavery of its ruler, the rendezvous and the prey of insatiable Provençals Poitevins, and papal emissaries.

Among the vassals who were settled on their estates must not these proceedings have aroused a suspicion that not only all their oft-promised privileges were concerned, but even their claim to the blessing of a home ? With common grievances must not prelates and barons have again sympathized in the desire to obtain at last better guarantees than the swearing of an oath, and the sealing of the great charter, which in its essential principles was constantly disregarded ? Their demeanour was surly and even menacing when they appeared upon the appointed days, still only the chiefs of the nobility and the dignitaries of the Church, for the purpose of granting subsidies in the name

of all the vassals of the crown, or ratifying a statute
by their assent, as at Merton in January, 1236.
Formally called together upon State affairs at regular
intervals, their importance undoubtedly increased, and,
as at other times, an imprudent absolutism itself gave
impetus to its growth. In official language these
deliberations were already styled Parliaments. Without constitutional authority, they repeatedly availed
themselves of the growing sympathy of the nation to
reject the shameless demands of the government,
retorting by loud complaints against the administration.
In order to break their opposition, and illegally to
secure the richest revenues for foreign favourites, the
great offices of State were conferred no longer upon
native nobles, but upon men of low birth, generally
Churchmen, who, in league with the Romish procurators,
sought to discover fresh pretext for tyranny.

Dull and gloomy discontent smouldered in the
country, for after Hubert was dead, and the race of
the great Earl Marshal had become extinct, no
courageous representative of national rights rose from
among the native nobility. The people would have
endured long with the patience of the Teutonic race,
had it not happened marvellously, amid the general
entanglement of European affairs in the middle of the
century, that a stranger became, through a peculiarly
romantic chain of circumstances, the champion of
national freedom.

CHAPTER I.

THE HOUSE OF MONTFORT BEFORE 1239.

ORIGIN OF THE RACE—THE EARLDOM OF LEICESTER—
SIMON DE MONTFORT IV—HIS RELATION TO ENGLAND
—HIS SON SIMON IN ENGLAND, 1231—MARRIES THE
KING'S SISTER, 1238—THE EMPEROR FREDERICK II.
HIS BROTHER-IN-LAW.

THE race which was called Montfort l'Amaury, from
its castle on a hill between Paris and Chartres, had
already, in earlier centuries, been from time to time
involved in the destinies of Britain. Tradition derived
its origin from that Judith, daughter of Charles the
Bald, who in 856 had married Æthelwulf of Wessex,
and after his death exposed herself to ecclesiastical
censures by a union with his fierce and turbulent son
Æthelbald. She contracted a third marriage with
Baldwin Bras-de-fer, Earl of Flanders. His great-
grandson, William of Hainault, was said to have
married an heiress of Montfort and Epernon at the

c 2

end of the tenth century, and to have become the
founder of a family that through nine generations
was represented in the direct male line.* Another
genealogical tradition connected the race immediately
with the royal house of Capet by making Amaury II.
a bastard of King Robert instead of the son of
William of Hainault.† It is certain that the Montforts
were counted among the bravest and most loyal
vassals of the French crown, and the situation of their
estates helped to place them in the foremost ranks of
the chivalry that always opposed a steadfast resistance
to the encroachments of the Dukes of Normandy, and
subsequently to those of the Counts of Anjou. In the
wars between Louis VI. and Henry I. of England,
Amaury IV., or Amaury I. as Count of Evreux,
appears as assisting his cousin Hugo, Lord of Montfort sur Risle, Waleram, Lord of Meulent, and other
refractory Norman nobles. His help was of no avail,
for in 1124 the King-Duke remained victorious, and
threw his prisoners into the dungeon at Rouen,
excepting Hugo, whom he took with him to

* L'Art de Vérifier les Dates, ed. 1818. 8vo. Vol. xi. 471. In
accordance with it, Histoire Littéraire de France, xvii. 205.

† Les autres (desquels l'opinion est plus certaine) dient à Bau-
douin, surnommé de l'Isle, Conte de Flandres, la fille du Conte
de Noyon, de laquelle le Roy Robert eut Amaulry, père de
Simon et Amaulry de Montfort, et dont est venuë la maison de
Montfort l'Amaulry, ne peut être esté Royne, mais seulement
amye du Roy. Du Tillet, Receuil des Roys de France, 1602,
p. 65.

England to suffer long and strict confinement at Gloucester. *

In 1140 Simon was succeeded in Montfort and in Evreux by his second son, Simon III., surnamed the Bald, a contemporary of Henry Plantagenet, and of the events whereby he confirmed his power in England and Normandy. As Simon was at the same time a vassal of this energetic prince and of the French king, he could only keep his own advantage in view amid their incessant rivalries, taking or changing sides with all the skill at his command. The marriage, which became of so much consequence to his descendants, with the sister and co-heiress of Robert de Beaumont, Earl of Leicester, he owed to a passing connection with England, probably at the time when the heir to the throne was concerting a widely extended conspiracy against his father with many English and Norman nobles, amongst others with Earl Robert of Leicester. According to Domesday Book the De Beaumonts had crossed the channel with the Conqueror from their family seat at Meulent, and had received the great English barony of Leicester in fee. Robert, the fourth and last earl of the race, survived until 1204. His sister Amicia bore her husband three sons: Amaury, afterwards Count of Evreux, Simon, Lord of Montfort, Guy, Lord of La Ferté Alais, and

* And Hugo of Mundford he sende to Engleland, and let hine don on ifele bendas on thone castel on Gleucestre. Saxon Chronicles, ed. Earle, 1865, p. 252. S. Lappenberg, Geschichte von England, ii. 273.

three daughters. The father died in 1181, the
marriage therefore must have taken place at least as
early as 1173. But the insufficiency of the documents
causes considerable obscurity with regard to the
dates, the degree of relationship, and even to the
hereditary right of Amicia.*

Again, with the second son of this marriage the
race not only continued to flourish in the ancient
inheritance, but reached at once the climax of its
glory. Simon IV. of Montfort was that hero of the
orthodox Church, equally famed as crusader, conqueror, and statesman, the most dreaded scourge of
all heretical enemies, especially those belonging to
another nationality. He had already reached the age
of manhood in 1202, when he desired to seek adventure by joining the Venetian crusade against Constantinople, but refrained in obedience to the prohibition

* Concerning the marriage of Amicia to Simon III., Dugdale,
Monasticon Anglicanum, i. 312, and Chronica Albrici Monachi:
Trium Fontium in Monum. Germaniae Hist. S.S. xxiii. 871.
Compare Anselme, Histoire Généalogique et Chronologique de la
Maison Royale de France, i. 314. Also, according to Rot. Lit.
Claus., ed. Th. D. Hardy, vol. i. 30, a. 1205, Amicie Comitisse de
Montford manerium de Winterburnstok cum pertinentiis quod fuit
datum ei in maritagium, and p. 70, August 28, 1206, Comitissa
mater Comitis Leicestrie, she was the wife of that elder Simon
and not of Simon IV.: the latter is an entirely untenable asser-
tion by an heraldic scholar in the Historic Peerage of England,
1857, p. 283. The biography of Simon the younger in the
Quarterly Review, vol. cxix. 27, calls Amicia Petronilla, a common family name with both the Montforts and the Beaumonts.

of Innocent III. Some years later his mother's right to the English earldom devolved upon him, the second son, and was confirmed by King John. He bore thenceforth the title of Earl of Leicester, although his enterprising nature quickly caused him to disregard the feudal allegiance it involved.* An ardent admirer† describes his noble and graceful appearance, his bodily activity, and his chivalrous temper. Eloquent and keen-minded, firm and immovable in all his purposes, heroic, brave, chaste, and devoted to the orthodox faith from interest as well as conviction, he united in himself all the characteristics of a northern French nobleman, as they are found variously distributed among individual members of his house during its

* In the document referred to of the 28th of August, 1206, John styles him Simon Comes Leicestric. Confirmation of the 10th of March, 1207, Rymer, Foedera i. 96. But as early as the 27th of December, 1207, the words occur: Terra illa fuit in manu Comitis Leicestric Simonis quem de terris suis precepimus disseisiri. Rot. Lit. Claus. i, 99. ;

† Petri Vallium Sarnaii Monachi Historia Albigensium, Recueil des Historicus des Gaules et de la France, xix. 22: Genere prae-clarus, virtute robustus, in armis plurimum exercitatus . . . . statura procerus, caesarie spectabilis, facie elegans, aspectu de-corus, humeris eminens, brachiis exertus, corpore venustus, mem-bris omnibus agilis et habilis, acer et alacer . . . facundia disertus, affabilitate communis, contubernio amabilis, castitate mundissimus, humilitate praecipuus, sapientia praeditus, in pro-posito firmus, in consilio providus, in judicio justus, in militiae exercitiis sedulus, in suis actibus circumspectus, in incipien-dis arduus, in perficiendis non defessus, totus divinis servitiis mancipatus.

long prosperity. Romantic, and at the same time
practical, he was a master spirit in an age of profound
agitation which gave birth to many new phenomena.

About the year 1190* he had married Alice, daughter
of Bouchard V. of Montmorency; she came of a noble
race, and was no less famed for her prudence and
piety† than for the courage and endurance she manifested by accompanying her husband on his great
conquering expeditions into southern France, though
most of their four sons and three daughters were then
infants, and the youngest was probably born at Lavaur
as late as 1211. In Lent, 1210, she joined her husband at Pezenas with fresh troops from the north; a
year later she and her eldest son Amaury appear as
principal witnesses when the wealthy Raymond of
Cahors was invested with the same castle, and again
on a similar occasion, April 23rd, 1212.‡ On the 24th
of June, 1213, the father and mother conduct the
still youthful Amaury to the altar of the church of
Castelnau d'Arri that he may be qualified to bear

* L'Art de Vérifier les Dates, xi. 481, says: Avant l'an 1191;
Vic et Vaissette, Histoire Générale de Languedoc, ed. 1842, v.
129: Avant l'an 1190. I know not on what ground, for it is difficult to determine the ages of the children, even approximately.

† Petri Vallium Sarnaii Mon. Hist. Albig. p. 23. In ea quippe
religio sapientiam et sollicitudinem adornabat, sapientia religionem et sollicitudinem informabat, sollicitudo religionem et
sapientiam exercitabat.

‡ Consensu et voluntate dominae Aelipdis comitissae uxoris
meae et consensu et voluntate Amalrici primogeniti filii mei;
May 12, 1211. Hist. de Languedoc, Preuves, v. 582, cf. 188.

arms in the holy war. On the eve of the battle of
Muret, against the King of Aragon, Alice has an evil
dream, but her husband calmly bids her leave such
presentiments to the superstitious Spaniards. In 1217
she defended Narbonne against Count Raymond of
Toulouse.* She was a woman of high courage,
altogether worthy of her husband, whom she survived
three years after he fell before Toulouse. She died on
the 22nd of February, 1221, and the dust of both
found a last resting-place in the family sepulchre of
Hautes-buyères, facing the castle hill of Montfort.
Thither Simon's bones were transported, after they had
first been interred with pomp and ceremony in the
cathedral at Carcassone as those of a saint and
martyr.

We do not here follow the history of the Albigensian
war, and those undertakings whereby its greatest hero
sought to extend his power. So long as he was supported by Innocent III. and the Lateran, he appeared
to have established successfully his own dominion in
the place of many Provençal dynasties, and carried out
his own purposes in defiance of England, Aragon,
Navarre, Castile, and Sicily; but even in his lifetime
a reaction set in against him, fostered in several
quarters, and not least by his liege lord the King of
France. We rather seek to trace his relations with
his English suzerain.

* La Contessa de Montfort, laquala era per hora dins la castel
Narbonés an granda garniso. Hist. de la Guerre des Albigeois,
Receuil, xix. 178.

After his mother's death the crown fief of Leicester
was divided between Saiher de Quency, Earl of Winchester, and the house of Montfort, and on the 10th
of March, 1207, King John invested Simon with the
third penny of the county and the office of **High
Steward of England,** which was associated with the
title to the earldom.* But he never actually entered
upon the inheritance which was recognised as his.
According to one chronicle the insurgent Barons of
England in 1210 desired to make him their leader, if
not even their king;† in the war between England
and France he sided with the latter; in his crusade
against the heretics he turned his arms first and chiefly
against Count Raymond VI. of Toulouse, John's
brother-in-law, and for these various reasons the
English King deprived him of his offices and estates,
and transferred them to Ralph, Earl of Chester.‡
But, in spite of deprivation and banishment, he continued to bear the title of Earl of Leicester, and was
so designated in 1209 by Innocent III. who, having

* Rymer, Foedera i. 96. Compare Hudson Turner, Manners
and Household Expenses of the XIIIth Century (Roxburgh
Club, 1841); preface, p. xi.

† Annales de Dunstaplia, ed. Luard, 1866 (Rer. Brit. med. aevi
SS.), p. 33, a. 1210, Rex . . . suscepit rumores de conspiratione
facta contra eum a baronibus suis, et quod elegerant Simonem de
Monteforti in regem Angliae.

‡ Not until the year 1215, according to Hudson Turner, l. c.
In 1217 Henry III. transferred to the Earl of Chester another
manor, Quod est de feodo Comitis Simonis de Monte Forti, not
Leicestrie. Rot. Lit. Claus. i. 326, b.

himself quarrelled with the English King, now confirmed his vassal in the conquered territories of
Beziers and Carcassone.* Simon habitually styled
himself at this time, Lord of Montfort, Earl of Leicester, and, by the grace of God, Viscount of Beziers
and Carcassone.† Others, however, as the Bishop
of Cahors, Cardinal Robert, and Innocent after
he was reconciled with King John, addressed him
simply as Count of Montfort.‡ It was not till later,
when his triumphs over his chief antagonist, Raymond,
had reached·their climax, that he assumed his titles,
Duke of Narbonne and Count of Toulouse, and
dropped that of Leicester, presumably at the request
of Pope Honorius III., because the curia was again at
peace with the King of England.§ Though the conquests were rapidly lost after the father's death, his
eldest son continued to bear the same titles, so that in
1220 he styled himself Duke of Narbonne, Count of
Toulouse, Earl of Leicester, Lord of Montfort, and

---

* Innoc. III., Epp. xii. 122–129. Hurter's opinion that the
Earl's title was a personal designation is erroneous. Gesch.
Innoc. III., II., 303, N. 834.

† For the documents see Vic et Vaissette, V. 571, 573, 574,
577, 591, a. 1209, 1210, 1214.

‡ Ibid. 583, 592, 597, a. 1211, 1214, 1215.

§ Ibid. 601, a. 1217, 1218. Once in the year 1216 he went into
North France upon affairs relating to his inheritance, but it cannot be said whether the English fief was the occasion. Pro eo
quod in fata concesserat Amicia mater sua. Chronologia Roberti
Altissiodor. Recueil, xviii. p. 283.

Constable of France, but at the same time he was addressed merely as Count of Montfort.* The English claims revived with greater distinctness when the proud but now unsubstantial conquests in southern France were ceded to Louis VIII. in 1224, and to Louis IX. in 1227. Amaury remained thenceforth Constable of France, Count of Montfort, and Earl of Leicester,† but all prospect that the last of these titles could ever again be made good seemed to have disappeared.

The duchy of Aquitaine, the possession of the Plantagenets with its dependent principalities, stood in imminent danger of being swallowed up by the crusade so long as the Pope gave his full support to the great Simon, and made no terms with England. John's seneschal, Savery de Mauleon, then held a most arduous post. At the synod of Lavaur, in 1213, the chief accusation brought against Count Raymond before the Pope was alliance with all the enemies of the Church,—the Emperor Otto IV., the Kings of England and Aragon, and the Sultan of Morocco.‡ Crusaders gathered together from the whole of northern Europe, from the Rhine and from Germany, but none came from England, with a single noteworthy exception; Walter Langton, brother of the Archbishop of Canterbury, placed himself under Simon's banner, and in 1211 was taken prisoner by

* Vic et Vaissette, 606.
† Ibid. 625, 645, 646.
‡ Innoc. III., Epp. xvi. 41.

the heritical Count of Foix*. But the treaty between
Innocent and John, though immediately directed against
the insurgent Barons in England, very soon produced
an effect in the south also. Not only was Simon
compelled by the Pope to release the infant Jaime of
Aragon, whom he had destined to marry one of his
daughters, but also the English at the same time were
able to gain ground once more. John even ventured
to recommend his nephew, the younger Raymond,
who styled himself by preference son of Queen
Johanna Plantagenet, to the Lateran Council, and it
was owing to change in the papal policy, still more
than to success of native arms, that the conquests of
the northern French were so soon checked. Not the
Popes, but Philip Augustus and his dynasty, out
of regard for their own feudal interests, recognised
the house of Montfort in the wide but insecurely
defended districts south of the Garonne. The Papal
Court had no desire to see a new dominion founded
north and south of the Pyrenees, or the whole district
absorbed in one great French monarchy, and therefore it
preferred to desist from the merciless persecution of
heresy, in order that the old dynasties might be preserved in Languedoc, Provence, and Aragon. In Aquitaine, as well as at home, it helped to preserve his possessions to the English sovereign ; the advancing power
of the northern French, after assisting the English
Barons and the orthodox crusaders, was pressed back

* Galterum de Langatone, fratrem episcopi Cantuariensis.
Petr. Vall. Sarn. Receuil, xix. 50.

on either hand, and it then became the interest of
the house of Montfort, never, after all its losses,
seriously estranged from Rome, to establish amicable
relations with the Plantagenets, as well as with the
Capets, during the period of treaties and truces.

The deprivation of Simon de Montfort was maintained under Henry III.,* until, at the time when a
sorry peace was concluded with the French in 1231,†
the Montforts themselves sought to renew the old
connection. The death of Ralph, Earl of Chester,
upon whom John had conferred the forfeited fief of
Leicester, so far as it was left entire, opened the way
on the 26th October, 1232. Amaury, as head of the
family, immediately made application on behalf of his
youngest brother Simon, who had already gone to
England. The intermediate brothers, Guy and Robert,
were dead.

We do not know the time and place of this remarkable man's birth, but it may be presumed that he was
born before his mother.Hastened to join her husband
in the south, therefore about 1208, and afterwards
grew up under her eye in the castle of Montfort.

---

* Henry III to Stephen de Segrave, July 28, 1218. Rot. Lit.
Claus. i. 366ᵇ. Audivimus, quod Comes Simon de Monte Forti
in fata concessit . . . plenam saisinam de omnibus terris in
balliva vestra que ipsum Simonem hereditaria contingebant de
Honore Leicestrie. Aug. 26, ibid. p. 399. Rex concessit P.
Winton, Ep. (des Roches) custodiam terre que fuit Comitis
Simonis de Monte Forti quam diu ei placuit.

† Geschichte von England, iii. 582.

When some twenty years old he had sought to attain
distinction in the unquiet days when Queen Blanche
ruled in the stead of her young son, Louis IX, but her
displeasure had compelled him to leave the kingdom.*
It is probable that he had already been active as
an English partisan in his own country, for just at the
time of the three years' truce he found an extremely
gracious reception at the court of Westminster. In
April, 1230, Henry assigned him a temporary pension
of 400 marks; on the 13th of August, 1231, he
accepted Simon's homage for his grandmother's
inheritance.† This was but the first step, in some
measure the naturalization of the stranger ; full
installation in his office and dignities involved a long
and tedious negotiation, for as England advanced
along the path of independent national development,
the monarch was less and less able to permit a divided
allegiance among his subjects.‡ It was chiefly for
this reason that Amaury determined to waive his own

* Chron. Guil. de Nangiaco. Recueil xx. 548, a. 1239, Simon
de Monte Forti, miles quidam de Gallia strenuissimus . . . .
infensus reginae Franciae matri regis piissimi Ludovici fugiit
in Angliam ad regem Henricum, quem ipse rex benigne sus-
cipiens dedit eidem in conjugio sororem suam cum Leicestriae
comitatu.

† Shirley, Royal and other Historical Letters illustrative of the
Reign of Henry III. (Rerr. Brit. med. aevi SS.) i. 362, 401. Also
Excerpta e Rot. Finium, i. 217. August, 1231, cujus homagium
rex cepit de honore Leicestriae.

‡ It is true that certain revenues (eschaeta) were also
granted to Simon in Normandy, donec terra nostra Angliae

claim to the English earldom in favour of his brother.

But years intervened before Simon could attain his object, and, being himself without property and burdened with debts, he was meanwhile supported by pensions from the revenues of Leicester.* Like his father he was adventurous and aspiring; twice he believed that he should succeed in forming a brilliant matrimonial alliance in his own country, but each time his expectations were ruined through the jealousy of the French court;† his energetic spirit then found at the English court fitting means of obtaining, together with the coveted earldom, a personal position and an opportunity for the profitable exercise of his talents.

His beautiful face, his noble figure and his chi-

et terra Normanniae communes fuerint, June 15, 1232. Shirley i. 107.

* Quod exitus terrae que de honore Leicestria usque in iiii annum post obitum ejus (the father's) sint ad acquietationem debitorum suorum. Rot. Lit. Pat. 20: Henr. III., membr. 4; July 28, 1236.

† Chronica Albrici Monachi Trium Fontium, Monum. Germ. Hist. SS. xxiii. 940. Quidam machinatores contra regem Franciae clam procuraverant matrimonium comitissae Flandriae cum viro nobili Symone de Monte Forti, fratre comitis Almarici, qui Symon alienatus erat a Francia eo quod esset suspectus in regis curia propter redditus quos habebat in Anglia et fidelitatem quam Anglorum regi fecerat. Quapropter istud matrimonium perdidit sicut et illud comitisse Bolonie perdiderat.

valrous bearing,* no less than his very considerable
intellectual endowments, won him the love of Henry
III.'s youngest sister, Eleanor, who was born in 1215 and
in 1224 had been espoused to William Earl of Pembroke, the younger, when she was nine years old and he
forty; but since the 15th of April, 1231, she had been
a widow.† Before Edmund of Canterbury and Bishop
Ralph of Chichester she had once vowed to take the
veil,‡ but this did not prevent the consent of even her
devout brother, King Henry, to the union that she
and Simon desired. The ring was not yet placed
upon her finger which would have sealed her as the bride
of Christ. On the 7th of January, 1238, the pair were
privately married in the royal chapel of St. Stephens,
the King himself leading the bride to her husband.§
When received into the council as Earl of Leicester,

* Vir in armis strenuus et armorum peritia callidissimus.
Guil. de Nangaco. Recueil, xx. 414. Sicut erat miles strenuus,
in corpore procerus et facie formosus. Chron. de Lanercost, p.
39: Bannatyne Club.

† Mrs. Green, Lives of the Princesses of England, ii. 48, 57.

‡ Thomas Wykes, ed. Luard, Annales Monastici. Rer. Brit.
medii ævi SS. iv. (1869) p. 65, under the year 1231. Quæ viro
suo defuncto aliquamdiu permanens in viduitate, in præsentia
Sancti Edmundi Cantuariensis archiepiscopi et Sancti Ricardi
Cicestrensis episcopi solemne votum castitatis emisit, cujus
postea prævaricatrix effecta, nupsit Simoni de Monteforti comiti
Leycestriæ.

§ Matthæus Paris, 465, ed. 1640. In parvula capella Regis
quæ est in angulo cameræ, tradente eam Rege per manum eidem
Simoni.

and brother-in-law of Henry III., Simon might have acquired immediately a controlling influence upon public affairs, had it not been that the ever wakeful opposition of the Barons was aroused against this new favourite, who was likewise an alien, whilst the clergy took exception to the doubtful marriage.

It was impossible to conceal the latter event, and both estates felt themselves to be deeply wronged, because the princess had been given without their consent to the foreign noble who had for some time been an object of envy and jealousy. The King's brother, Earl Richard of Cornwall, openly raised the standard of revolt at the head of the nobility, seeking to call the men of the Cinque Ports under arms.* The majority of the Barons with the Earl Marshal Gilbert at their head tumultuously demanded Simon's re- moval; none listened to the mediation of the Papal Legate, and when the King's court met during Lent,

---

* Prohibition addressed to them by Henry, February 3, 1238 : Eo quod tradidimus nuptui comitissam Pembrochiæ sororem nostram Simoni de Monte Forti. Shirley, Royal Letters, ii. 15. Matth. Paris, Historia Minor (Compendium of the Great Chro- nicle). ed. Sir F. Madden (Rerr. Brit. med. ævi SS.) ii. 404. Commotum est regnum vehementer, eo maxime quod rex, præter suorum magnatum consilium et assensum præsertim comitis Ricardi, procuravit illud tam arduum matrimonium inter Simonem de Monte-forti et Alienoram, contra etiam voluntatem et con- silium sanctissimi archiepiscopi Edmundi, in cujus præsentia dicitur ipsa Alienora votum fecisse continentiæ vidualis, vestibus utens tinctura carentibus. Cf. Stubbs, Constitutional History of England, ii. 55, 56.

and other grievances were brought under discussion, it was decreed that Simon should remain excluded from the royal council. A proposal of certain reforms appeared to satisfy even his brother-in-law, Earl Richard, but the scruples of the Church only grew the more serious. If Eleanor had given but a preliminary promise to remain single, her marriage was neverthe-less a grave offence against canonical ordinances; none but the Pope could subsequently release her from the vow and pronounce pardon.

In March Simon set out for Rome, to avert the threatened disgrace and displeasure. A rich citizen of Leicester had advanced him 500 marks, the money necessary for the Papal court.* On his way thither he waited upon his great brother-in-law, Frederick II., who had just won the battle of Cortenuova, and was now ceaselessly striving to break the obstinate resist-ance of the Lombard towns which were in league against him. One would gladly know more about the personal intercourse of these two men.† The brief mili-

---

* Matth. Paris, 468, Historia Minor, ii. 405, 406. The King's safe conduct, dated the 27th of March. Rot. Lit, Pat., 22 Henr. III., membr. 8.

† From Matth. Paris, without continental notices, it can only be conjectured that Simon met the Emperor in May on the occa-sion of the diet in Cremona, and, after leaving the Papal court, did service at the siege of Brescia, like many other foreign nobles. Compare Böhmer, Reg. Imp. 1198–1254, p. 179, 180. Schirr-macher, Kaiser Friedrich der Zweite, iii. 28 *et seq.* Winckel-mann, Geschichte Kaiser Friedrich's des Zweiten, ii. 94 *et seq.*

tary service rendered by the adventurous knight to the
mighty ruler in his fruitless struggle against municipal
freedom was requited by commendations to the Pope,
which might still be serviceable at this time, before
the irreparable breach between Frederick and the
Vatican. On the 10th of May, Simon obtained the
wished-for dispensation from Gregory IX. ;* and, notwithstanding the opposition of the Dominicans and
Archibishop Edmund, the Legate Otho was directed
to release Eleanor from her vow. Simon travelled
home joyfully, received an affectionate welcome
from King Henry on the 14th of October, and
then hastened to Kenilworth castle, where six weeks
later his wife bore him a son, an event hailed with
rejoicings at court where it was still feared that the
Queen would be childless.† On the 2nd of February,
1239, Montfort was at last formally installed in the
earldom of Leicester, and thereupon admitted among
the Barons of the realm and the counsellors of the
crown.‡

---

* Super matrimonio, quod inter te ac nobilem virum S. de
Monte Forti Comitem Leicestrie (ac nobilem feminam E. filiam
regis Anglie) in facie ecclesie intelleximus esse contractum,
nobis et fratribus nostris sunt a diversis diversa relata, per que
non vidimus contra jam contractum matrimonium presumendum,
vi. Id. Mai. Double copy in Monum. Brit. ex autographis Rom.
Pont. Mus. Brit. MS. Add. 15, 354, p. 81.

† Matth. Paris, 471, 475, 481.

‡ Matth. Par. 483. Die vero Purificationis S. Virginis contulit
Dominus Rex comitatum Legriae Simoni de Monte Forti et in-

vestivit, vocato primo comite Almarico primogenito fratre ejus et pacificato, ne super hoc aliquando moveret questionem. Rot. Cart. 23 Henr. III. 32, 34. Amaury's renunciation. Rymer i. 203. dated an. 16 Henr. III. (123½), but certainly a later copy, for Cardinal Otho (in England from 1237 to 1241) appears among the witnesses.

CHAPTER II.

EARL SIMON OF LEICESTER ALTERNATELY IN FAVOUR AND DISFAVOUR.

FIRST RUPTURE IN 1239—THE BISHOP OF LINCOLN AND THE FRANCISCANS—CRUSADE TO PALESTINE, 1240— SIMON ACCOMPANIES THE KING TO GUIENNE, 1242— OPPRESSION OF ENGLAND BY THE POPE AND KING— SIMON'S RETIRED LIFE, WITHOUT PARTICIPATION IN POLITICS — HE IS MADE GOVERNOR OF GUIENNE, 1248—THE REBELLIOUS GASCONS AND THE INTRIGUES AT COURT—SIMON IN HIS NEED COUNSELLED BY THE FRANCISCANS — INVESTIGATIONS AND PROCEEDINGS AGAINST HIM, 1252—FRESH BREACH WITH THE KING—THE EARL HIMSELF ASSERTS HIS RIGHTS IN GASCONY — HENRY III. AT BORDEAUX APPEALS TO HIM FOR HELP, 1258—SUCCESSFUL EXERTIONS OF HIS CLERICAL FRIENDS.

THE period of harmony and happiness did not last long, for soon the Earl was driven anew by the King's temper and the political circumstances of England and Europe to an unsettled and adventurous life.

On the 16th of June an heir to the throne, Prince
Edward, was born at Westminster. He was baptised
by the Legate on the fourth day, Simon assisting at
the ceremony as godfather and Lord High Steward.
The atmosphere appeared perfectly calm, but when
the Queen was about to be solemnly churched in
London on the 9th of August, an angry outbreak suddenly occurred between the King and his brother-in-
law, without any palpable reason. Henry called Simon
an excommunicated person, and forbade him and his
wife to be present at the ceremony, because he had
once criminally consorted with her. Astounded, and
overwhelmed with abuse, the Earl and Countess fled
across the river to Southwark, where the town palace
of the late Bishop of Winchester had been recently
assigned them as a residence. But the King commanded them to be driven thence also, and remained
inexorable when they ventured to appear before him
in tears. "You seduced my sister before marriage,"
he cried. "When I made the discovery I gave her
to you, to avoid scandal, sorely against my will. Then
you went to Rome to remove the impediment to marriage, and with presents and endless promises you
bribed the Papal court to grant you the forbidden
thing. When this reached the ears of the Archbishop
of Canterbury, he discovered the truth to the Pope;
but before Romish greed the truth has no chance
against redoubled promises. Now that you cannot
pay, you have incurred excommunication; and, to fill
the measure of your baseness, you have by means of

false testimony made me surety without my knowledge
or advice." Rendered speechless by indignation,
Simon embarked the same day with his wife and a few
companions, and sailed down the Thames to seek refuge for awhile in France.*

For more than a year Henry III. had regarded his
sister's marriage with approval, he had publicly given
it his royal sanction, and forwarded the journey and
petition to Rome as far as he was able. But the
catastrophe did not result from his habitual fickleness,
neither was it occasioned by the factious proceedings
of the aristocracy, for in them Simon had hitherto
taken no part. The true cause lay rather in the deadly
enmity between Pope and Emperor which had just
broken out afresh,† for Frederick II. had been excommunicated on Palm Sunday, the 20th of March,
1239, and a threatening war cloud was gathering over
Rome. Though the English King looked up to his
imperial brother-in-law with admiration and awe, and
had sent him men and money during the previous
year,‡ he was now constrained to yield obedience to
the ecclesiastical power under whose guardianship he
stood. To the strict Papal party at court the Earl,
who but the year before had been so cordially received and accredited by the Emperor, appeared an
inconvenient member of the royal council. It was
necessary to remove him by the basest means, and, with

* Matth.Par. 497.
† Biography in the Quarterly Review, cxix. p. 31.
‡ Matth. Paris, Historia Minor, ii. 408.

lamentable weakness, the King lent his aid, accusing
the relative, whom he had hitherto treated with marked
affection, of involving himself in a dishonourable money
transaction, and forcing the Princess to become his
wife by previous seduction. These accusations are
not only falsified by the King's whole deportment, but
also there is not the slightest indication that the Papal
dispensation granted the year before had been now suddenly revoked. A contemptible fiction was seized
upon to screen a political necessity. In 1232 a device,
as gross and shameless but obviously the same, had
helped to ruin the venerable Hubert, Earl of Kent,
who was said to have necessitated his marriage with
Margaret, daughter of the Scotch King, by previously
dishonouring her.*

That a prince should so insult his own sister appears
incredible, yet it was in accordance with the feebleness
of his character, with the influences that surrounded
him, and the spirit of the age. That Eleanor followed
her husband spoke loudly for their innocence, and a
yet clearer proof was the friendship and testimony of
one of the noblest men in England, with whom the
pair were already intimately connected.

Robert Grosseteste, a native of Suffolk, of humble
birth, had risen to the highest dignities of the Church
and made himself illustrious as a pious and zealous
pastor, as a scholar and as Chancellor of the University of Oxford. He was more than all these, for
among the English clergy there was no one who so

* Compare Gesch. v. England, iii. p. 596.

fully understood the constructive and destructive
tendencies of the age, no one who watched more
faithfully over discipline and doctrine among priests
and laity, and no more courageous champion when the
rights of the national Church were to be defended
against the avarice of the court of Rome and the
tyranny of the crown. Mainly through his help the
Franciscan friars were rapidly naturalized in this
country, founding theological chairs in the universities, and developing their peculiar mission in spite of
opposition from the secular clergy and the monas-
teries. He was convinced that the moral want of the
time could be best supplied by means of their zeal for
reform ; and in alliance with them he strove himself by
word and pen and undaunted action to save the souls
and confirm the minds of men and to defend the
right. He had already been brought into connection
with the house of Leicester, when he was archdeacon
of that town.* In 1235 he was raised to the bishopric
of Lincoln, and thenceforth administered the widest
and most populous diocese in the kingdom. It extended over a considerable part of central England,

---

* Grosseteste's letter to Margarita de Quincy, Comitissa Win-
toniæ, is correctly attributed by Luard to the year 1231, Roberti
Grosset. Epistolæ, 1861 (Rerr. Brit. med. ævi S.S.) p. xxxv.
p. 33, for Robert was Archdeacon of Leicester until 1232; but
the Dominus Leicestriensis, against whom the Jews of the town
were protected, was not Simon of Montfort, but Ralf of Chester.
Upon Grosseteste generally, see Pauli, Tübinger programme of
the year 1864, p. 11, *et seq.*

and included Oxford, with the parent house of the Franciscans, and also those lordships which, after many changes, had again been assigned to a member of the house of Montfort.

Simon and his wife, both ardent and sincere in temper, had from the first given heed to the warning and advice of this spiritual guide.* A genuine friendship grew up and resulted in a connection between the Earl and the Franciscan order, as remarkable as that once existing between his illustrious father and the scarcely established Dominicans. This source of consolation did not fail when the husband and wife were abandoned by their own kindred, and driven from the country in shame and distress. In replying to Simon's written account of the heavy trial that had come upon him, the Bishop quoted the apostle's words of comfort : "No chastening for the present seemeth to be joyous, but grievous ; nevertheless, afterward it yieldeth the peaceable fruit of righteousness unto them which are exercised thereby." He reminded him of the fruits which would not fail to follow, and pointed out the noble meaning

---

* The letters of the Bishop are without dates, as was then well-nigh universal. His earnest intercession with Simon, in Christo carissimo domino de Monteforti, for one of these too harshly punished townsmen of Leicester, Luard, p. 141, must belong approximately to the year 1238. It breathes all the earnest conviction of the writer: *Quia igitur vestram ingenuitatem brachiis caritatis arctius amplectimur. . . . ut sitis exemplum clementiæ et mansuetudinis et non magister crudelitatis.*

of his family name with an inclination to dwell upon the etymology of words which often appears in his writings. From the deep depression that he now suffered he would climb to the summit of the strong mountains whereon Christ is enthroned.* Lastly, he promised, in accordance with the Earl's request, to think much of him, to intercede for him with the King, and faithfully to comfort his dependants, especially two who had been commended to his peculiar care. In these and all other matters he was ready to do whatever would, as he hoped, tend to his friend's honour and advantage.

Thus the stern and zealous prelate, the best and noblest of his order, not only held the Earl and Countess guiltless, but also used every means in his power to bring about a reconciliation with the King, and probably with the Pope and his representatives likewise. It was chiefly through his intercession that the breach was quickly healed. Simon returned at the beginning of April, 1240, and the King vouchsafed him an honourable reception at court.† The pregnancy of the Countess had caused her to remain behind in France.

Immediately upon his return, Simon commenced preparations for a crusade to Palestine, providing himself with money by the sale of woods and lands. The

---

* In cacumen montis fortis, hoc est Christi, qui est mons in vertice montium et virtus Dei Patris ; Luard, p. 244, n. 1239.

† Calend Aprilis . . . receptus est cum honore a rege et a regalibus. Matth. Paris, 516.

undertaking could scarcely be a consequence of the recent quarrel, for nothing indicates that he intended by this means to propitiate those who censured his marriage. Grosseteste would not urge such a course, nor the Minorites, for they, with an almost methodistic system of self-examination, held that penance consists rather in turning away from all sinful living than in performing outward works. It is more probable that he, like other great barons of the realm, had an earlier crusading vow to fulfil. The Pope some years before had granted a dispensation to him, and the Earls, Richard of Cornwall and William of Salisbury, the more willingly because the expedition then commanded to the east was calculated simply to further Hohenstaufen interests, and was therefore regarded with extreme disfavour at Rome, even before the breach with the Emperor.* Latterly the Curia had been zealously exhorting everywhere to a crusade against Constantinople. But a host of English nobles, headed by the King's brother, were now of another mind ; to them Simon joined himself ; they started between Ascension and Whitsuntide, journeyed through France, and embarked on the Mediterranean for Acre, where they expected to arrive in the autumn. The army, led by Earl Richard, found the remnant of the little Christian State miserably disorganized in consequence

---

* Imminet eidem regno periculum, si tuo auxilio et consilio hoc presertim relinquitur tempore destitutum. Gregory IX. to the three earls, V. Kal. Mart. 1238, MS. Add. Mus. Brit. 15,354, p. 399.

of the heavy losses which its army had just suffered
at Gaza, on the 13th November, from the superior
force of the Egyptian Sultan. Among many nobles
of Western Europe, Count Amaury of Montfort, was
there taken prisoner by the Mohammedans.* How
far Simon took part in his brother's deliverance, and
in what manner he otherwise distinguished himself in
the Holy Land, is nowhere narrated. It is certain
that he was in the English crusading army, and that
his wonted spirit and judgment attracted attention in
the east, for on the 7th of June, 1241, the barons,
knights, and citizens of the kingdom of Jerusalem
petitioned Frederick II. to appoint the Earl of
Leicester vicegerent of Palestine during the minority of King Conrad.† But Simon returned to
England about this time. The Earl of Cornwall had
left Palestine on the 3rd of May, and during the
summer he landed at Trapani, visited his sister, the
empress, in Sicily, and afterwards her husband, on the
continent.‡ If Simon, the other brother-in-law, took
the same route he would probably be present on this
occasion, perhaps himself bearing the petition from

* Chronica Albrici Monachi Trium Fontium in Mon. Germ. Hist.
SS. xxiii, 948. Cf. Wilkins, History of the Crusades, vi. 604 *et seq.*

† M.S. Cotton. Vespas. F. I., quoted by Hudson Turner,
Manners and Household Expenses, etc., p. xix. Quil nos baut a
bail mon sire Simon de Montfort Conte de Leicestre jusqe alage
de nostre seignor le Roi Conrad.

‡ Matth. Par. 568. The meeting took place at the end of June
in Terni or before Rieti. Böhmer, Reg. Imp. 1198–1254, p. 190.
Schirrmacher, Kaiser Friedrich der Zweite, iii. 224.

Jerusalem. Their father's name may have made participation in a crusade incumbent upon the Montforts; but the Earl of Leicester's adventurous spirit was no more captivated by the idea of oriental glory than his father had been by the prospect of taking part in the conquest of Constantinople. The elder Simon yielded implicit obedience to the prohibition of the great Pope; the younger, on the other hand, was not in the best repute with the Curia, and repeatedly became involved in the policy of the mighty Hohenstaufen Emperor. Even during this expedition his eyes could not fail to be opened afresh to the growing opposition to the temporal power of the Papacy.

It may be inferred that during these years his personal fate was determined by the alternate predominance of imperial and Papal influence at the Court of Westminster. After his return from the crusade, he retained Henry's favour the more easily because the death of the aged Gregory IX. (August 21st, 1241), was followed by an interregnum of nearly two years, excepting only the three weeks of Celestin IV.'s pontificate, and this vacancy of the Holy See left its trace even on the domestic policy of England. When no longer watched over by a legate, King Henry was compelled to be the more on his guard against the demands of the estates. He now sought to raise a barrier against them by systematically promoting his wife's grasping kindred. The situation was not one in which he could cherish personal animosity against the Earl of Leicester, who, as a foreigner, was himself likewise obnoxious to many of the nobles. Moreover, his dynastic ambition, zealously encouraged by favourites, plunged him into a foreign war, and it was obviously desirable to ' be on friendly terms with two of his brothers-in-law, Frederick II. and Earl Simon.

The King of France, Louis IX., had gradually extended his power over the provinces south of the Loire, and at last installed his brother Alphonso as Count of Poitou. This measure was felt bitterly as a challenge, and as a disgraceful insult to the crusading Earl of Cornwall, who still bore at least the title of a Count of Poitou; moreover, after some hesitation, the neighbouring Count de la Marche, step-father of the royal brothers, came forward as a partisan of the Plantagenet claims, and by his intrigues and the suggestion of assistance from Toulouse and Aragon, he inflamed the passion for military glory at Westminster. War was at once determined upon; the unsuccessful expedition to Britanny, in 1230, and the present truce with France seemed wholly forgotten. Towards the end of January, 1242, the king summoned all the magnates of the realm to London to discuss urgent business of State, but, as he would grant no concessions, they drew up an energetic protest and refused his demand for a subsidy.* Even

* The writ omnibus episcopis, abatibus, comitibus et baronibus in Reports from the Lords' Committee touching the dignity of a Peer, iii. p. 7, a die Sti. Hilarii in 15 dies ad tractandum nobiscum . . . de arduis negotiis nostris, statum nostrum et totius regni

then Henry adhered obstinately to his purpose, and succeeded at least in extorting money from some individual barons, abbots, and priors, and compelling a considerable number of the former to accompany him in person.

In May he embarked on his ill-considered voyage to the Garonne, accompanied by the Queen, his brother, seven earls, and three hundred knights. He first encamped northward in Saintes, summoned the warlike nobility of his domains in Southern France to appear under arms, and even sent for troops from Ireland and Wales. On the 22nd of July the English were unable to prevent the passage of the Charente, at Taillebourg, by Louis' army, and they were defeated in battle because the Poitevins, who had invited them to cross the Channel, went over to the enemy with Hugh de la Marche at their head. Much valuable booty fell into the hands of the French. The English army would have been annihilated and the King taken prisoner if the Earls of Leicester, Salisbury, and Norfolk had not valiantly covered the retreat to the Garonne.* The Court afterwards remained for a

nostri specialiter tangentibus. Matth. Par. 579, die Martis prox. ante Purif. B. Virginis (January 28). Compare Geschichte von England, iii. 647 and Stubbs' Constit. History, ii. 58–60.

* Henry III.'s report to the Emperor Frederick, Rymer, i. 206, Sept. 19 ; but the year 1232 is an error. The date appears from the Rot. Vascon. 26 Henry III. membr. 5, of which, unfortunately, only a few sheets have been printed, but never published. Matth. Par. 591–596.

E

considerable time at Bordeaux, and the good understanding between the King and Simon was confirmed,
in spite of the hostile influences which the Count of
Toulouse and the King of Aragon constantly sought
to exercise against the house of Montfort. The King
repeatedly made provision for his entertainment, and
as counsellor he ranked only second to Earl Richard. *
After Richard and most of the other nobles had
returned to England, where the estates again obstinately refused to defray the expenses of the war,
Simon maintained his confidential position in a country
which had once lain within the circle of his father's
conquests, and where the self-governing fiefs had since
those days been relieved from all the restraints of a
centralizing government. He made use of the time to
observe keenly the party tactics of the nobles, the
position of the towns, the relation of the English
crown to these untrustworthy vassals, and the constantly changing temper of the people. Henry
embarked for England in September, 1243, after
concluding a truce for five years with France. The
whole of Poitou was surrendered; but, for the present,
at least, he secured the Duchy of Guienne. Simon
probably followed the king home, and the custody of
Kenilworth Castle was soon afterwards committed to
him, doubtless as a sign of royal favour. The Earl and

* Quingentas marcas de dono nostro, July 2 ; quinquaginta
marcas de annuo feodo, Sept. 8. Evidence at the investiture of
one of Richard's vassals, Aug. 3, Rot. Vascon. 26 Henry III.
membr. 2, 3, 11.

Countess had already resided there, and a few years later it was granted to the latter for life.*

For several years Simon remained a silent spectator of the growing evils of the King's misgovernment. The prelates, earls, and barons summoned to Westminster in 1244, made another fruitless effort to promote worthier appointments to the high offices of State, and a more frugal administration of the exchequer. At the time when Pope Innocent IV. undertook the life and death struggle with the Hohenstaufen Emperor, and the Church, as well as the princes and peoples of the west, were stunned by the world-shaking transactions at Lyons, Henry III. was again more willingly than ever under the direction of Rome; but, in proportion as he yielded to it in his weakness, the quarrel with his own vassals acquired greater intensity. The clergy were indignant at the boundless demands of the Papal court. Extremely ingenious in the invention of provisions, taxes, and perquisites, and in conferring foreign benefices upon insatiable Italians, it had just discovered in England an inexhaustible source of wealth and a means of meeting the enormous cost of the great war. The nobles saw with growing anger that lay rapacity kept pace with this clerical system. The queen's uncle, Archbishop Boniface, was joined, as occasion served, by his brothers, Amadeus, the reigning Count of Savoy, and Thomas. A fourth, Peter, established him-

* Rot. Lit. Pat. 28 Henry III. membr. 8, Febr. 13, 1244; 32 Henry III. membr. 11, Jan. 9, 1248.

self firmly in England, and conducted negotiations
with the courts of Lyons and Paris in the interest of
the dynasty, without regard to that of the nation.
Unlike the earlier Plantagenets, Henry was not without sentiments of piety; and when his mother Isabella
died, in 1246, he interested himself zealously on
behalf of his numerous step-brothers and sisters. Two
of them were altogether provided for in England, to
the constant vexation of the native nobility. The
elder, William of Valence, an arrogant and voluptuous
knight of the Provençal type, caused the earldom of
Pembroke to be assigned him; for Aimar, the second,
no benefice was accounted rich enough until he was
appointed to the noble bishopric of Winchester, even
before he had reached the canonical age.

Amid such oppressions and spoliations the opposition which had long existed naturally grew stronger.
The Church repeatedly made complaint to the Pope
himself through the mouth of procurators; and the
courageous Bishop of Lincoln, who at home never forgot
his office and vocation before high or low, went twice
to Lyons that he might appeal personally to the con-
science of the Holy Father. Grosseteste always preserved an independence which, while it was eccle-
siastically blameless, by its national character recalled
the memory of Stephen Langton. He also saw in free
discussion and the decisions of the great council of the
realm the only legitimate means of inducing the
sovereign to consider his position. And at this time
the importance of the almost periodical assemblies,

already called parliaments,* steadily increased. The
spiritual and temporal lords protested more and more
fiercely from year to year against the shameless avarice
of the Papal court, and the long-standing national
grievances. For wasteful expenditure they desired to
substitute carefully regulated finances, under the
superintendence of the chief tax-payers; instead of
the crowds of foreign favourites and low-born officials,
they desired to see great State functionaries appointed
by agreement between the King and his tenants-in
chief, lay and clerical.

For five years the Earl of Leicester watched these
profitless proceedings without joining any party; he
was untroubled in his personal relations, and happy in
his family. His wife had already borne him three
sons; the two elder were seen accompanying their
parents to one or another famous abbey at the time of
the Easter solemnities, when he shared in the worship
of the monks, and thanked them in princely wise for
their princely hospitality.† United in closest friend-

---

* First officially Rot. Lit. Claus. 28 Henry III. membr. 13,
1244. Parliamentum Runemede quod fuit inter Dom. Johannem
Regem patrem nostrum et Barones suos Angliæ. Cf. Ann. de
Dunstaplia, 164, a. 1244. Further Matth. Par. 696, a. 1246 con-
venit ad parliamentum generalissimum. Cf. Geschichte von
England, iv. 668; Gneist, Geschichte und heutige Gestalt der
Aemter und des Verwaltungsrechts in England. 2nd edition, 1866,
i. 293, and for the parliaments from 1244 to 1248, Stubbs' Const.
Hist. ii. 61–66.

† On the visit to Waverley, in Sussex, on Palm Sunday, 1245,
Annales Waverl. Luard, Annales Monastici (Rer. Brit. med. ævi

ship to the Bishop of Lincoln and the Bishop's trusty friend, Adam of Marsh, the learned Franciscan teacher at Oxford, he confided to them* all his anxieties concerning the widening schism between the King and the estates, and the position of the Church, threatened as it was by the secularising tendencies of the age. Already Adam acquired the position of father-confessor at the Earl's court, in small things as in great. A zealous correspondent, he was the medium of epistolary intercourse between the friends. When the Bishop's cook died, he begged Eleanor to choose a fit successor from among her domestics.† But soon the pastor was charged with graver commissions.

In 1248 the King determined upon sending the Earl of Leicester to Gascony, but not with the object of ridding himself of him, for at this time they were on the most friendly terms with one another. So lately as the preceding October, Simon had returned from a mission to the French court, the object of which was to prolong and confirm the truce concluded five years

SS.) ii. 336. In the year 1263 Simon was admitted by the prior of Dunstaple into the brotherhood. Ann. de Dunst. Luard, Ann. Monast. iii. 226.

* Ipsius consilio tractabat ardua, tentabat dubia, finivit inchoata, ea maxime, per quæ meritum sibi succrescere æstimabat. Will. Rishanger, continuator of Matth. Paris, ed. Riley, Rer. Brit. med. ævi SS. 36.

† Ipsa autem non tantum de beneplacito vestro non est molestata, etc. Adam de Marisco to Bishop Robert, Brewer, Monumenta Franciscana, p. 170. Rerr. Brit. med. ævi SS. 1858. Adam's letters are collected in a codex, but all are undated.

earlier. He had been present at the February parliament, and had heard the tumultuous demands that the
offices of justiciary, chancellor, and treasurer should
be conferred upon such men as the estates could
approve, but he had taken no part in the violent opposition. Inspired, like some others, by a flickering
outburst of enthusiasm, he had just taken the cross,
with his wife and their whole family,* but this could
not prevent his compliance when the King called upon
him to accept an eminently arduous and responsible
post for the long term of six years,† conferring upon
him the high rank of viceroy (locum tenens), instead
of the ordinary title of seneschal. After he had com-
pleted the necessary preparations, in other words, had
borrowed money from the London citizens, he hastened in October to Bordeaux, travelling through
France, where the government appeared to give but a
hesitating assent to the proposals of peace from England.

The position of affairs in the duchy was more perilous than before. The ever-restless native nobility
defied the authority of the Plantagenets under the
leadership of the powerful Vicomte Gaston de Béarn,
whose artful mother had obtained considerable grants
from Henry III. in 1242. From the south, King
Theobald of Navarre pressed upon the disordered pro-

* Matth. Paris, 739, 742.

† Rot. Lit. Pat. 32 Henr. III., membr. 2, Sept. 7, 1248. Matth.
Par. 838, Confecit ei chartam suam de custodia per sex annos
continuanda.

vince, whilst, even in spite of the peace, the progress
of the French monarchy made itself constantly felt cu
the north. Also, the internal confusion in England
produced an effect even here ; for the government and
seneschals were incessantly changed, according to the
King's caprice, and greatly to the injury of all conti-
nuity in political and financial affairs. Already a
hostile faction in the towns was considering the expe-
diency of transferring the source of their wealth, the
exportation of wine, from England to Spain. Simon's
actual task was to avert the immediate loss of Aquitaine, the province which Eleanor of Poitou had
brought to the English crown a century before. He
devoted himself to it with such promptitude and energy
that, after Gaston had been brought to submission, the
unruly knights of the duchy became mindful of their
fealty, and the King of Navarre acquiesced in the decision of an umpire upon certain boundary disputes.*
The Earl caused universal astonishment by arriving at
court in December, with proofs of the complete pacification of the province, and received the thanks of the
sovereign in due form.†

In February, 1249, he returned to the south, and
whilst at Paris, where he had important commissions to
discharge, he addressed a remarkable letter to the King,

---

* Rymer, i. 269, Feb. 6, 1249.

† Grates vobis referimus copiosas de sollicitudine nec non et
laboribus immensis, negotiis nostris terræ nostræ Wasconiæ
vigilanter a virilitate vestra multotiens impensis. Rymer i. 271.
Cf. Matth. Paris, 757, 767.

the only one that is preserved from his pen. It describes the condition of Gascony, and gives a first glimpse of the difficulties of his position between the rebels of southern France and the busy intrigues of the English court. He* states, that during the recent disorders many Gascon noblemen had forfeited their property; it could never be restored to them by the authorised tribunals of the country, and, according to the latest tidings from Bordeaux, they and their adherents had sworn to regain it by force. A revolt might be confidently expected towards Whitsuntide, and Simon would be exposed to great personal danger; for, as representative of the rights of the crown and of the common people, he was hated by the nobility of the country.† Before he proceeded thither, the King must therefore furnish him with fresh instructions, and, above all, with indispensable military supplies, for not a penny from the revenues of the country was at his disposal; they were absorbed by the imposts of the French King. Moreover, an ordinary army and ordinary generalship would avail little against a people who, like robbers or free-lancers, fell upon the enemy, and destroyed his property in numerous troops of twenty, thirty, or forty men. For all these reasons, Simon urgently desired to have another interview with

* Donnée à Paris la veille de Pasques (April 8). Although the signature is lacking, no one but Simon can have written the letter. Shirley, Royal Letters, ii. 52.

† Por ce que je sui si mauvoleu de les graunz genz de la terre, por ce que je sostien voz dreitures et de la poure genz contre aus.

the King before proceeding southward; all the more
because Henry would hear various dark accusations,
implying that his brother-in-law was himself the instigator of the apprehended revolt. The most necessary provisions had been already made for the royal
castles and garrisons on the Garonne, and the Earl's
negotiations with the Paris parliament took a favourable course, he therefore crossed the Channel once
more, chiefly for the purpose of counteracting the
effect which the expected machinations of his enemies
might produce upon the fickle-tempered King.

After having thus, as he believed, secured his ground
at home, he defeated Gaston and his accomplices a
second time during the summer, and sent them prisoners to London. He followed up this success by
planting strong posts all over the country, and the
King appeared to signify his approval by granting him
the Irish revenues and the proceeds of a great sale
from the royal wine stores, to enable him to complete
the security of Gascony.* But by the very messenger
who brought these welcome communications, the King
announced to his viceroy that he had set free the
Vicomte de Béarn and the Knight Arnauld de Hasta,
and permitted them to return home, because they had
penitently submitted, and sworn eternal loyalty.†
Either from wilful folly, or malevolence instigated by
others, Henry himself broke in upon his deputy's
vigorous work. In 1250, but not till then, Simon took

* Patents of 28th Nov. and 28th Dec. Shirley, ii. 55, 56.
† Shirley, ii. 56, 57, Dec. 27, 28. Cf. Matth. Paris, 775.

Egremont, Gaston's strongest castle, subdued another dangerous rebel, the Vicomte de Fronzac, and extorted due respect from the haughty guilds of Bordeaux, who had likewise assumed a hostile attitude towards him. On the other hand, there was no lack of testimony to his integrity ; the citizens of Castel d'Uza represented to the King that they had first obtained a hearing from the Earl of Leicester in an old suit against the Lord of Tartas, to which former English governors had always turned a deaf ear.*

Nevertheless, the Earl was overwhelmed with difficulties. Guienne was widely separated from its Duke by the channel and the entire kingdom of France, and it was still well-nigh impossible to retain it in face of the spirit of unbridled independence. The supplies furnished by the crown were instantly consumed, like a drop of water upon burning stone, and Simon had long been unable to maintain his position without drawing upon his own private resources. He caused his English forests to be felled, and devoted the proceeds and the revenues of the fief of Unfranville, which he held in wardship, to the payment of his troops, and the support of the fortresses he had been obliged to erect. It is possible that he aggravated the difficulty of his undertaking by excessive severity, either de-

---

* Hanc veritatem et querelam ostendimus multis ballivorum vestrorum, qui nullum ibidem consilium posuerunt, donec per Dei gratiam Dominus Simon de Monte Forti, Comes Leicestriæ, venit in Vasconiam cui hanc veritatem ostendimus et querelam. Shirley, ii. 58.

signedly or because the faithlessness of the race he
was trying to subdue filled him with indignation. But
the Prince whose sovereign rights he had undertaken
to defend did most to ruin his work. For after Gaston
and his comrades were set free, they artfully contrived
to keep the way open to Henry's suspicious ear, whilst
they renewed the rebellion at home, as if it were
directed against the viceroy alone. To defend his
cause against them, and to induce the King's government to grant more continuous support, the Earl of
Leicester had made another visit to England in the
winter. He appeared before the King at the feast of
Epiphany, 1251, reminded him of his own experiences
among the southern French in 1242, and pressed for
supplies of men and money. The characteristic reply
was, " By God's Head, thou speakest truth, sir Earl ;
and since thou servest me so doughtily, I will not deny
thee sufficient help. But grave complaints have
reached me that thou hast thrown into prison, or even
put to death, people who came to thee peacefully, or
whom thou hadst thyself summoned." Simon replied
that the notorious treachery of his accusers must prove
their falsehoods, and the King complied with his wishes
so far as to renew his authority, and grant him 3000
marks. The Earl added moneys of his own, and levied
several hundred Brabant soldiers.*

It was during this brief sojourn that Simon made
some remarkable regulations for the conduct of
his household affairs, and again rejoiced in a free

* Matth. Paris, 779.

interchange of thought with his trusted friends. The Bishops of Lincoln and Worcester, the two Franciscans Adam of Marsh, and Gregory of Bosell, were his frequent guests.* By word and by pen they discussed the "signs of the times," and such stupendous events as the death of the great Hohenstaufen Emperor, Louis IX.'s disaster at Mansura, the desperate condition of the Holy Land, and the growing grievances in Church and State, as well as the Earl's personal trials.† The devoted Adam probably found in the duties of his Oxford lectureship an excuse for tarrying long at Kenilworth; he learnt to his great joy, upon trustworthy authority, that the King and Queen, Earl Richard, and other distinguished nobles and prelates again showed signs of a more amicable disposition towards Simon.‡ The same zealous friend and pastor was indefatigable as a medium of communication, and found Simon's heart always open to the religious and world-regenerating ideas of this reforming band. Eleanor wished this time to accompany her husband to Gascony, and Adam

---

* The learned John of Basingstoke, who had studied in Athens and understood Greek, was also one of this group. Simon had to lament his death in 1252, gemitus et lachrymas multiplicavit comitis memorati. Matth. Paris, 835.

† It is difficult to arrange Adam's many letters, but I assign to this date, Nos. 144 and 145 in Brewer's Monumenta Franciscana, p. 276 et seq., as they can only have been addressed to Simon whilst he was in England.

‡ Longe sereniorem solito, sit benedictus Deus pacis et dilectionis, conceperunt benevolentiam. To Simon, No. 146.

aided them in placing their young sons under Robert Grosseteste's care and training.* There is no subsequent letter in which he does not report to the parents of the children and their reverend guardian.

Simon embarked early in spring, better equipped than before, and a third time succeeded in quelling the insurrection. Adam continued to send him intelligence of passing events, and the disposition of the court, mingled with judicious advice upon his own conduct. When Simon gave himself up for lost, driven, as he sometimes was to despair by the untrustworthiness of the King, who seemed to respect neither the ties of blood nor his own plighted word, the pious Franciscan not only pointed him to the consolatory books of the Old Testament, Job and Proverbs, but would also narrate an encouraging conversation with the King, whose confidence in the Earl's integrity might be preserved unshaken, if those who surrounded him did not prevent it.† The same messenger, John de la Haye, an often-mentioned servant of Simon's, bore also a letter from Adam to the Countess, reminding her that amid the cares, conflicts, and expenditure in which her husband had

---

* Dominus Comes Leycestriæ, si contingat eum maturius redire in Vasconiam deliberatione cum domina comitissa et mecum super hoc habita, proponit, etc. To Grosseteste, No. 25; compare Rishanger, ed. Riley, 36; eique suos parvulos tradidit nutriendos.

† Si in hac parte ipsum favorabiliter sua fulcirent latera.

involved himself for the sake of preserving her
brother's possessions, it was for her to use her
influence with both to promote charity and calmly
considered measures.* The wish of the husband and
wife to have with them a father-confessor from the
brotherhood which they regarded with so much
affection, was also a subject of discussion, but it
was difficult to carry out the project. Bosell had
already prepared to undertake the journey, when
he was unfortunately prevented by work for the
Archbishop of Canterbury. Then again, there were
evil tidings in the form of a long letter of consolation,
with digressions upon the troublous condition of
Christendom and of England in particular. It told of
increased bitterness on the part of the King, evidently
consequent upon certain expressions of the Earl's, who
could with difficulty repress his proud and passionate
words, and was therefore exhorted to greater reticence,
" because the fool's heart is in his mouth, but the wise
man's mouth is in his heart."† Another journey
to England was now deemed necessary, and the
faithful adviser constantly insisted, especially to
the Countess, upon the need for watchfulness and

---

* I associate Nos. 140 and 161, because the same messenger is
named in both, but Brewer, p. 297, would refer the latter letter to
1252.

† The long letter, No. 143, written after the 18th Oct. (1251),
when Adam relates that he had excited the King's anger by a
sermon.

discretion.* After Simon had taken all such pre-
cautions as were possible for the protection of his
fortresses, he and his wife went in November through
France to London. The King would scarcely have
gone to welcome them if his step-brother, Guy of
Lusignan, had not been one of the company.†

Meanwhile the Gascons were again in movement,
not only with arms in their hands, but also with
increasingly bitter complaints against the man who
could, if it were by any means possible, enforce among
them the restraints essential to public order. They
artfully described him as the worst traitor to the
crown, because he enriched himself by extorting their
property from nobles and citzens with unheard-of
violence, whilst the King, incessantly urged by the
Pope to undertake a crusade, was now helplessly
embarrassed.‡ When Simon complained that men
long convicted of malice and knavery received more
credence than he, the servant of the crown, the
King replied drily that, since he was conscious of
innocence, he could but desire an impartial investigation. He had come to seek further supplies, and

* De profectione vestra erga regnum Angliæ cavendum est
omnino ne fiat sine magna deliberatione et provisione discreta.
Adam to Eleanor, No. 160.

† Matth. Paris, 810.

‡ Letters of complaint from the corporation of La Réole and
the Vicomte Raymond de Soule against Simon's administration,
and especially against his seneschal William Pigorel at the
earliest, Feb. 1252. Shirley, ii. 72 *et seq.*, compared with Matth.
Paris, 814.

especially compensation for the very considerable advances he had himself made.

On the 4th of January, 1252, eleven barons of high rank, but some of them ill-disposed, were actually appointed arbitrators to give judgment upon the amount of his pecuniary claims.* But instead of dealing fairly with him in this affair, Henry at the same time nominated two commissioners, who were sent to Gascony in order to institute formal proceedings against him. The two emissaries were the Master of the Templars in England, Rocelin de Fos, a Gascon by birth, and Henry of Wingham, who had once himself been seneschal at Bordeaux and was now one of the royal secretaries.† But the Englishman and the Frenchman drew opposite conclusions from their investigations, and though they were joined by William of Valance, the King's malicious half-brother and the head of the foreign party, the only result was a written accusation drawn up by the knights and some towns and fortified places of Guienne. It was to be delivered at Westminster by a company of distinguished delegates, with Archbishop Girald of Bordeaux, a man of very doubtful loyalty, at their head. The commissioners further put a stop to the

* Patent, Shirley, ii. 68. Likewise the Protectio quamdiu fuerit in servicio regis in Vasconia. Rot. Lit. Pat. 36 Henry III. membr. 11, Febr. 22nd.

† Letter to Queen Blanche of France, an infringement of the truce being also discussed, and authorization of January 6th. Shirley, ii. 69, 70.

F

struggle between Gaston and Simon's troops around
the fortress of La Réole, and obtained a royal
command that Simon, who had hastily followed them
in order to prevent one-sided proceedings, should
appear in London at a prescribed date after Easter.*
It might be difficult for his accusers to prove individual cases in which the harshness and tyranny
alleged against him had been exercised for his
own advantage, and not in the King's service, yet the
current of adverse opinion was already so strong that
these accusers easily found a place among his judges.
They arrived in England at the same time as he,
and would have attacked him at once had it not been
necessary to await the report of a second commission
despatched by the King to the Garonne for the
purpose of collecting further evidence. It was
composed, like the first, of one Englishman and one
Gascon, Nicolas de Molis, who had likewise been
seneschal in 1244, and Drogo de Valentin. These
men brought back much testimony evidently favourable to the accused; and though Henry desired his
ruin and had just liberated one of his bitterest
enemies, the unruly Arnaut of Egremont, he was
compelled to leave the course of justice free. In the

* Report of Fos and Wingham, erroneously referred to the
year 1253 by Champollion Figeac, Lettres de Rois, etc., i. 116.
Shirley, ii. 76, gives the correct date, March 6th, 1252.
Petition of the Gascons, Petunt quod dominus comes Leycestriæ
presens sit in Anglia, etc. Letter No. 1604 in the Public Record
Office. Henry's writ to Simon, March 23rd, a die Paschæ
in unum mensem. Shirley, ii. 81 ; cf. Matth. Paris, 828, 832.

week between Ascension and Whitsuntide the proceedings commenced, and the Earl of Leicester stood
opposed to his angry enemies before the assembled
Council of the realm.*

Simon read no friendly greeting in the King's face,
but only suppressed animosity. The Gascons, on the
other hand, were encouraged by the favour shown
them, and began with loud and violent complaints,
supporting them by references to the previous ad-
ministrations, which they described as rich in blessings
to the country. Simon in reply denied the credibility
of men who revolted against every kind of authority. The Earl of Cornwall had some years earlier
experienced the faithlessness of the same race, as
well as the inconstancy of the King, who had left him
also unsupported upon similar grounds, and to him
and to other previous governors, Simon appealed. The
defence produced a most favourable impression, not
only upon sure friends like Bishop Walter of Worcester, but also upon the most influential members of
the Council, as the Earls of Cornwall and Gloucester,
so that they showed themselves disposed to defend
the honour and the estates of their peer, whose justice
and disinterestedness were as unimpeachable as his
heroism. But they assisted him rather with good
will than with decisive words and deeds, and Simon

---

* Matth. Paris, 836 : Circa Pentecosten, paucis ante diebus;
compare Ann. de Dunstaplia, 184. According to Adam's account
to Grosseteste: Circa festum ascensionis Domini (May 9th).
Brewer, Monum. Francisc. 123.

was left practically alone in the task of proving by
documents and witnesses the blamelessness of his
whole course of action, and showing that he had provoked these accusations by seeking to bring to obedience a turbulent people who waged war against all
law and justice.* His enemies became more and
more embarrassed and entangled amid their own lies
during the many days occupied by single debates, and,
to the satisfaction of the prelates and barons, a decision
in vindication of slandered innocence was impending
when the King, who relapsed into personal abuse at
every opportunity, provoked his brother-in-law to an
unexampled quarrel. When reminded by the Earl of
the compensations which were due, and his own most
sacred promises, Henry said : " 1 am in nowise bound
to observe promises to a knave and traitor such as
thou, because thou hast withdrawn thyself from all
contracts." Simon had hitherto controlled his impetuous temper with admirable moderation,† but now
he let loose his indignation, called the King a liar, and
said the hour when he spoke such words would have
been an evil one (mala hora) had not his diadem protected him. " Can one ever believe thee as a Chris-

* Nec Deum timentes, nec hominem reverentes, sine rege
sine lege agentes, foedera violantes, affectionem non curantes . . .
idem comes studiis quibus valuit coercere curabat." Adam de
Marisco, l.c.

† Per omnia moderantiam mansuetudinis cum magnanimitatis
maturitate et ad suum Dominum et ad adversarios suos obser-
vans. Ibid.

tian? Hast thou ever confessed thy sins? Or if thou hast, was it with bruised and penitent heart?" To which Henry replied with burning anger: "No act of my life do I repent so sorely as that I permitted thee to come to England to win lands and honours and grow fat and insolent." He would have gladly caused him to be seized and thrown into the Tower, but he feared the assembled peers. They were able by their intervention to moderate the indecorous character of the proceedings, but they did not venture upon a vigorous encounter with the monarch's habitual autocratic caprice.* The King was base and revengeful, but powerless to command; Simon's energy was proudly impatient of resistance, and collision between them produced a violent explosion; the scene left an impression that seeds of mutual distrust sown years before had borne their fruit, and that peace and reconciliation could never be established by ordinary means between men whose natures were so antagonistic, especially because their outward position with regard to one another was incongruous.

The King's caprice even prevented any decisive result from the present contention. Simon prayed for

---

* Compare the scene in Matth. Paris, 857, with Adam, p. 127: Post noctis unius intervallum reditur ruptis loris æquitatis et justitiæ contra comitem Leycestriæ ad minarum sævitias: tumultuante regis iracundia. The Franciscan reports to Grosseteste the information which he received directly from the Bishop of Worcester; but the monk of St. Albans also frequently had the testimony of eye-witnesses in writing the last years of his great chronicle.

fresh equipment and the most complete authority to
terminate the war in Gascony, with the condition that
he and his followers should receive compensation for
their losses. On the other hand, he offered to resign
the post which had been conferred upon him for six
years if, under the guarantee of the great Council of
the realm, the same security were granted to him and
his against all loss, especially against prejudice to their
honour. The King would hear nothing of either pro-
position, and the Council preserved a cowardly silence,
whilst, by his own absolute authority, he issued a
series of proclamations commanding both the contending parties to keep the peace until he or his eldest
son should appear in Gascony at Candlemas. As
conservators of the truce, Rocelin de Fos and Nicolas
de Molis were commissioned to hold the enemies apart
during the interval ; the town of Bordeaux was charged
to keep the peace, the wardens of the corporation
being elected in equal numbers from the two parties.*
In the judgment of well-disposed patriots † these were
senseless measures, well calculated to ruin the Earl,
but no less likely to issue in the loss of the province,
and to cost Henry the personal esteem of his subjects.

Simon submitted to the King's decision in spite of
its imprudence, and after the course that matters had

* Writs of the 6th and 16th June ; Shirley, ii. 89, 90, 391.

† De aliis pluribus ineptiis, nisi divinitas subveniat, plurimum
nocituris. Adam, l.c.

taken, Henry, on his part, could not prevent the Earl's
departure for Bordeaux on the 13th of June,* for the
purpose of solving the difficulty on his own responsibility. His accusers, who had sworn his death, had
immediately hastened away likewise, enraged by the
bearing of the English nobility and Council. It was
rumoured that they were encouraged by certain words
in which the King expressed a wish that this lover
and instigator of war might be satiated and recompensed as his Father had been before in the same
southern region.† It was not accidentally that at the
same time the governorship of Gascony was conferred
by royal patent upon Prince Edward, though still in
his nonage, whilst the hostile factions were enjoined to
keep the peace until the King arrived with his son.‡
The secret expectation that the hated governor would
work his own ruin § was wholly disappointed. Simon
resumed the war with his wonted courage and good
fortune, evidently purposing to obtain for himself the
justice that was denied him, and finding no lack of
assistance among his French fellow-countrymen. His
military skill proved superior to all the craft of his

---

* Feria quinta post festum beati Barnabæ. Adam, l.c.

† Matth. Paris, 844.

‡ Rot. Lit. Pat. 36 Henr. III., membr. 6, June 9, and Rymer,
i. 282, June 13, the day on which Simon embarked for Boulogne.

§ Evidenced by the command to investigate Simon's expenditure for the castle of Cusac and to restore Blancfort to its rebel
owner; August 10. Shirley, ii. 91, 92.

enemies; he not only succeeded in rescuing his hard-
pressed adherents, but also captured five of the rebel
ringleaders and sent them triumphantly to the King.*
It was not until he had vindicated his honour, and redeemed at least a part of his pledge, that he left the
country and sojourned for a while in France. He was
there in December when Queen Blanche died, and, her
son Louis being still absent in the East, the princes
and peers discussed the appointment of a new regency.
In their perplexity they would have brought Simon
forward, but fate had already attached him too firmly
to his second home, although it repulsed him so often.
Twice he unhesitatingly declined the most honourable
proposals.†

He might then watch with triumph, if he were so
disposed, how his worst predictions were fulfilled
during the next year; how the King of Castile threatened the English supremacy, and Béarn immediately
threw himself into his arms, with other Gascon nobles
who had hitherto artfully preserved a semblance of
loyalty to the crown; how Henry III., unmindful of
his repeated crusading vows, involved himself in fresh
money difficulties with the clergy and the baronage,
and set out upon an expedition altogether profitless
and fool-hardy. In October, 1253, Simon had the most
perfect satisfaction possible, for, when the King found
himself utterly helpless among the Gascons, he at last
sent for his brother-in-law to come under a safe conduct, and bade him bring whatever horsemen and

---

* Matth. Paris, 852, 853.   † Matth. Paris, 865.

bowmen his military reputation would enable him to gather together.* It speaks much for the Earl's magnanimity that, in the critical position of the two kingdoms, he lived a whole year as an exile in France without making use of his connections there to revenge the injuries he had received from his brother-in-law, the English King. Though a man of the sword, he was the friend of the most zealous preachers of peace in all Christendom. We still have their testimony that amid his heaviest trials, they did not cease to care for his spiritual well-being, and to check the impetuous ardour that threatened to ruin him and the good cause represented by him.

So early as the end of 1251, Adam of Marsh had written to Grosseteste that now, if ever, the Earl and Countess stood in need of his sagacious counsel. Both had long seen and dreaded the approaching catastrophe,† and both sought to influence Simon by word and by pen when he was conducting his own affairs in England.‡ When he returned to Gascony for the last time in the summer of 1252, Adam not only exhorted him to persevere in his noble zeal for the faith, but also informed him affectionately of the approaching delivery of his wife, whom he had left pregnant at

---

* Champollion Figeac, Lettres de Rois etc., i. 90; Oct. 4, 1253. Compare Geschichte von England, iii. p. 697, *et seq.*

† Epp. Ad. de Marisco, Nos. 22, 34.

‡ No. 135: Studeat, oro, vestræ discretionis diligentia cum effectu, Divinæ voluntati, secundum quod literæ præferunt incunctanter, adhibere consensum.

Kenilworth,* and of the health of his sons and the venerable Bishop of Lincoln. Grosseteste, Walter of Worcester, and Adam himself were working zealously to free the Earl from his difficulties, even looking to the Pope for help.† By their advice Simon had addressed himself to Rome, and Innocent IV. yielded to this intercession when he ordered an investigation against Archbishop Girald of Bordeaux, the bitterest and falsest of his enemies.‡ On his deathbed at Bugden in October, 1253, Grosseteste § bequeathed as his last greeting to Simon an injunction not to cherish anger against his King and liege lord on account of his violent words, but magnanimously to assist him in his perplexity. Thus these men again helped to save the royal family from bitter strife, and the realm from the immediate loss of a valuable province. They encouraged Simon once more to draw his sword generously in the King's service, and they obtained from the Pope bulls of excommunication ‖ against the muni-

* No. 136; compare No. 158 : Letter of congratulation to Elea-nor on the birth of a daughter, the youngest child as Mrs. Green points out, The Princesses of England, ii. 104.

† Locutus fui de negotio subventionis vobis faciendæ per indulgentiam Apostolicam ; Ep. 141. Also No. 161 may be placed here, a letter to the Countess which treats of magnificis eventibus domino comiti et vobis per Dei clementiam concessis.

‡ Breve to the Bishop of Clermont : Inn. IV., Ep. x. 642, (MS. Mus. Brit. Add. 15, 357) ; iii. Non. Apr. 1253.

§ Cui comes tanquam patri extitit familiarissimus ; Matth. Paris, 879 ; cf. 876.

‖ Rymer, i. 294, Dec. 21, 1253. Champollion Figeac, Lettres de Rois, etc. i. 99.

cipal officers of La Réole and the Vicomtes of Béarn, Chatillon, and Fronzac, which largely contributed to the final subjugation of the country.

A sort of amicable settlement of money claims was now arranged between the two brothers-in-law. In several considerable sums the King repaid what Simon had spent in his service, and compensated him at least in part for the remaining years of his government.* But this could not be called a reconciliation, and the Earl had already retired once more to France in the spring of 1254, when Henry, then at Bordeaux, concluded the important betrothal of his heir to Eleanor of Castile.

* Payment of 7000 marks, according to ₊Rot. Liberate, 38 Henr. III. membr. 8, 4. Also Rot. Lit. Pat. 37 Henr. III. membr. 11. Cf. Champollion Figeac, Lettres, i. 94, 95.

CHAPTER III.

THE EARL THROWS HIMSELF INTO THE POLITICAL OPPOSITION.

HENRY III. IN BORDEAUX AND PARIS ; THE SICILIAN CROWN
—THE KING AND EARL UPON TOLERABLY FRIENDLY
TERMS—THE DISTRESSED CONDITION OF ENGLAND—
RICHARD OF CORNWALL, KING OF THE ROMANS—
VICTORY OF THE ESTATES AT WESTMINSTER, 1258—
PARLIAMENT AT OXFORD IN JUNE—THE PROVISIONS OF
OXFORD—EXPULSION OF THE ALIENS—THE GOVERNMENT
OF THE BARONS—THE FIRST OPPOSITION ON THE PART OF
THE KNIGHTHOOD—PEACE WITH FRANCE NEGOTIATED BY
SIMON, 1259—THE KING AND EARL IN ENGLAND AND
FRANCE, 1260—RESTORATION OF THE MONARCHY, 1261
—KING AND EARL APPEAL TO THE MEDIATION OF
FRANCE, 1262—HENRY HIMSELF AGAIN AT THE FRENCH
COURT—LOUIS IX. DECLINES THE MEDIATION, 1263.

FOR a time the Earl of Leicester now almost disappeared from public life. His friendly relations
with the King were not re-established, neither did
he join the opposition party among the English
Barons. He lived in retirement with his family in

their French home, without professing permanent
allegiance and citizenship, or taking any part in
the remarkable conferences and treaties, the political
significance of which he could not fail to recognise.

Just at that time Henry's dynastic ambition led ✓
to extensive continental alliances, perilous to the
last degree to English independence. Whilst the
King was still at Bordeaux, the Spanish marriage
of the heir was followed by an eager acquiescence
in the craftiest designs of the court of Rome. Pope
Innocent IV. aimed at uprooting the last of the
Hohenstaufen lineage from southern Italy, by calling
a foreign prince to the throne of Naples and Sicily ;
and, after Richard, Earl of Cornwall, the possessor of
the rich tin and copper mines in that county, had
declined his proposals, he had selected Henry's
younger son Edmund, a boy of nine. The father's
delight was boundless, although the sums which
his kingdom had hitherto contributed towards the
furtherance of the Pope's temporal policy, must
inevitably be doubled in consequence. In the form of ✓
crusading grants, foreign exactions pressed more and
more heavily upon England and her dependencies.
Alexander IV. not only adhered to his predecessor's
design, but some years later, with Henry's zealous
co-operation,* he succeeded in enticing Earl Richard
to accept the elective crown of Germany in the

* The subject is well treated by A. Busson, Die Doppelwahl
des Jahrs 1257, und das römische Königthum Alfons X. von
Castilien : Münster, 1866, p. 10 *et seq.*

ecclesiastical interest.   The house of Plantagenet
did in fact rise to a European dignity and consequence
almost unparalleled at that epoch, but these deceptive
and visionary prospects were inevitably counterbalanced
by injury to the foundations of its real power.   " England appeared to be no longer a free kingdom,
applying its resources to its own ends; with all its
riches it was at the service of the Pope of Rome, and
the throne was an organ of the hierarchy."*

Other political designs were directed towards Paris.
It was only in consequence of Louis IX.'s continued
absence in the East, that the English had been left
unrestrained in Gascony.   Now the condition of his
kingdom, and the many complications among the States
of the West, called for his presence at home, where at
last he arrived in September, 1254.   The English
court had hitherto remained at Bordeaux, and it
was now immediately resolved to return home by
way of France, the inducements being partly devo-
tional sentiment, partly love of art, but chiefly schemes
of family policy.   In December, during this brilliant
visit to Paris, which must have again swelled the
amount of the English debts, the four Provençal
sisters were seen there together, the Queens of France
and England and the consorts of Richard of Cornwall
and Charles of Anjou.   Louis's noble and gentle
temper made personal intercourse easy, but no progress
was made towards an adjustment of the many points

* Ranke, Englische Geschichte, i. 98.   Details in my Geschichte
von England, iii. 696, 700, 707; and Stubbs' Constit. History, ii.
68–71.

in dispute, especially those relating to feudal rights, which caused incessant discord between the two kingdoms.

It is remarkable that although the Earl and Countess of Leicester were probably in the neighbourhood, he did not take part in these negotiations concerning foreign affairs,* and even Eleanor, the only surviving sister of the King, had no place in the circle of royal ladies. It was not till the 10th of May, 1255, when Henry had returned home and the Earl of Leicester was tarrying in France upon his own business that he, with Peter of Savoy, was again charged with the onerous task of renewing the French peace, which in July was accordingly prolonged for three years.† At this time the Countess had already returned to England, where she lived in solitude at Kenilworth. Her brother the King rejoiced her now and then with a present of game,‡ but the ostrangement between them was by no means forgotten. It had, on the contrary, become more marked since Eleanor, as well as her husband, had been among the creditors of the crown. When Henry purchased the county of Bigorre in Guienne, she had assisted him by the loan of 1000 marks. As

* A secret mission to Scotland in August, 1254 (Green, Lives of the Princesses of England, ii. 111), appears to be wholly unauthentic and based upon a misunderstanding.

† Simon's commission, Rot. Lit. Pat. 39 Henr. III. membr. 8 ; Peter's, Shirley, ii. 107 ; here it is said of Leicester, Qui pro quibusdam suis negotiis ad partes Franciæ se jam transtulit. The treaty, Rymer, i. 321.

‡ Rot. Lit. Claus. 39 Henr. III. membr. 10 ; 40 Henr. III. membr.7.

in many other cases, he was unable to pay the debt,
but referred her, July 8th, 1256, to his own debtors,
Roger Earl of Norfolk, or a Jew named Adam; this
was but an empty consolation, the more so because
Earl Richard's claims had long taken precedence of
all others. Bigorre remained mortgaged to the
Montforts, and many other arrears were still due
to them from the days of the government in
Gascony.*

Notwithstanding all this, the relations with the
court seemed gradually 'to improve. Simon was
among the chiefs of the nobility who on the 16th
of August, 1256, guaranteed the transfer of the fief of
Huntingdon to the young King Alexander III. of
Scotland.† The disputes with the clergy and
baronage of the realm had become more violent, and
Henry doubtless restored Simon to favour in order to
secure his support. On the 11th February, 1257,
several manors were granted him in fee, and on the
20th he was again nominated peace commissioner in
conjunction with the learned lawyer, Robert Waleran,
receiving at the same time express permission to
enter upon the heritage claimed by him in France,
if King Louis would put him in complete or partial
possession of it. On the same day he obtained leave
to dispose of his present property by testament,
the King as debtor, swearing for himself and his heirs

* The evidence from the Rot. Lit. Claus. Green, Princesses,
ii. 111, 112.

† Shirley, ii. 120.

never to contest the provisions he might make.* This spirit of compliance showed itself again in the summer of 1258, when the law was called upon to determine whether the village of Huddon appertained to the county of Berkshire or the barony of the Earl of Leicester.† But at that time Simon had chosen his side, and it was against the King his brother-in-law.

Since Henry's return from Gascony, the ill humour of the Lords had continually increased. He had recently incurred debts to the amount of 350,000 marks,‡ and immediately began to borrow again from his brother, to make illegal amercements upon the city of London, and to extort their usurious riches from the Jews, and from the officers of the exchequer in England. From the gulf in which he was sinking more and more deeply, he expected the estates to rescue him by voluntary aids. Hence, in return, the great council ✓ or Parliament, summoned at Easter, 1255, had again demanded a share in the choice of the three most important State functionaries, the Great Justiciary, Chancellor, and Treasurer, and that these officers should not be dismissed without consent of parliament. Although under different obligations to Pope and King, the Prelates and Barons declared themselves in closest alliance ; § but, as the court still showed no

* Documents in Shirley, ii. 121. 392.   Also Green, ii. 113.
† Shirley, ii. 393 ; July 5th, 1258.
‡ Matth. Paris, 913.
§ Ex parte universitatis ; Matth. Paris, 902.

G

signs of yielding, the fruitless negotiations were postponed till autumn. In the interval, Henry concluded'
the treaty concerning the Sicilian crown, and thereby,
with inconceivable rashness, made the Pope his largest
creditor. In order to conquer the districts already
occupied by King Manfred, he not only accepted the
most humiliating obligations on his son's behalf, but
also swore to send troops and to pay the totally imprac-
ticable sum of 135,541 silver marks.* Nevertheless,
it was with unbounded joy that he presented the young
Edmund to the reassembled peers in October, as King
of Sicily and Apulia, the boy wearing on his finger the
ring conferred by the Pope. Upon the question of
contributions, Master Rustand, the plenipotentiary of
the Curia, would not make terms with the assembly of
the clergy, or with their procurators, but only with
each individual person. Nevertheless, the greater
number were faithful to their secular allies, and the
estates as such refused every proposal because they
had not been called together in a body, as Magna
Charta expressly stipulated, and the affair of the
Sicilian crown had been concluded without their
consent.† The same attempts were repeated next
year, with the same result. In 1257 the clergy granted
an extraordinary aid upon a renewed confirmation of
the Great Charter, but three weeks later they con-
curred with the barons in unanimously refusing to

* Rymer, i. 316 et seq.
† Sine consilio suo et assensu baronagii sui; Matth. Paris,
902, 913; Annales de Burton, 360. Cf. Stubbs' Const. Hist. ii. 71.

conquer southern Italy for the Roman court with
English blood and gold ; although ingenious Papal
agents miserably impoverished the country, and by
threats of interdict and excommunication, sought
gradually to reduce both King and kingdom to submission.

As ill luck would have it, serious contentions broke
out at the same time with Scotland, where the unruly
nobility had driven their young king, Alexander III.,
to seek help and protection from his father-in-law of
England ; and in Wales, also, after Henry's eldest son
Edward had been invested with the Marches, the
national Prince, the youthful and aspiring Llewellyn,
rose in rebellion at the head of the native mountain
tribes, to assert the independence of their country.
Owing to lack of money, and the already dubious attitude of the gentry, the expeditions against both countries were inefficiently conducted ; both ended dis-
astrously, and the Scotch and Welsh even combined
in a military alliance.* Some slight advantage over
semi-barbarous enemies had been obtained by earlier
and more capable governments of a politically organized
State, but even this seemed now to be forfeited. In
every relation, by folly and fickleness, by obstinacy
and vanity, Henry had trifled away the affection of his
people and the honour of his kingdom.

But he was innocent of another disaster, which,
nevertheless, was equally potent in nourishing the
spirit of discontent and insubordination. The wet

- * Their treaty of March 18, 1858 ; Rymer, i. 370.

summer of 1257 ruined the corn harvest; wheat rose✓
during the winter to ten times its ordinary price, and
a general famine broke out among the common people,
who suffered largely from the other distresses of the
time.* It was impossible to overlook the dangers
whereby the monarchy and the progress of national
development would be threatened, if the passive but
persistent opposition of the Barons should now become
active, and the lower classes in town and country,
rough and ignorant, and still half-bound to the soil,
should become possessed by vague and uncompre-
hended ideas, and rise in a destructive insurrection.
Isolated convulsions of this kind had hitherto been
easily repressed ; the Anglo-Saxon peasant inherited
from his fathers the habit of endurance and toil in the
sweat of his brow, and he brooded on in stolid silence
in his old condition. But what if now a hero should
appear, who, with patriotic enthusiasm and political
acuteness, knew how to guide all classes towards a
goal which promised at once material ease and public
peace, in place of bitter want and universal shame ?

Since Stephen Langton, no great leader had appeared upon the thorny road whereby political rights
are attained.   Through John's humiliation before
Innocent III., the Bishops were fettered by a double
relationship to the Pope, and constant jealousies among
the Earls and Barons permitted no one man to achieve
distinction in the still very undeveloped assemblies.
The authority of the crown and its experienced judi-

* Geschichte von England, iii. 714.

cial and administrative officers was supreme in all
affairs of business. Earl Richard, the King's brother,
suffered frequent injuries like the rest, and might
perhaps have exercised an influence at once commanding and conciliatory, but his character lacked solidity,
and his position forbade him to disregard the dynastic
interests of the Plantagenets whenever they were
seriously at stake. His royal brother had for years
been mortgaged to him if to any one in the kingdom,
but his own hands were tied in consequence. Now,
on account of his world-renowned wealth, Richard had
been elected King by the Papal party in Germany,
without bringing any serious burdens upon the crown
and its vassals, as in the case of the Sicilian crown.
He left England in the spring of 1257, and thus
deprived the prelates and barons, temporarily at least,
of his personal counsel.

Such was the general position of affairs when the
Earl of Leicester came forward, and in a few years
made himself the leader of a popular movement. Personally, he was not unprepared for the position, but
forces of very diverse character supported and favoured
him. What induced him just at that moment to emerge
from his retirement? Through his marriage, his relationship to the King was well-nigh as close as that
of the other foreign nobles who domineered over the
country; but, unlike them, he carefully abstained from
dishonourably enriching himself with revenues and
offices, or from interfering precipitately in the public
business of the realm. His disinterested acceptance

of responsibility in Guienne, and the prudence and
courage he there manifested must rather have won
him the long-withheld esteem of the native English
Barons. He did not belong to the insatiable parasites,
but to the creditors of the court. Neither could it be
unobserved that, though Henry repeatedly restored
him to favour after gross ill-treatment, there remained
an unconquerable mutual repugnance between the two,
founded in Henry's mind upon that dread of ability
common with incapable despots, and in Simon's upon
long-increasing distrust. It may be that in proportion
as he was compelled to distrust this relationship, it
became easier for him to join the opposition party,
although there was no sign of closer personal connection with any of the prominent nobles.

More effect was produced by home and family
politics, in which the Countess played an active part.
Her nature was ardent and enterprising, whilst the
King, her brother, was capricious and dependent upon
promptings from without; sympathy between them
was impossible. Not only had he sinned against her
womanly honour, he had also curtailed her inheritance
long before; for when she was the widow of the Earl
Marshal, and still a minor, he had contrived that
instead of the 2000 marks assigned her, only £400
should be yearly paid as jointure, and, without her
knowledge, he had affixed her seal to the agreement.*
The matter had been before a court of law for many

---

* Rot. Lit. Claus. 17 Henr. III. membr. 9 dorso. Numerous
facts in Mrs. Green's Lives of the Princesses, ii. 116 and 453.

years, and various other claims had been added ; for, in his constant embarrassments, Henry applied to his sister, whose admirable financial management was as remarkable as his incompetence. Though she was scarcely received at court, and seldom treated as became her royal birth, she never failed to assert her rights as a member of the house when any opportunity occurred, such as a cession of territory, or transfer of fiefs. In all these matters her husband was her best counsellor. It was part of the destiny of their lives that, living in familiar intercourse with the band of Minorites, who were struggling against the deep moral corruption of the time, they both saw the duties of King and bishops and nobles in a totally different light from that in which they appeared for the most part to those dignitaries themselves. The Franciscan doctrine of lowliness and humility opened their hearts to sympathize with the position of the common people, and they, in short, attained views of life very rare in their time and station. The family was inspired by peculiar religious and political convictions. To their sorrow, they had lost their best support in 1253, by the death of Robert Grosseteste, who never wearied of preaching forbearance and patience under wrong. Four years later, the faithful Adam of Marsh died ; he appears latterly to have been less intimately connected with the Earl's household than before.* The only

* According to Brewer, Monumenta Franciscana, p. xcix., Adam must have died in 1257, at latest in the spring of 1258. It is remarkable that there is no letter to the Earl and Countess in his collection after their last return from Gascony.

wholesome check upon Simon's ambition and self-
confidence, perhaps upon their common desire to
retaliate upon their enemies, was thus removed.
Though the noble convictions and principles which
they had derived from that connection remained unchanged, it certainly was not an accident that now,
when Leicester was fifty years of age, and had out-
grown priestly advice, he entered upon a new course
of public life, where he was no longer protected against
arrogance and other obvious perils.

The peers and lieges of the realm were summoned
to Westminster, as was customary, fourteen days after
Easter, 1258, to discharge urgent business, this time $\vee$
in connection with the Welsh war, and the rigorous
demands of Rome.* The Earl of Leicester appeared
among them. It is scarcely probable that he had-
accomplished a mission to Italy, upon which he had
been appointed during the previous summer with
Peter of Savoy and John Mansell, a clerk of the
Treasury. In any case they had made so little use of
the authority granted them, to return the Sicilian
crown in the last extremity into the Pope's hands,†

* Rymer, i. 370, May 2 : pro negotiis nostris arduis . . . .
proceres et fideles regni. Among the attesting members of the
royal council there appear, besides Prince Edward, no native
barons except the Earl of Warwick, and no judges. On the
other hand, there are two of Henry's step-brothers, Peter of Savoy,
and such obsequious officials as John Mansell.

† Rymer, i. 360 ; June 28, 1257. Probably the journey was
never taken, and Rot. Lit. Pat. 42. Henr. III. membr. 15, where
the King acknowledges a debt to the Earl of £1198. 14s. 10d. has
no connection with it.

that in January, when the King was sorely embarrassed, he, nevertheless, wrote to the Cardinal-Deacon
Octavian, that the estates did indeed withhold their
consent, but, if the Papal court had patience, he would
still fulfil all his obligations.* Immediately afterwards,
the sharpest menaces had proved that the Pope was
in earnest; the displeasure of the assembled estates
was full to overflowing. The Earls of Leicester and
Gloucester made no attempt to conceal it, both not a
little encouraged by Richard's absence in Germany.

In extreme ill-humour, the King again had recourse
to abusive language, and his malicious half-brother,
William of Valence, the son of the same Hugh de la
March, who in 1242 deserted to the French at Pons,
dared to call the Earl of Leicester an old traitor and
liar. " No, no, William," he replied wrathfully, " I am
neither a traitor nor a traitor's son. Our fathers were
of a very different stamp." The personal and political
quarrel between these two foreign nobles would have
been decided on the spot by the sword, if the King
himself had not separated them. In the fierce debates
Simon most frequently acted as spokesman to the
assembly, and gave expression to that which was in
the hearts of all,† charging the unhappy King with
reducing the realm to such destitution by mortgaging
it to the Pope, and by granting enormous favours to

---

* Shirley, ii. 126, undated, but not later than the beginning of
February.

† Non tamen regi, sed universitati præcordialiter est conques-
tus, exigens instanter sibi justitiam exhiberi. Matth. Paris, 968.

his minions, that it was now impossible to shake off
even such contemptible enemies as the Welsh. Nothing was gained by discussion, or by the old plan
of soliciting the prelates singly; and, on the 2nd of
May, Henry was at last compelled to make concessions
which were tantamount to a complete overthrow of the
present system of government. The estates promised
a national subsidy on condition that the Pope should
moderate his demands, and the King pledged himself
in return to reform the administration of the realm
before Christmas, with the advice of his faithful
estates and in presence of a Legate. But on the same
day, in the tumult which the movement caused, a writ
was issued bidding the Parliament meet again four
weeks after Whitsuntide, at Oxford, an unusual and
neutral place, where a committee of twenty-four—
twelve chosen by the Crown and twelve by the Barons
—should propose the essential features of a comprehensive reform; their decision the King swore upon
his soul to accept without gainsaying. * So, at last,
after long and miserable restraint, the dam was broken
through, as in King John's days, but the question
remained whether the waters could again be brought
under control as speedily as then.

On the appointed day, the 11th of June, the Barons,

---

* The documents in Rymer, i. 370, 371, 372. The words of
the writ are: Ad hoc parliamentum nostrum Oxoniæ, quod erit
in unum mensem post festum Penticostis.   Stubbs' Select
Charters and other Illustrations of English Constitutional History, 2nd ed. p. 380, 381.   Const. Hist. ii. 73, 74.

great and small, arrived in Oxford, to assemble there
in the Dominican Convent. Some hundred nobles
marched, armed and mounted, towards the town with
their horsemen. The summons against Wales, and
the insecurity of the French truce, afforded the pretext; but, remembering the events of 1215, they had
secured the harbours in order to guard against any
stroke from abroad.* Their equipment really expressed a steadfast determination to abolish the
grievances under which the kingdom groaned. The
King, who lodged in the neighbouring Castle of
Woodstock, and his party, consisting chiefly of
foreigners and churchmen, were compelled to give
way. Yet as their representatives upon the committee
of twenty-four, they for the most part elected themselves; two bishops, Henry's step-brothers, his
nephew, the eldest son of King Richard, the Earl de
Warenne, who had married a half-sister, the Earl of
Warwick, and some low-born and submissive tools of
the government. Among those elected by the opposite party were Walter of Cantilupe, Bishop of Worcester, Grosseteste's saintly friend; the Earls of
Gloucester,† Hereford, Norfolk, and Leicester; and,

---

* Matth. Paris, 970.

† According to the patent of June 22, in Reports of the Lords'
Committee touching the dignity of a peer, i. 103, Richard of
Gloucester was chosen by the King; but the contemporary
reports, especially the documents in the Annales de Burton, 447
(newly edited by Luard, Annales Monastici, Rer. Brit, med. ævi
SS. i. and described even in those Reports, i. 105, as authentic

among the knights and barons, also a cousin of the last Peter of Montfort. With passionate delight in constantly repeated elections, the twenty-four then nominated four out of their number who were to appoint a royal council of fifteen members. The Barons succeeded in carrying ten candidates for the council; whilst on the king's side, only the Arch-, bishop of Canterbury, the Earls of Warwick and Winchester, Peter of Savoy, and John Audley were chosen. Thus the faction of foreign favourites and subordinate clerks was completely defeated, and an elected government and a constitutional ministry established. Of its members an overwhelming majority were hostile to the present system, and practically wrenched the government out of the King's hands. Simon was superior in rank to all, except the two prelates of Canterbury and Worcester; and already he was pre-eminently distinguished by his zeal in establishing an entirely new *régime*. Probably the measures and decisions of this memorable parliament were for the most part originated by him.

The committee of twenty-four did not now retire, but proceeded to act in the name of all the tenants-in-chief (*per le commun*), first presenting a series of petitions for the abolition of abuses in feudal matters and in the administration of justice; and marking the

documents) place him distinctly on the other side. Moreover, the late date of the patent is noticeable. Perhaps the two parties contended for the doubtful earl, who from the first could hardly work harmoniously with Simon.

national character of the movement by the demands that all royal castles should be taken out of the custody of aliens, and committed to natives; and that heiresses should only be given in marriage to their countrymen. They pressed for a reduction of the exactions arising out of the high rents of the sheriffs, and many other dues augmented by the crown itself, and urged that measures should be taken against the Jews and usurers of whom many embarrassed nobles and gentlemen became the prey. From such memorials the committee drew up new constitutional articles, the so-called Provisions of Oxford,* enforcing in the first place inviolable observance of the oft-confirmed charters. They reserved to themselves the long-disputed right of appointing the Great Justiciary, the Chancellor, and the Lord Treasurer. This encroachment upon the province of the executive would have been prejudicial to the vigorous centralization that had been carried out in judicial business since the reign of Henry III., and would have substituted the feudal pretensions of baronial justice for the legal system developed by the crown judges. The Great Justiciary, until Hubert de Burgh, was the highest officer of State, and the King's representative as the sole and personal fountain of justice. Since that time he had been superseded by the personal absolutism of the monarch ; and now he was to be reinstated by the

---

* The petitions in Latin, and the Provisions of Oxford in French, Annales de Burton, p. 439, *et seq.* ; and Stubbs, Select Charters, 382 *et seq.*

Barons themselves, but for a contrary purpose, as the most important guarantee of their political rights. The position accorded to their nominee, Hugh Bigod, brother of the Earl of Norfolk, recalls that held by the justicia in Aragon.

A special resolution ordained that Parliaments should be regularly summoned for the 6th of October, the 2nd of February, and the 1st of June. Besides the King's fifteen appointed counsellors, only twelve nobles (*prodes homes*), elected in the name of the whole, were to meet on these occasions to transact the general business of the realm as far as the King's rule extended. This restriction of number was nominally to save expense to the community, * but really to limit the assembly in accordance with the character of a baronial court. The whole community was bound to acquiesce in the decisions of these oligarchic representatives.

Yet another committee of twenty-four members was elected to consider the subject of a national tax, evidently with reference to the Pope's demands. They came, however, to no understanding, for the rapid revolutionary changes were just reaching their climax. A separate article ordered the election of four knights in each shire † to take note of local grievances for the next Parliament. Oaths were prescribed for all the elected commissions, for the new

* Pur esparmir le cust del commun. Annales de Burton, 452.

† Quatuor discreti et legales homines, qui quolibet die, ubi tenetur comitatus, conveniant, etc. Ibid. 446.

officers, and for the wardens of castles. Without the
possibility of making resistance, Henry was compelled,
candle in hand, to swear to the laws which were forced
upon him. In a series of charters wrung from him
under the pressure of existing circumstances, he confirmed the oath for himself and his son ; made himself
surety for the confidential adherents who were left to
him, and enjoined upon the sheriffs the abolition of
their oppressive practices.* His humiliation could go
no further.

But this result would not have been attained without
a decided exercise of force. On the 22nd of June the
victorious party had determined the fate of the royal
fortresses. These had been entrusted almost exclusively
to foreign favourites, to whom the King's first-born son
Edward, Henry, the son of King Richard, and the Earl
de Warenne adhered. Although Leicester, whose position by birth was similar to theirs, set them an excellent
example by delivering up his castles of Kenilworth and
Odiham to the King, they raised a vehement opposition.
Young Henry declared that he could not acquiesce in
the decree in his father's absence. Simon retaliated
upon the insolent William of Valence for his recent
abuse by crying : " Either the castles or thy head."
To escape the storm Valence and his brothers, Guy and
Geoffrey of Lusignan, suddenly left Oxford with their
retainers, and joined their brother Aimar, the Bishop

---

* Shirley, ii. 127, June 26 : Fiat reformatio et ordinatio status
regni nostri ; p. 129, August 4, similar French writ ; to the sheriffs,
Annales de Burton, 456.

elect, at Wolvesham castle, near Winchester. The
Barons, on their side, now raised the session and followed them in arms, taking the King with them and led
by Simon, for he had caused the custody of the castle
of Winchester to be assigned to him on the same 22nd
of June.* A convention was framed there in July, and
the whole coterie were banished from the kingdom, including William, although he was Earl of Pembroke,
and also the Bishop Aimar. Before this was effected,
the Abbot of Winchester and a brother of Gloucester's
had been poisoned at a banquet at their instigation.
When removed from the King's council, their insolent
demeanour had brought upon them the national
vengeance, all their possessions, titles, and honours
were accounted robbery and forfeited; their royal patron
was compelled himself to pronounce sentence of deprivation. Their fall was followed by the submission of
Edward, Henry, and Warenne.†

Such coercion did not meet with universal approval,
and the disaffected were not slow to perceive that
it would furnish the desired occasion for a reactionary
attack upon the Provisions.‡ Was it not in fact, the

* Rot. Lit. Pat. 42 Henry III. membr. 6.

† The principal source of information, besides Matth. Paris
and the Annal. Winton. ed. Luard, p. 95, is the letter of an eye-witness de curia regis in Annales de Burton, 443 ; also a number of
documents : compare Gesch. v. England, iii. 720 ff., and Stubbs'
Const. Hist. ii., 78, 79.

‡ This opinion is expressed by the so-called Thomas Wykes,
p. 119. almost the only royalist historian : Quintus articulus
omnino illicitus fuit et præcipue detestandus. He must have ⁿ

greatest anomaly, a grave offence against the new law,
that an alien by birth, such as the Earl of Leicester,
should imperiously press to the front as spokesman in
a patriotic movement; that he had taken possession of
Winchester, one of the keys of the realm, and despatched his eldest son, Henry de Montfort, to Boulogne
in pursuit of the exiles, for the purpose of rescuing the
treasures which they had carried off? The humiliation
of the King, and the attempt of the vassals to conduct
a constitutional government themselves, threatened to
issue in the dictatorship of one man. But, for a time,
nothing was more popular than the expulsion of the
foreigners from fiefs and benefices, and the transfer of
fortresses to native governors in the name of the State.
The national peace far outweighed in consequence the
vigorous and permanent transformation of the constitution. Hence, the prevailing opinion among contemporaries was almost enthusiastic approval of the new
measures; it was later, when their fruit would not
ripen, that the opposite party gave the derisive name
of the "mad Parliament" to the Oxford assembly.*

had before him an original numbered draught of the Provisions, such as has not been preserved to us. According
to Luard's edition, he nearly copies the Osney Annals down to the
year 1258, but differs entirely from them in the period of the
Barons' war.

* The chroniclers of St. Albans, Winchester, Waverley, and
Dunstaple were entirely favourable to the Barons: Ferociter pro-
cedunt Barones in agendis suis, utinam bonum finem sortiantur.
are the words of the above-mentioned letter in the Annals of
Burton. The expression insane parliamentum apud Oxoniam,

In the summer of 1258, when the promoters of the new
laws proceeded forthwith to put them into execution,
the greater number could scarcely overlook the dangers
of the situation which they had themselves created :
though with a measure of distrust they relied upon
Montfort's sagacity for the solution of all domestic and
foreign perplexities. The Papal agents were promptly
sent home with an answer thoroughly characteristic
of the temper of the secular vassals : The Sicilian crown
had been accepted without their sanction, and therefore they were not bound to pay the heavy price.* No
one was better qualified than Simon to bring about an
enduring peace with France. This, chiefly, because of
the King's vain hope of winning back Poitou, or even the
Norman duchy, had been hindered for more than twenty
years by a succession of unsatisfactory truces, almost
more effectually than by war itself. The King's administrative council and the committee of delegates, in
which Simon was for a time the master spirit, believed
that they neglected no means of making their work
lasting. From Winchester they hastened to London,
in order to secure the City as their fathers had done in
1215. The King was forced to issue a series of writs,
appointing new sheriffs to the counties, and subordi-

afterwards so common, is first found in the London Chronicle,
written in the reign of Edward I. by the Alderman Arnold Thedmar, an adherent of the crown, of German descent. ' Liber de An-
tiquis Legibus,' p. 37 (Camden Society.)

* Letter of the fifteen counsellors to the Pope in Annales de
Burton, 457 ; Matth. Paris, Additament, 215 ; and Rymer, i. 373.

nating their office to the will of the community.*
Every provision was to be actually put into execution.

And yet the provisional government, though it was
carried on till the end of 1259, and with some inter-
ruptions even to the spring of 1263, almost immediately
proved unequal to the performance of its promises
upon the most essential points. Hugh Bigod, the Great
justiciary, was not an erudite lawyer; and baronial justice
could not in any measure replace the system that had
been founded by the crown as the basis of the realm,
and required skilful administrators, well versed in the
common law—men who in the thirteenth century still
sought to learn from the jurists of Bologna, at least
formal principles for the support of the national juris-
prudence. The Barons further believed that they had
cut off one nerve of the monarchy by persecuting its
loyal and experienced officers, but in doing so they
robbed themselves of indispensable instruments, without whom the new government inevitably lapsed into
confusion. The higher clergy, with the exception of a
few friends of reform, had estranged themselves from
the nobility, and, because the claims of the Pope were
so sternly ignored, most of the prelates were necessarily
omitted in the many elections of committees. And,
lastly, the crowd of smaller vassals had never been
bidden as a body to Parliament, as had been once
promised in Magna Charta, and they were by no means
content to be of no importance beyond their own
shires, whilst the great Barons deported themselves as

* Ann. de Burton, 456. Rymer, i. 375.

if their oligarchic rule were to last for ever. Hence, the
first attempts at administrative reform, under the
judicial and financial authority of the sheriffs, naturally
aroused opposition among the holders of small fiefs,
who, though they gladly welcomed a release from royal
oppression, did not consider themselves represented in
national matters by a committee elected exclusively
from among the great Barons. With all the elections
and siftings for the various commissions, none were
provided with representatives except the *élite* of the
tenants-in-chief.

These malcontent views, grounded upon the memory
of universal political rights in primitive times, made
themselves immediately apparent, though quietly and
cautiously. After the constituent decrees passed at
Oxford, the Parliament, since moved to Westminster
in October, 1259, felt itself to be in truth a legislative
assembly, as it announced the ratification of the new
laws to the nation through the provisional government
of fifteen and in the King's name. It is remarkable that
the two vernacular idioms, French and English, were
first used about this time.* The sovereign was virtually divested of his free authority, and the great
Barons, as rulers and legislators, took the government
of the realm into their own hands through the instrumentality of the fifteen ministers and twelve representatives whom they elected.† On the other hand, it was

---

* See the names of the council and the different commissions
collected and arranged by Stubbs, Const. Hist. ii. 82.

† The remarkable patents of October 18th, 1258, Rymer, i. 377.

on this account the more significant that the knighthood, the *communitas bacheleriæ Angliæ*, as they styled themselves, ventured to draw up a protest and present it to the young heir, who regarded the whole movement with marked disfavour. Full of loyalty to the King since he had submitted to the conditions laid upon him, they accused the Barons of acting for their own advantage only, and doing nothing for the good of the realm. If the position of affairs remained unchanged, Prince Edward himself, seemingly in concert with Earl Simon, openly threatened a counter reformation.*

To their own loss, moreover, the great Barons overlooked a numerous class of peers by the recognition of whom the whole movement might have gained real popularity and vigour, had they so chosen. The twelve delegates proceeded as if no one could disturb their rule, and issued from Westminster a long series of statutes in French and Latin for regulating the administration of justice. In the Parliaments which were

378. Geschichte von England, iii. 909, 910; and the excellent monograph by Alexander F. Ellis. The only English proclamation by Henry III.

* Annales de Burton, p. 471: Festivitate S. Edwardi regi et confessoris in quindenam S. Michaelis, the 13th and not the 6th October. Many of the documents in these annual registers are loosely arranged, and it remains uncertain whether the year was 1258 or 1259. Gneist, Geschichte und heutige Gestalt der Aemter und des Verwaltungsrechts in England, 2 ed. i. 305, dates 1258; Stubbs, Const. Hist. ii. 81, 1259, in accordance with the Provisions of the Barons, see Statutes of the Realm, i. 8, and Select Charters. 400.

assembled, according to the Provisions, for more than
a year, this zealous law-making ceased, but still the
self-chosen ministers and peers governed in the stead
of the King and the community,* and when Richard,
King of the Romans, visited England, they exacted from
him an oath to accept the newly enacted measures.
At the same time they experienced daily increasing
difficulty in conducting foreign affairs and in preserving
union among themselves.

Earl Simon was the only man who stood forth pre-
eminent among them all, the only man before whom the
King trembled. If he had really been dictator instead
of one among many, he might have steered clear of
many perils. But the possibility always remained that
whenever any schism occurred among the Barons themselves, the Earl's adversaries, of whom there was no
lack, would go over to the King's party. Upon one
occasion, during the stormy summer of 1258, the King
was surprised by a tempest on the Thames, and sought
shelter in Simon's lodging. He then told him to his
face,—him who had torn from him his kinsfolk and
favourites, and forced upon the court the practice of
economy and thrift : " I have great dread of thunder
and lightning, but, by God's Head, I fear thee more
than all the storms in the world."† And the peers of

* Le cunseil le Rey et les duze esluz par le cummun de l'Engle-
terre saluent tute gent, are the words of their address of
March 18, 1259 ; Rymer, i. 381. In November the itinerant
Judges were despatched to the counties per consilium magnatum nostrorum ; Shirley, ii. 141.

† Matth. Paris 974.

highest rank feared him no less. Not only did his
quite peculiar connections and his impetuous and imperious manner excite their mistrust; he did not fully
sympathize with the exclusive attitude of the nobility,
who anxiously debarred the knights and citizens from
all participation in public affairs. Add to this, that
almost without their concurrence, the negotiations with
France on the part of the new government were
chiefly entrusted to this born Frenchman. His return
from the continent was eagerly awaited by his friends
in the spring Parliament of 1259, but when he arrived
late in the session, an altercation immediately followed
with Richard de Clare, Earl of Gloucester and Hertford,
the man who everywhere stood next to him in rank.
Although Gloucester had been for years a champion of
constitutional rights, he had recently betrothed his son
to the daughter of Guy of Lusignan, one of the King's
half brothers, and according to one statement had even
been chosen by the crown to the committee of twenty-
four. We are ignorant of the special occasion of the
outbreak between him and Simon, when the latter cried
passionately : " I will have nought more to do with such
turncoats and deceivers."*   But we know that popular
opinion already pointed to the Earls of Gloucester and
Norfolk, and some other prominent nobles, as waverers
or even renegades from the good cause.†

* Matth. Paris, 986.
† O Comes Gloverniæ, comple quod cœpisti :
    Nisi claudas congrue, multos decepisti . . . .
    O tu, Comes le Bygot, pactum serva sanum :
    Cum sis miles strenuus, nunc exerce manum. . . . .
Th. Wright, Political Songs (Camden Society), p. 122, 123.

Simon had immediately hastened back in wrath to
France, where his presence was indispensable to the
conclusion of the long-sought peace. Normandy and
the counties of Anjou, Maine, Touraine, and Poitou
were at last formally ceded to Louis IX., and
the points in dispute concerning the feudal relation
in Guienne were determined.* The two States and
peoples were thus placed upon a more satisfactory
footing with regard to one another, than at any
time since King John's humiliation ; but the negotiations were disturbed, not only by the compensation due to Simon for the services he had rendered, but also by his direct dynastic claims. It was
not without reason that the Countess again accompanied her husband abroad. He made use of his
power to compel the King to discharge his debts out
of his strictly administered revenues, and Eleanor also
hoped now to receive the whole of the jointure bequeathed by her first husband.† It is remarkable that
Simon, on this occasion, resigned the eventual title to
Toulouse and Beziers that he derived from his illustrious father ; ‡ and the King of France did not pro-
ceed to ratify the instrument of peace until he had
received a renunciation from all agnates of the house

* Rymer, i. 383 et seq.

† £200 to Simon, Rot. Lit. Pat. 48 Henr. III. membr. 15.
Eleanor was to be indemnified by certain royal manors ; and the
King redeemed his pledge on Bigorre at least for seven years.
Mrs. Green, Princesses, ii. 117.

‡ Vic et Vaissete, Histoire de Languedoc, vi. 110, and Preuves,
p. 522 ; Simon's deed dated Paris, December, 1259.

of Plantagenet, consequently from Richard and his sister. But Eleanor and her husband, doubtless not undesignedly, raised many difficulties with reference to the county of Agenois, once received by Raymond of Toulouse as dowry with his wife Johanna, daughter of Henry II.; through her granddaughter it passed to Alfons, brother of Louis IX., when he, by marriage, acquired possession of Toulouse as well as this fief. After his death, Eleanor, as cousin of the present Countess, again asserted her claim to the province, which was lapsing to the French crown. Probably her object was less to preserve an ancient fief of Guienne to the house of Plantagenet, than to assist the constantly-reviving schemes of the house of Montfort for securing dominion on French soil.* It can scarcely have been accidentally that the Earl of Gloucester was appointed one of the arbitrators on the English side in this case. The peace could not be concluded in its entirety until the end of the year, and then not until Henry III. had escaped from his guardians and their disagreements, and repaired to the French court. Throwing himself into Louis's arms, he skilfully took advantage of Simon's dubious demeanour, and encouraged the suspicion that he sought to profit by the general confusion, and to acquire undue power for himself and his house, perhaps even the crown of the realm.†

* All the authentic documents in Mrs. Green's Princesses, ii. 111, *et seq.*

† Comes autem Leycestriæ huic paci opposuit, proponens quod

A dangerous double game immediately commenced between Henry and Leicester, each seeking to elude and outdo the other in dealing with the English nobility and the French King. On the 4th of December, as soon as they had signified their concurrence in the Anglo-French peace,* Simon and his consort sailed from the French coast, and landed with a stately train of horsemen, which excited universal attention. On the 10th of February, 1260, the Earl was entertained like a prince by the Abbot of St. Albans.† He had come to make sure of his adherents, to protect the Provisions of Oxford from the intrigues of his opponent Gloucester, and, if necessary, to defend with his sword the constitution which was founded upon them. His sudden boldness and decision would be inexplicable if the Court had not been engaged in extensive intrigues during its apparent triflings at Paris. After he had at last made terms with his brother-in-law, King Louis, and whilst he remained in a foreign country, Henry appeared to consider himself perfectly free from restraint, at least in dynastic matters. On the 16th of January he despatched a message to the clergy and nobility of Sicily, to the effect that, with the hope of support from the Pope, he was disposed to

processu temporis contingere posset quod eædem terræ simul cum regno Angliæ ad filios suos vel hæredes jure hæreditario descendere possent, says the royalist Thomas Wykes, 123. Compare Geschichte von England, iii. 736.

* Rymer, i. 392.

† Matth. Westmonast. 371.

renew his suit for the crown of that kingdom on behalf
of his son Edmund.* On the same day he addressed
a communication to the Great Justiciary, Hugh Bigod,
informing him that unforeseen difficulties necessitated
his continued absence, and demanding that no parliament should meet until his return.† The sagacious
Louis IX. was favourably disposed towards the Earl of
Leicester, and it was not easy for Henry to attach him
to his interests. He had trifled away several months
on the coast of Boulogne before he found courage to
give him notice that suspicious exportations of arms
and horses were carried on by Simon's orders.‡ His
entire destitution, and his great dread of disorderly
scenes at home, led him to postpone his return until
the money stipulated in the treaty of peace was paid.‖
But, on the 23rd of April, he landed suddenly at Dover,
for a rumour had reached him that, at a Parliament held

* Negotium Siciliæ quod assumpsimus secundum effectum
nostri desiderii veluti proponebamus hucusque prosequi nequi-
vimus. Shirley, ii. 147.

† Ibid. ii. 148. The same again to the other members of the
council on the 19th of February, p. 153.

‡ Rymer, i. 396: Per quod motum animi ejusdem comitis evi-
dentius perpendere poteritis qualiter erga nos se habeat. The
date April 28 is erroneous. A similar warning to King Richard,
who was then in England, against an enterprise of the step-
brothers from Poitou, April 18, l. c., has the appearance of a
feeler.

‖ According to Rot. Lit. Pat. 44 Henr. III. membr. 5, he received on the Monday after the feast of St. Peter and St. Paul
14,583 livres tournois for himself, and 5000 marks for King
Richard.

in London, in spite of the royal prohibition, Simon
was attaching Prince Edward to himself, and that the
latter had declared his intention of abiding by the oath
he had once sworn. Henry feared, therefore, that his
son might be induced to aid in his dethronement; and
for fourteen days he struggled against the desire to
admit him to his presence, conscious that if he saw
him, he should be unable to restrain the impulse to
embrace him.* It may be that Edward wavered for
a moment, impressed by the sacredness of his oath,
but very soon after the King's return the constitutional
party were compelled to give up their hopes of him
and many others. A mission to Gascony filled the
young and enterprising Prince with other thoughts.
We do not know how far Simon ventured towards so
hazardous a measure as a combination with the heir
against the father, but it is plain that he now gave
way before Henry; perhaps because he had dared too
much, and could no longer rely upon his followers.
At the marriage of the Princess Beatrix with the heir
of Brittany, on the 13th of October, he did not discharge the functions of steward, but Henry, son of the
King of the Romans, officiated in his stead.† The

* Ann. de Dunstaplia, 214. Will. Rishanger Chronica, ed. Riley,
p. 9 : Iratus valde, a patris absentavit se conspectibus, adhærens
Baronibus in hac parte, sicut juraverat. According to Thomas
Wykes. 124, King Richard, Edward, and the Barons, contradicted
the rumour under their respective seals. Compare Geschichte
von England, iii. 738.

† L'atorne Simon de Montfort Conte de Leicestre a servir pur
li. Rymer, i. 402.

King, evidently well advised, succeeded in misleading
his subjects by the wording of his proclamations
against the importation of foreign mercenaries and
war materials, conveying the impression that he intended faithfully to observe the Provisions of Oxford,
whilst, at the same time, he took up his residence in
the Tower with his consort, and gave orders for its
fortifications to be put into a state of thorough efficiency. The breach had already widened considerably,
and Simon's influence greatly declined when Henry
could venture to summon the Barons of the realm,
no longer, we may be sure, the elective committee
that had been forced upon him, to meet for the autumn
Parliament in the royal fortress. The peers declined
to assemble in any other place than Westminster,
where their meetings had been held from time immemorial,* but they thus themselves invited the long-
prepared attacks upon those Provisions which three
years earlier they had defiantly issued from an unac-
customed place.

When the regular parliaments and concord among
the nobles came to an end, the present system of
government was shaken in town and country. The
court sought by aid of its partisans among the knights
of the shire to recover the power of appointing sheriffs.
When Hugh Bigod, perhaps driven to despair by the
course which the movement had taken, voluntarily
resigned his high post, and the constitutional peers

* Ubi parliamentum tenere consueverunt, et non alibi. Ann.
de Dunst. 217.

put Hugh Despenser in his place, both were harassed
by royalist soldiers, the one at Dover, the other in
London. These troops had taken possession of the
bridges and gates in the city, and pledged all the male
inhabitants to support the King. A mandate of the
14th of March, 1261, ordered the arrest of all persons
who falsely asserted that the King intended to impose
taxes by his own authority, or arbitrarily to alter the
laws of the land.* Six weeks later William of Valence
was already restored to favour, and to the possession
of his estate, together with the castle of Hereford.†
In the old form used before the revolution of 1258, a
Parliament was summoned to meet in Winchester at
Whitsuntide, the 14th of June, and there, at last, the
decisive blow was struck.

Pope Alexander IV. followed the example of Innocent III.'s dealings with King John, and absolved
Henry from all the obligations that had been forced
upon him. Whilst the Barons were united, the Curia
had kept silence for some years, and had not despatched
the Legate, for whose assistance Henry prayed so
earnestly when, in 1258, he was compelled to submit
to the estates. But the secret intercourse between
him and Rome was kept up without intermission. His
necessities forced him to crave remission of the large

---

* Chiefly Liber de Antiq. Legibus, 45, 46, and Rymer, i. 405.
Also Thomas Wykes, 125 : Cœpit proponere plures articulos
contra Barones, et rationes prout sibi videbatur satis efficaces.
quod non tenebatur observare Provisiones Oxoniæ.

† Rot. Lit. Pat. 45 Henr. III. membr. 13, April 30.

sums for which he stood pledged on account of the
Sicilian transactions, and to pray that for God's sake
the Pope would not insist upon the reinstalment of
Aimar of Lusignan in the see of Winchester.* Fortunately, Aimar had died on the 13th of December,
1260, when the breach was widening between Leicester
and Gloucester, and in the interval, the Sicilian affair
had again been put in train at Rome. Then, on the
13th of April, the bull was published at the Lateran,
which enabled Henry to meet his Parliament in better
spirits, and to make perjury easy to himself and all
who would follow him. The bull anathematized the
violence that had been put upon the power and freedom
of the kingly dignity under pretence of reforming the
realm; and, by virtue of apostolic authority, it cancelled the Provisions in their entire compass, with all
the oaths taken under the new government. "For
the sacredness of the oath, which ought to confirm
faith and truth, may not become a cement of violence
and iniquity." Several prelates, John Mansell among
them, were authorised to absolve the King and his
house, and all persons, whether priests or laymen, from
their oaths.†

Although no formal negotiations took place at Winchester, the Earl of Gloucester and other moderately
disposed men now came over publicly to the King's

---

* Ad vitandum enorme periculum quod nobis et regno nostro
occasione ipsius posset imminere. Still from St. Denis, January
18th, 1260. Shirley. ii. 151.

† Rymer, i. 404, 406.

side, and Henry again ventured to nominate the Great
Justiciary, Chancellor, and Treasurer upon his own
sole authority. To reinstate his sheriffs in the several
counties was more difficult. Conferences on the subject were called to Windsor, London, and Kingston,
but the opposite party took their stand upon the
Provisions of Oxford, and would recognise none but
their own officers; in vain the King commanded
his lieges to expel the present sheriffs, in vain a mixed
committee for months discussed a compromise, until,
as a desperate resource, King Richard was requested
to arbitrate. At Easter, 1262, he delivered his judgment, to the effect that the King alone had power, as
of old, freely to appoint and dismiss all judicial and administrative officers. Hereupon a desultory war broke
out in the country, and both parties strove to inflame
it and make it general by importing French mercenaries. An amnesty was proclaimed for the Earls of
Norfolk, Leicester, and Warenne and eleven other
nobles, who had all belonged to the committee of
twenty-four, on condition that they signed and sealed
a renunciation of the Provisions by Whitsuntide, 1262,
but neither this measure, nor the renewal by Pope
Urban IV. of the bull promulgated by his predecessor,
produced the desired effect.* The court party had
long recognised the fact that without other assistance
neither Papal mandates nor the means at the disposal

* Shirley ii. 192 ; Oct. 18, 196; Dec. 6. Rymer, i. 411 ; Dec.
7. Compare Geschichte von England. iii. 742, and the detailed
survey in Stubbs, Const. Hist. ii. 84-86.

of the King's adherents were sufficient to coerce and
subdue the defenders of the statutes of 1258, with the
support which they could fall back upon in the
country.

The Earl of Leicester, the leader of the constitutional party from the time when Gloucester and others
had renounced fellowship with him, did not give up
the game as hopeless. For a while longer he maintained a defiant attitude, relying upon his foreign
horsemen, whose importation the King vainly forbade,
and with the Countess he resumed the contest for the
jointure.* We do not know whether he appeared in
person at Winchester, London, or Kingston, but he
went to France as early as the summer of 1261 ; it was
rumoured among the people that he had sworn a vow to
live in poverty and exile rather than be faithless to the
truth,† but the real object of his journey was to appeal
as a claimant of equal standing to the same foreign
power as the King, his adversary.

On the 14th of March, before he ventured to emanci-
pate himself by Papal aid, Henry had agreed with
Simon and Eleanor to refer their personal quarrel to
the decision of the pious and upright French King,
and if he declined the office, to Queen Margaret, as-

* Datum est intelligi quod Simon de Monteforti comes Leycestriæ nititur introducere in regnum nostrum gentem extraneam
cum armis contra nos. Rymer, i, 406 ; May 28, 1261. Compare
Mrs. Green, Princesses, ii, 129.

† Ann. de Dunst. 217, dicens, se sine terra malle mori, quam
perjurus a veritate recedere.

I

sisted by the renowned French jurist, Pierre le Cham-
br'elain.* The verdict was expected by the end of
June, for Margaret's reply promised to despatch the
business as soon as the parties appeared, either in person or by their attorneys. But Louis IX., who was
impartial towards the Earl as well as towards Henry,
perceived that the dispute to be decided went far beyond certain money claims, and the publication of the
bull at Winchester confirmed his opinion to certainty.
Already on the 21st of April, he pronounced the
statements of the two parties to be irreconcilable.†
Soon afterwards, however, on the 20th of July, Henry,
now admitting the political differences,‡ again solicited
the queen's mediation. A little later the Earl of
Leicester hastened privately to the French court, where
he was known and esteemed, that he might there advance his own and his adherent's cause. A letter of the
2nd of September from Henry to Louis expressed the
alarm awakened by this news,‖ and begged earnestly that

* Nos Henris, par la grace Deu rois Dangleterre, et nos Simon
de Muntfort et Alienor, cuens et contesse de Leycestre. Now
printed, Shirley, ii. 168. Also the letter to Louis of the 17th of
March, p. 170, 171. Upon Pierre de Fontaines compare Histoire
Littéraire de France, xix. 131 et sq.

† Green, Princesses, ii, 121; compare Shirley, ii. 173.

‡ Pro facto nos et barones nostros, et specialiter S. de M.
comitem L. et Alienoram comitissam L., sororem nostram contin-
gente; Rymer, i. 407. Also the Patent of the 5th of July, Shirley,
ii. 176, which appoints Hugh Duke of Burgundy and Pierre le
Chambrelain as mediators.

‖ Ob quam tamen causam, cum id de nostra conscientia non
processerit, penitus ignoramus. Rymer, i. 409,

neither Simon nor others of his party might be admitted
until the royal messengers arrived to explain the position
of affairs to Louis. There were no immediate results,
because at this time the prospects of the royalists in
England certainly appeared to brighten. It was not
till all amicable attempts to propitiate the fourteen
Earls and Barons had signally failed, that a dread took
possession of the King's soul lest Simon should con-
trive his ruin whilst at Paris, where he seems to have
passed the winter. To his terror he learnt that the
Barons were even seeking to influence the court of
Rome,* as if they were still the rulers of England.
He sent urgent commands to his procurators immediately to anticipate and counteract their attempts. On
the 17th of May, 1262, Louis IX. himself communicated to him that, to his great regret, he saw no means
of making peace for him,† whereupon Henry hastily prepared to go himself to France. His brother-in-
law Louis had given him friendly aid in his pecuniary
necessity, and shut his eyes to the proceedings of the
Count of St. Pol and other French noblemen who were
embarking their squires and soldiers for England to
assist in the subjugation of his refractory subjects;
Henry therefore hoped by his presence to secure at last

* Cum ... quidam de regno nostro agentes in curia Romana in
nostri juris et honoris præjudicium diversa suggerere et contra
nos impetrare præsumant et intendant. etc. May 26th 1262. to
the procurators Hemingford and Lovel. Shirley, ii. 210.

† Ad præsens non invenire possumus aliquam viam pacis;
Rymer, i. 416, and Champollion Figeac, Lettres, i. 135,

a favourable verdict, if not the open and permanent
support of the French crown.

Other reasons urged him to set out speedily upon
this journey. His heir, Prince Edward, who was
strolling from one to another of the knightly courts
of southern France and Burgundy, in the company of
his two young cousins, Simon and Henry de Montfort,
still appeared to shun his father and his policy of
restoration. In July the entire English Court, including Edward and his brother Edmund, the Sicilian
candidate, met in Paris, and concord was re-established
in the bosom of the royal family; but an interview
with the Earl of Leicester, proposed by Queen Margaret,* for the purpose of discharging the duty that she
had undertaken, was prevented, on the one hand, by
an obstinate fever which confined Henry to his bed at
St. Germain, whilst Montfort, on his side, withdrew
skilfully and craftily. The King's absence was to him
a welcome summons to show himself in England, as it
had been two years earlier. Moreover, his rival,
Richard of Gloucester, had died on the 15th of July,
and his son and heir, Earl Gilbert, prevented by his
mother from taking an oath of allegiance to the King,
had adopted the cause of the Barons.† Through the
faults, the weakness, and the falsehood of the opposite
party, Leicester's prospects, sufficiently gloomy
hitherto, appeared to brighten once more. Henry

---

* Champollion Figeac, Lettres, i. 136 ; compare Green's Princesses, ii. 122.

† Instigante matre sua ; Thos. Wykes, 140.

fully recognised the danger of this new move; and, as
the Justiciary and Chancellor were governing the kingdom in his absence, he hastily notified them of the
Earl's departure, that they might prepare to oppose his
design ; he announced to them also his own resolve to
desist from these proceedings against Simon, since no
progress could be made towards a conclusion of the
compromise negotiated by the French Queen.*
Nevertheless, he remained abroad until the 20th of
December, fruitlessly endeavouring to obtain effectual
support from the court of France. He sent for the
crown jewels that he might deposit them with the
Templars as pledge for an indispensable loan. Even
after his return, he trusted that Louis would make
terms in his favour with the Earl of Leicester, and
that after all the troubles Simon had already brought
upon the kingdom, the work that had been set on foot
might not end in yet greater calamity.† Again, on
the 5th of February, 1263, he wrote to Queen Margaret
to stimulate her zeal, which was somewhat doubted
even in France.‡ Then the unhappy prince fell as
from the clouds ; for, under the date of the 16th, his

* Quia compromissum nuper initum inter nos et comitem
Leycestriæ coram Regina Franciæ non processit nec habemus
in consilio per illam viam ulterius procedere contra eum, Oct. 8th.
Rymer, i. 422.

† Henry to Louis, Jan. 18, 1263, through John de Chishull,
Archdeacon of London, and Imbert of Montferrant. Shirley,
ii. 234.

‡ Shirley, ii. 235, 239.

ambassadors informed him of a communication from
King Louis, to the effect that he had conferred with
the Earl of Leicester, who declared in reasonable
terms that, though the King's intentions were of the
best, there were those about him who had no desire
for a pacification, and would even prefer that none
should be concluded. The Earl, therefore, could not
honourably enter into the agreement, and he had
besought the French King to give himself at present
no further trouble.*

No disappointment could have been more bitter if
Henry really deceived himself with the hope of being
thus rid of his worst enemy. Twice he had so far
humiliated himself as to allow him to pass for his
equal. Twice he had applied to a tribunal which well-
nigh bore the character of a family council, and yet at
the same time had to take cognisance of a question the
national defenders of which could least of all recognise
the King of France as supreme arbitrator. Louis's
tardiness suggests the possibility that permanent dis-
union in the insular kingdom appeared desirable in his
eyes. As Henry still did not venture to appeal to
him in the political dispute likewise, he let both parties

* Idem comes prædictum dominum regem Franciæ rogavit
quod, ad præsens, circa præmissa ulterius non laboravit. Report
of the ambassadors Chishull and Montferrant. Data Parisiis in
crastino cinerum. This report is dated 1262 by Rymer, i. 416,
and I followed his authority in Gesch. von England, iii. 744.
Now, because of the dated letter of January 18th, which mentions
the same messengers, it is referred to the following year. Shirley,
ii. 242.

go their own way without direct interference ; but he
gave the Earl a new pretext for defending the sinking
cause of the English estates by all available means,
especially by calling to its aid those popular forces
which had long been aroused in its favour. Simon
employed them with an incomparable boldness which
was to make his name glorious then and in after ages.

CHAPTER IV.

THE CIVIL WAR AND MONTFORT'S PROTECTORATE.

ORGANS OF POPULAR OPINION—SIMON AT THE HEAD OF
THE KNIGHTHOOD—MARCH TO LONDON—THE KING
FORCED TO RECOGNISE THE PROVISIONS—TAKES UP
ARMS IN VAIN—LOUIS IX. GIVES AN ARBITREMENT IN
THE KING'S FAVOUR, AMIENS, JANUARY 23, 1264—
CONCURRENCE OF THE POPE—OUTBREAK OF THE CIVIL
WAR, HENRY III. IN OXFORD, SIMON IN NORTH-
AMPTON—LONDON ON THE SIDE OF SIMON—BATTLE
OF LEWES, MAY 14—KING AND REALM IN THE POWER
OF THE VICTORS—ADMINISTRATION OF THE EARL—
CONCEPTIONS OF A CONSTITUTIONAL COMPACT.

THE lower nobility, the lesser crown vassals of
Norman descent, as well as the Anglo-Saxon gentry,
were much exasperated by the haughty neglect of
the great Barons, and many of them, who had been
trained in judicial and administrative offices, remained
loyal to the crown. Among the great merchants of
the City there was also a strong royalist party to which

belonged many an honourable alderman, such as
Arnold, Thedmar's son, the author of some interesting
memoirs on the contemporary history of the town.
The heads of the clergy, at least, abstained as far as
they were able from participation in the struggle.
But the great body of knights, citizens, and clergy had
long been eager to uproot the abuses which grew out
of the union of monarchical and Papal absolutism,
and were injurious to all alike. Even the peasant, the
drudge of all, was beginning to listen to voices which
proclaimed to the people through the mouth of skilful
teachers the dawn of a better time. A great longing
for an alleviation of their lot prevailed in all classes ;
the greed and tyranny in high places appeared as a
common enemy,* against whom the day of revolt was
at last breaking. The idea of remedying the evils of
the time by a general and peaceful national measure
struck deep root. The Franciscans, the mendicant
friars in general, and the humbler secular clergy, had
been the first to proclaim the need for moral regenera-
tion and social reform. They were admitted to the
courts of the great and the cottages of the poor ; they
carefully observed the course of events and awakened
new and eager aspirations at the universities. Now
certain organs of public opinion originated among

* Mundi status hodie multum variatur,
Semper in deterius misere mutatur ;
Nam qui parcit nemini, quique plus lucratur,
Ille plus dilectus est et plus commendatur.
                    Wright, Political Songs, p. 47.

them, chiefly in the form of political rhymes—rough
but popular—full of bitter satire, but no less full of
sound and wholesome truth. The predominance of
Latin betrayed the clerical pen. Popular staves in
English were addressed to the ear of the multitude,
who could not read, and yet began to concern themselves with public interests. The habits of study and
discipline practised by the learned brotherhoods at
Oxford were closely connected with the aspirations
whence sprang those political theories that, some
years earlier, had found expression at the same place
in legal reform. The same popular pulse beat in the
religious as in the political movement, and no man
had greater share in either than Simon de Montfort.
In proportion as he won the confidence of knights
and citizens, of the middle classes, as we should say,
he could the more easily assert that position of power
and authority towards which violent ambition doubtless spurred him. Though itself without legal warrant,
it was in the eyes of many the sole remaining way of
escape from the tyranny of an unlimited and faithless
monarchy.

As early as the summer of 1261, when the committee
of the estates were still struggling desperately with
the King for the right to appoint sheriffs, the experiment had been tried of inviting three knights from every
shire, representatives of the knighthood (Bachelleria),
to the Barons' Parliament at St. Albans on the 21st of
September.* Henry thwarted the project by forbidding

* Stubbs, Select Charters, 405 ; Const. Hist. ii. 85.

the counties south of the Trent to comply with the decree, and summoning the delegates of the knights to appear before him at Windsor instead.* This experiment came to an end when concord ceased among the Barons, and the King was apparently successful; now, when Henry's situation had again become critical it was not easy to revert to it. Such a course of action must first be initiated as would win back the confidence of the country, which the great nobles had repeatedly forfeited, and no man was able to do this but Leicester. He had to convince the people that the Provisions of Oxford had never been given up by their authors, and that they would redound to the advantage, not of an oligarchical confederacy, but of the whole community. For this purpose he chose a fortunate moment when he had been freed from his formidable rival by the death of the elder Gloucester, when, in consequence of the same event, the Prince of Wales had made another incursion upon the western marches, and when King Henry, having failed to shake Louis's impartiality, returned home more helpless and destitute than ever. The Earl's personal presence produced an exactly opposite effect to the King's. His ardent words and his talent for

---

* Cum ex parte episcopi Wygorniensis, comitum Leycestriae et Gloucestriæ, et quorundam aliorum procerum regni nostri vocati sunt tres milites de singulis comitatibus nostris, quod sint coram ipsis apud S. Albanum in instanti festo S. Matthæi apostoli, secum tractaturi super communibus negotiis regni nostri. Sept. 11th, 1261. Shirley, ii. 179.

organization reunited the scattered fragments of the
party, and youths of knightly birth* above all looked
up with enthusiasm to their hero when, at the beginning of 1263, he collected his forces and assumed the
attitude of an independent commander about to interpose between Prince Edward and Prince Llewellyn of
Wales.   Edward had at last given heed to his father's
reproaches, and left the festivities of the continent in
order to defend the border districts conferred upon
him.   On behalf of himself, his son Henry, his cousin
Peter de Montfort, and other knights and barons,
Simon published a declaration on the 4th of March,
under the seal of Bishop Walter of Worcester, to the
effect that they would abstain from hostilities against
the Prince until mid-Lent, and were ready to negotiate
a friendly accommodation with him.†   With reference
to the Provisions, King Henry promised once more to
accept a committee composed of Norfolk, Leicester,
Hugh Bigod, and Philip Basset; but this again was
merely a feint to gain time whilst his energetic son
received oaths of allegiance in all the counties, and
Henry imported as many foreign mercenaries as
possible for his own army, whilst the ports were
closed to those of the opposite party.

* Juniores Angliæ . . . tanquam cera liquescens ductiles
ad quamlibet formam cum quibusdam baronibus, says Thos.
Wykes. 134.

† Et alii barones et milites sibi adhærentes . . . quo magis
inter ipsum et nos cum commoditate majori valeat tractari de
pace. Shirley, ii. 245.

Then Earl Simon ventured publicly to take up arms. He ordered his forces to meet in Oxford at Whitsuntide, and here the English nobility gathered in yet greater numbers than in 1258. The Earl de Warenne and, at first, even Henry, Richard's son, did not absent themselves. As if the native chivalry could at last avenge themselves upon the venal foreign instruments of an insupportable despotism,* they pressed forward along the Welsh frontier from one fortified place to another, chastised Bishop Peter of Hereford, a Savoyard of Aquabella, and drove away the foreign sheriffs and governors of castles; who for the most part adhered to the King. Prince Edward could not march against them, for Simon left the Welsh prince unchecked, and succeeded in winning the sympathy of the towns. Violence and plunder could not be avoided, but adventurers rushed the more eagerly to join the army; it soon extended its avenging march across the island to the eastern counties, and then turned threateningly towards the south, where lay the most important strongholds of the crown. The greatest enthusiasm for the leader prevailed in the ranks. It was probably at this time that some knight or noble composed the song which celebrated his name, 'The Strong Citadel,' above all other because he loved the right and hated wrong. The whole nation greeted him jubilantly because he had imprisoned the Bishop "who would

---

* Indignati Angligenæ . . . ad expellendum alienigenas . . . uno animo properabant. Ann. de Burton, p. 500.

have devoured all English people. Therefore he should have lordship."*

Simon encamped his army at Dover, whence he could best command the Channel, and in June he sent a writ under his seal to the citizens of London, by the hand of the knight Roger Clifford. He thereby invited them to proclaim the Provisions of Oxford, which had been issued to promote the glory of God, loyalty to the King, and the weal of the whole realm.† In a tumultuous popular assembly the citizens set aside the hesitation of royalist aldermen of the ruling families, and vehemently cheered their Mayor, Thomas Fitz-Thomas, when he proposed to comply with the Earl's request. Again the King's cause was ruined. He had shut himself up in the Tower with his family and court when an accommodation was proposed to

* Il est apelé de Monfort,
    Il est el mond et si est fort,
        Si ad grant chevalerie ;
    Ce voir, et je m'acort,
    Il eime dreit, et het le tort,
        Si avera la mestrie.

    El mond est veréement,
    Là ou la comun à ly concent
        De la terre loée :
    C'est ly quens de Leycestre,
    Que baut et joius se puet estre
        De cele renomée.
                    Wright, Political Songs, p. 61.
    † Liber de Antiq. Leg. 54, statuta facta ad honorem Dei, ad fidem Domini regis, et ad utilitatem totius regni.

him from various quarters. On the 29th of June the
Bishop of Winchester addressed the King's Chancellor,
Walter of Merton, with an urgent request that he
would help in promoting the peace of the kingdom.
On the same day King Richard was negotiating with
the army, which in the meantime had taken up a
position on the Thames above London. At court he
urgently advised that some restraint should be put
upon his nephew Edward, who had violently broken
into the Temple and taken £1000 from the treasure
chest.* But, on the following day, Richard announced
that the Earl had eluded a conference, and withdrawn
between Reading and Guildford,† evidently in order
that the pressure of the capital might work with
greater effect. He was not mistaken, for in a few
days the unchained fury of the populace forced the
most hated of all the counsellors, John Mansell, to a
precipitate flight down the Thames and across the
Channel. Through all changes he had been the soul
of the resistance at court, and innumerable benefices
had been sacrificed to his greed. Henry, son of the
King of the Romans, pursued him, and was taken
prisoner by a French nobleman, whereupon his father
threatened to make terms independently with the
Barons, unless the King would consent to negotiate,

* Two letters of Richard's, Rymer, i. 427. The second also
Shirley, ii. 247. Compare Ann. de Dunst., 222.

† Shirley, ii. 248. On the 16th a royal safe conduct had
been despatched for Simon. Rot. Lit. Pat. 47 Henr. III.
membr. 8.

and himself guarantee Henry's release.* The King
immediately gave his word, with his usual intention of
disregarding it. Meanwhile, Edward, with some faithful troops, had succeeded in seizing the royal fortress
of Windsor, and his mother, Queen Eleanor, intended
to join him by water. Her strength of will was much
greater than her husband's, and precisely for that
reason, and on account of her Provençal and Savoyard
kinsfolk who had taken up their abode in the country,
she was the special object of popular hatred. On the
13th of July, as she sailed through London Bridge,
the people compelled her to turn back by scornful
abuse and actual violence.

The Earl of Leicester had waited for such events as
these, and on the 15th he entered the capital at the
head of his army, like a conqueror, amid shouts of
rejoicing and ringing of bells. The gates of the
Tower were opened to him now, and the King, reduced
to submit to his will, again assented to the humiliating
Provisions. Delegates elected by the two parties were
to consult together as to what must be added to the
Provisions, and what taken away, for the good of the
sovereign and the kingdom.† It was a significant fact

---

* Richard from Berkhamstead, July 10th; Rymer. i. 427. The
King from the Tower, also July 10th; Rot. Lit. Pat. 47 Henr.
III. membr. 7.

† Ita quod per quosdam electos ad hoc statuta Oxoniae per
dicta eorum deberent augmentari vel diminui, prout utilitati
regis et regni expediret. Ann. de Dunst. 224. A royal order
of the 18th commands Edward to deliver up the Castle of Dover

that the servants of the Church, the Bishops of London, Lincoln, Coventry and Lichfield, as well as Worcester, used their influence in furtherance of this agreement. When Prince Edward had hastened from Windsor towards the Welsh border, and narrowly escaped capture by the citizens of Bristol, Worcester even induced him, though in extreme ill-humour, to turn back to London. There, in St. Paul's church, on the 9th of September, the spiritual and temporal peers assembled in Parliament, swore to recognise the constitution which the conquerors proposed. The King once more took up his residence in Westminster, after he had dismissed his officers, and again confirmed Nicolas of Ely and Hugh Despenser as Chancellor and Great Justiciary; but Simon de Montfort actually ✓ governed the kingdom in his name.*

Nevertheless, his success was as insecure and as short lived as it had been five years earlier, and he was compelled to yield still oftener to the opposition of others. The nobility of Northern England did not give him their support, but rather invited the King to throw himself into their arms. Prince Edward, who had wildly attempted much more than he was

to the Bishop of London. The opening words are, Quia pax inter nos et barones nostros reformata est et firmata. Rymer, l. c.

* The great seal was delivered up to Nicolas of Ely on the 19th of July at Westminster in præsentia S. de Monteforti Comitis Leicestriæ et aliorum Magnatum Angliæ. Rot. Lit. Claus. 47 Henr. III. membr. 6. For the proofs of these events, see Gesch. v. England, iii. 749, and Stubbs, Const. Hist. ii. 86, 87.

able to accomplish, only acquiesced in his fate under
compulsion, and became almost immediately the rally-
ing point for many knights and barons who, ill-
pleased by the recent violent changes and the
imperious and illegal position of him whom they
had placed at the head of affairs,* already contem-
plated another revolution. Even of those who had
made themselves prominent by their vehemence in the
persecution of aliens, some now deserted, as Leiburne,
Vaux, and Bigod. The restless Henry, King Richard's
son, who after his return from the French coast had
been commissioned, with some others of these nobles,
to pledge Edward to observe the Statutes,† presently
declared to Leicester that he should never again draw
his sword against the two Kings, his father and uncle,
against his blood relations. He requested his dismis-
sion, promising at the same time not to appear in
arms against the Earl, who replied : " Your sword
troubles me not, Lord Henry, but your instability.
Go, therefore, and come again with thy weapons, for I
surely do not fear them.‡

Under these circumstances King Henry meditated
another meeting with Louis IX., a project which he
could not have entertained if it had been possible for

---

* Comes quippe Leicestriæ omni pœne nobilium regni
caterva submixus erexit sibi cornua superbiæ, moliendo grandia,
cogitando sublimia, nec permisit ejus improbitas quod aliquatenus
flecteretur ad pacem, writes the royalist Thos. Wykes, p. 136.

† Rymer, i. 430.

Will. Rishanger, Chronica, 13, ed. Riley.

him who had assumed the direction of the government
to prevent the journey. Although when the royal family
were formally invited to Boulogne, the Barons caused
the King to swear that after a brief conference he
would return with all speed, and although he himself
requested the Earl to accompany him,* even Simon's
presence could not prevent an attack upon his
authority being concerted at the instigation of the
Queen. She remained behind in France, whilst
Henry, immediately after his punctual return home,
began to disturb the peace that he had been
compelled to conclude by demanding a compensation
for the dispossessed foreigners, and dismissing the
counsellors who had been forced upon him. The breach
was then soon complete. At the beginning of
December the father and son found themselves so
far prepared, that they could march suddenly from
Windsor against Dover, and, after an attack upon this
most important key of the kingdom had failed,
attempt by a bold and rapid movement to regain
possession of the capital. Being in correspondence
with four prominent burgesses, they had chosen
the moment when Simon was absent at Kenilworth
Castle, the defence of which, after it was well fortified
and provisioned, he had intrusted to his wife.† He

* Henry to Louis, Aug. 16th, barones nostri ex certis causis
volunt securitatem sibi præstari de reditu nostro festino : Rymer,
i. 429. Henry to Simon, Sept. 16th, invitation to be in Boulogne
on the 23rd ; Shirley, ii . 249.

† Green, Princesses, ii. 124.

K 2

narrowly escaped capture by the enemy in Southwark as he hastened back, but the Londoners
voluntarily opened the gate of their bridge to him
and stifled the disaffection which was striving to
make itself felt in their midst. The King now
commanded them in vain to expel the Earls of
Leicester and Derby (Robert de Ferrers), with their
troops, from the town.*

Thus violence and treachery, defiance and cowardice,
were again matched against one another. Though
agitated and excited, the liegemen of England still did
not venture to wreak their fury upon their own
flesh and blood, but at the same time they and the
crown were equally unable to devise for themselves
any expedient whereby to secure peace. Now,
at last, Louis IX. declared himself ready to bring
the affair in its entire compass under the consideration
of his tribunal. Probably the last royalist rising had
been intended to prepare the way for this arrangement,
and the meeting at Boulogne had laid the basis.†
On Sunday, the 16th of December, Henry III.,
Prince Edward and their adherents, declared from

---

* Quatinus . . . ad perturbationem predicti regni nostri
cum equis et armis commorantes visis litteris istis sine dilatione
aliqua amoveatis ab eadem, Dec. 8th. Now printed, Shirley, ii.
250.

† Archbishop Boniface, the Queen's uncle, was also in Paris,
in sermonibus publicis tam apud Prædicatores quam apud
Minores regis Angliæ comitis que Leicestriæ processus gestaque
declaravit. Nicolai Trivet. Annales, 254 (Engl. Hist. Society).

Windsor that, if the verdict upon the Provisions of Oxford and all contested points arising thence were given before Whitsuntide, they would accept unconditionally the decision of the French King. Leicester and his party had been obliged to execute a deed of similar purport on the 13th.* From these documents the inconstancy of the individual Barons and the groups they formed, are more evident than before. To the King adhered, besides his son and nephew, the heads of the most noble houses, as the Earls of Norfolk, Warenne, and Hereford, William of Valence, who was not to be driven away, and twenty-six others; amongst them the northern Barons, Percy, Nevil, Vaux, Marmion, Bruce, and Baliol, but also Bigod, Basset, Leiburne, and many another who had once declared himself a supporter of the Statutes of Oxford. With Simon, on the other hand, besides the Bishops of London and Worcester, were the Great Justiciary Despenser, two young Montforts, the cousin Peter, and seventeen more. The list included such names as Humphrey de Bohun, the heir of Hereford and Essex, Basset, Ross, Grey, Vescy, Lascy, and Vipont. Younger sons predominated in this company, and natives of the southern part of the island.†

---

* Super provisionibus, ordinationibus, statutis et obligationibus omnibus Oxoniensibus, et super omnibus contentionibus et discordiis quas habemus et habuimus usque ad festum Omnium Sanctorum. The deeds, Rymer, i. 433, 434; and Shirley, ii. 251.

† See the references in Stubbs, Const. Hist. ii. 87, 88.

Immediately after Christmas the King and his son,
with a numerous following, repaired to Amiens, the
place named in the writs. Earl Simon had likewise
started from Kenilworth and reached Catesby in
Northamptonshire, but there he broke his thigh bone
by a fall from his horse, and was thus compelled to
remain at home.   On the 31st December, Humphrey
de Bohun the younger, Henry and Peter de Montfort,
Adam of Newmarket, William Marshall, William le
Blond, and three clerks experienced in affairs, were
deputed to represent his cause.* Louis heard the
advocates on both sides, and on the 23rd of January,
1264, he solemnly and formally delivered his judgment, the so-called Misa of Amiens.   He cancelled
the Provisions, already declared null and void by the
Pope, with all constitutional law that might be
deduced from them, because they were derogatory
to the power and dignity of the crown, and had
caused dissension in the kingdom, spoliation of
the Church, and great injury to all private persons,
whether lay or clerical, native or foreign.   The
observance of them, or even continued legislation
based upon them, was forbidden, and all covenants that
the King had been forced to make were repealed.
Louis further ruled that all fortresses must be restored
to Henry without any pledge or security, and

---

* Ann. de Dunst. 227, and Simon's credential from the Paris
archives printed in the Chronicle published by Halliwell under
the name of Rishanger (the Chronicle of William de Rishanger
of the Barons' War, Camden Society, 1840), p. 122.

absolute liberty accorded him to choose either alien or native ministers for all offices whether high or low, and to appoint and dismiss them at will. No guarantees remained against the complete restoration of the monarch's personal authority, except that the charters and franchises granted before 1258 were left untouched by the Misa, and an amnesty was promised for all that had occurred since that date.*

All contemporaries must have foreseen that the verdict of St. Louis, of him who had augmented his own kingdom and was regarded as the glory and ornament of monarchy, would surely be favourable to unlimited sovereignty. Moreover, as Henry's brother-in-law, he could not be an impartial judge. But did the Barons really entertain the hope that he would decide in their favour? Was their acquiescence in this transaction merely apparent? Or was there not incitement to renewed resistance in the sentence which annihilated their work? The application made by Henry to an alien King was practically an indirect petition for help, and brought more disgrace upon him in the eyes of the nation than they, the representatives of national independence, could incur by refusing to accept this foreign decision. And if they yielded all other points and again trusted to their ancient privileges, the unconditional return of insatiable foreign parasites would be a transgression

* The judgment in Rymer, i. 433, Stubbs, Select Charters, 106, also in the Paris archives and in a communication to the City of London in the Liber de Antiq. Leg. 59.

against the law of nature, and no arbitrator in the
world could insist upon it. Not only was the national
party incensed by so unreasonable a demand; the
royalists in England themselves called it hasty and
imprudent.* The many voices which did homage to
the popular cause attributed the blame, according to
the rumour of the day, sometimes to the two Queens
of England and France, sometimes to direct bribes to
which Louis had yielded.† There were even distant
hints at his secret wish to sow the seeds of new and
disastrous strife.

If he really allowed himself to be bought, it was for
a prize situated in a totally different place, and not only
costing the King of England nothing, but even greatly
relieving his embarrassments. On the 28th of July,
1263,‡ Pope Urban IV. had released Henry from all
obligations undertaken by him on account of the Sicilian crown promised to his son Edmund, and at the
same time he cast his eye upon Louis's brother, Count
Charles of Anjou, as the fittest person to overthrow
the last offshoots of the Hohenstaufen family. The
Misa of Amiens declared expressly that the Holy
Father was ever the supreme arbitrator of the fate of

* Forte minus sapienter et inutiliter quam deceret eructatione
si quidem improvisa suum præcipitavit arbitrium. Th. Wykes.
139.

† O rex Francorum, multorum causa dolorum.
Judex non rectus ideo fis jure rejectus.
M.S. Cott. Otho D. viii. quoted by Blaauw. The Barons' War,
1844, p. 98.

‡ Rymer. i. 428.

kingdoms. His jurisdiction extended over the Norman
State of the north, where the devout King must be protected against the eager desires of his subjects for
parliamentary government, and over that of the south,
where an unruly and ever accursed race of princes was
to be expelled. As neighbour and suzerain the French
King had always a word to interpose in the constitutional struggle, and his real power was great enough
to restrain the two parties from open and bloody war
up to this date. But the decision in the last instance
lay with Urban. Quite in accordance with the tactics
of his predecessor, who had justified Henry III.'s first
perjury in anticipation, and in some measure as preliminary to the repeal of the Oxford articles by the King
of France, Urban had during the summer of 1263 repeatedly reminded the English that all which they attained by conspiracy was as tares sown by the Evil one,
and therefore long ago condemned by the Holy See.
On the 27th of November, as arranged in a diplomatic
agreement, he issued a mandate for the preaching of a
crusade against the English rebels, and wrote threateningly to the Earl of Leicester, " the ringleader of the
revolt, who had so basely degenerated from the example of his illustrious forefathers, the zealous promoters of a righteous peace."* The same messenger
carried the tidings that Guido, the Cardinal Bishop of

* Primus inter actores turbationis hujusmodi . . . nam cum tui
progenitores sicut de ipsis habet fama laudabilis pacis zelatores
extiterunt . . . . immo dampnabiliter degenerare videris
ab illis. Urbani. IV. Epp. iii. 188, 199. according to the copies in
M.S. Add. Mus. Brit. 15,361. Also Raynaldi a. iii. § 83, 84.

Sabina, one of the most redoubtable representatives of Papal policy, was about to arrive as Legate. The verdict of Amiens was officially confirmed at Rome in the middle of March, almost immediately it was known.* It is easy to see how all the circumstances dove-tailed together, and France and the Court of Rome, as allies of the English crown, believed that they could cope with the constitutional pretensions of the estates, which threatened to be inconvenient to all three.

King Henry did not venture to land in England until the 15th of February, when he knew that the Cardinal-Legate was on his way, and after he had received considerable pecuniary assistance from Louis. He learnt with great uneasiness that though some of his adversaries had laid down their arms, terrified by the rigour of the sentence, others now first felt themselves bound to maintain the Provisions of Oxford, because all earlier franchises, especially the Magna Charta, were confirmed by the Misa of Amiens, and the Provisions were simply the natural outgrowth of these.

The Earl of Leicester said, and his words circulated far and wide, that he and his four sons would stand firm, although he had never found in strange lands, among Christians or heathen, such faithlessness and treachery as here in England.† On the Welsh border, where

---

* The Acts of the Curia in this affair collected in my Geschichte von England, iii. 758, 759.

† The Chronicle ascribed by Halliwell to Rishanger, p. 17, 18.

tho Montforts now openly allied themselves with Prince
Llewellyn, disorders had broken out, so that, as early
as the 4th of February, the royal sheriffs in Worcester,
Stafford, and Shropshire were ordered to destroy all
bridges over the Severn, with the single exception of
that at Gloucester.* When the King returned from.
France, the Earl of Leicester, his family and retainers,
had already taken up arms and secured the most important passages across the river. Early in March Prince
Edward hurried to oppose them, and fought valiantly
for the possession of Gloucester; on the 13th he withdrew in order to effect a junction with his father at
Oxford.

The choice of this city, where Henry summoned the
baronage of the realm to meet in Parliament, and
which also offered a convenient pivot for his military
operations in the civil war, was peculiarly significant
in contrast to the events which had taken place there
six years earlier. But one serious difficulty required first to be removed, the temper of the university, by which the Barons had doubtless profited at
that time. The new spirit had been planted by the
energy of the friars, Franciscans and Dominicans.
It was devoted to practical social reform, and imbued
with their doctrine of a stern religious need for change
of nature. The thoughts freely interchanged among
such men as Grosseteste, Marsh, and Montfort, rising
to the highest questions in Church and State, struck
deep root. Just at the middle of the century the

* Shirley, ii. 254.

place attained for the first time the dignity of a
national school. Students, eager for knowledge, from
the opulent classes in all parts of the kingdom,
crowded thither to be trained in the sober but popular
scholasticism of the Minorites.* The projects and
ideas which had inspired their fathers found a still
more vehement acceptance among the younger generation. The wandering scholars, infected by the universal spirit of violence, were engaged in a furious
fight with the citizens at the time when Prince Edward
marched past on his way to Gloucester.† Probably
this was the immediate reason of a stringent order
issued by the King to the Chancellor and University
on the 12th of March, as soon as he arrived at Woodstock. He desired to meet the estates at Oxford upon
most solemn business of State, but among them would
be many unruly fighting men, probably the Barons
expected from the Scotch border, and therefore the
scholars were commanded to leave the town and repair
for a while to their homes, all their rights being as-
sured to them.‡ The true reason, the fear of the

* See in general my Tübingen Programme of 1864, p. 21, and
an excellent passage in J. R. Green's 'Short History of the
English People,' 144.

† A. Wood, Hist. et Antiq. Oxon., p. 111.

‡ Nos attendentes quod sine gravissimo periculo ibidem morari
non possetis, maxime cum in tanta congregacione multi indomiti,
quorum serviciam de facili reprimere non possemus ibidem fuerint
accessuri, vobis mandamus firmiter injungentes, quatinus ad
pacem et. tranquillitatem vestram salvandam a dicta villa ad
propria sine dilacione divertatis. Rymer, i. 435.

great number of able-bodied students and their rebellious temper, was suppressed. A contemporary
reckoned their number at 15,000.* The error of
driving away such multitudes into the arms of the
enemies of the crown, could not fail to work its own
punishment.

At Oxford and at Brackley, a few miles to the
north-east, where the Earl of Leicester was encamped
with his followers, brief but active negotiations seem
to have been carried on once more, through the
mediation of the clergy and a French ambassador.
According to one positive statement, the nobility
promised to acquiesce in the Amiens sentence if the
King would give up the article in favour of aliens.
The terms were even drawn up, stipulating that,
among all his countrymen, none should be permitted
to return except Boniface, the Archbishop of Canterbury.† But the King's evil counsellors induced him
to withdraw this concession, and on the 20th of March,
the last day on which he issued safe conducts to the
opposite party, he summoned the long prepared troops

* Erat enim clericorum numerus, quorum nomina scripta
fuerunt in matriculis rectorum, excedens XVM. Rishanger, ed.
Halliwell, p. 22.

† Copy of a record by the town clerk of London in MS. Mus.
Brit. Add. 5411, fol. 66ᵇ.: quod saltem unicum et solum remittat
articulum, viz., quod alienigenis ab Anglia remotis per indigenas
gubernetur, et omnibus statutis provisionibus et ordinationibus
regis Franciæ aquiescat. Also the agreement concerning the
Archbishop in præsentia illustris regis Angliæ, de consilio procerum et magnatum ejusdem regni. Rymer, i. 438.

to appear under arms on the 30th, because a serious contest threatened danger to crown and kingdom.* A few days later the army marched from Oxford to Northampton, where Simon's men had withdrawn behind the walls. On the 5th of April, Edward ordered an assault and succeeded in entering the town through the treachery of the French Prior of St. Andrew's monastery, the Barons and the band of students, who fought under their own banner,† making an heroic but fruitless resistance. The young Simon de Montfort was taken prisoner, with fifteen bannerets and forty knights, whilst his father escaped with the rest from the pursuit of the royal army, turning first towards the east and afterwards towards the south.

But this disaster was more than counter-balanced elsewhere. In the city of London every measure tending towards submission was rejected, the party of progress, the *Bacheleria*,‡ had unquestionably the upper hand, and the numerous inhabitants took up arms under their own constable and marshal. Here Hugh Despenser still ruled as Great Justiciary, doubtless in concert with the Earl of Leicester. On

* Four documents, Rymer, i. 436, 437 ; March 13, 18, 20. In the last are the words : Cum jam in regno nostro gravissima turbacio sit suborta, ex qua periculum regni et corone Anglie, quod absit, de facili possit imminere.

† Walter de Hemingburgh, i. 311 (ed. Engl. Hist. Soc.) habebant enim vexillum per se et in sublime contra regem erectum.

‡ Innumera multitudo ribaldorum quos bachilarios vocitabant. Thos. Wykes, 138.

the 31st of March, the great bell of St. Paul's rang
an alarum, and the populace poured out to devas-
tate King Richard's magnificent parks at Isleworth,
and the neighbouring estates of William of Valence,
Walter of Merton, and Philip Basset. Within the
city they fell upon the Jews, and searched for their
stores of money deposited in the Temple. A nobleman who had slain the wealthy Kok Abrahamson
offered half the plunder to the Earl of Leicester. The
people also laid hands upon the officers of the royal
courts at Westminster.* The insurrection and the
acts of devastating violence went on under Simon's
eyes, for by Palm Sunday (the 12th of April), he had
advanced as far as St. Albans, summoned thither by
the preparations which the enemy were already making
to cut him off from the coast.

From Oxford a detachment had marched upon
Rochester, led by the Earl of Warenne, who had
recently become once more an ardent royalist. On
the 19th Simon stormed and took the town, but the
old castle, built by Bishop Gundulf, the Conqueror's
great architect, resisted all his siege appliances.
The Easter season closed ; then tidings arrived that
Prince Edward, who had hitherto occupied strong
quarters in Leicester and Nottingham, the domains of
Montfort and Derby, was now completely in accord
with the Barons of the Scotch border, and was leading
forward the King's main army by forced marches.
The Londoners urged the Earl of Leicester to return
for the defence of their city on the 26th. Rochester

Thos. Wykes, 140–143. Lib. de Antiq. Leg. 61, 62.

must therefore be given up, and under these circumstances the King thought to make himself master of
the Cinque Ports, Sandwich, Dover, Winchelsea,
Romney, and Hythe. But the inhabitants, endowed
from time immemorial with certain baronial rights for
coast defence and navigation, proved no less defiant
than the Londoners. They manned their ships and
put to sea, that they might not be employed in a
voyage up the Thames against the capital. The
people of Kent and Surrey showed themselves altogether unfriendly; provisions were soon unattainable,
so that horse and man must starve.

At length the King led his army into Sussex, and
on Sunday, the 11th of May, he fixed his head-quarters
at the Priory of Lewes, a noble position where the
Ouse broadens into an arm of the sea. As an off-
shoot of Cluny, the community was well inclined towards foreign connections, and as a Benedictine
foundation, thoroughly royalist in sympathy.

All attempts upon London had meanwhile been
suspended. The riches of the capital even then promised
success to the cause it espoused, and for many years
the system of arbitrary amercements by the crown,
the innumerable discourtesies of the court and its followers towards the citizens, and the complete in-
difference of the government to the interests of the
flourishing transmarine commerce, had fostered resentment and ill-will. For these and other reasons the
citizens regarded the cause of the Barons as their own,
and looked upon the Earl of Leicester as the states-

man and popular hero who would unite the military and commercial classes, and lead them to victory.

After agreeing with the nobles and citizens to offer peace once more upon condition that the Statutes of Oxford were accepted, Leicester, on the 6th of May, marched southward at the head of his troops, to whom a strong band of some 15,000 Londoners had now joined themselves.[*] On the 12th of May, they encamped upon a woody ridge a few miles above Lewes, near the village of Fletching. A brief and courteous letter to the King, under the seal of the Earls of Leicester and Gloucester, besought him to give up certain counsellors, his enemies and theirs. It was conveyed by the Bishops of London and Worcester to the monastery, where they also discharged their special oral commission. But Edward was eager for war, and, in this case, King Richard also. They would listen to no terms, although £30,000, even 50,000 marks to the King of the Romans personally, are said to have been offered as compensation for the devastation and destruction of property.[†] They persuaded the King to declare that Simon de Montfort and Gilbert de Clare were his enemies—with-

---

[*] Rishanger, ed. Halliwell, p. 27. Lib. de Antiq. Leg. 62.

[†] This is the subject of the ballad, or rather satire, which has been so often printed, the oldest in the English language :

> The Kyng of Alemaigne, bi mi leauté
> Thritti thousend pound askede he
> For to make the pees in the countrée.

Percy, Reliques of Ancient English Poetry, ed. 1810, p. 90. Wright, Political Songs. p. 69.

out even deigning to give them the title of Earl—
because they and their confederates had brought war
and rebellion into the land, and henceforth he cared
nothing for their safety and friendship. In a separate
written declaration, Richard and Edward, the lords,
and knights, on their side, took upon themselves the
responsibility of advising the King, and offered to prove
their own loyalty, and the treachery of the opposite
party before the royal court of justice.*   After this full
renunciation of obedience and esteem, the two armies
made ready on the 13th for battle.

The bloodless strife of words was at an end, and there
remained no appeal but to the sword. Among the
patriots all were inspired by one sentiment, one faith,
one will, and by love to God and their fellow-men†
which robbed death for their country of all terror.
Every one relied with implicit confidence upon Simon's
energy, and the military genius‡ of which he had once

* These three letters are not found in the rolls of chancery, the
keeping of which was much disturbed by the war, but they are
preserved in most of the annals of the time. First printed from
the continuations of Matthew Paris. Rymer, i. 440. See Gesch.
von England, iii. 766, 768—notes.

† Per omnia una fides, una voluntas fuit, amor et Dei et proxi-
mi. Rishanger, ed. Halliwell, p. 34.

‡ Tum propter ejus constantiam, tum propter belli notitiam.
Tantus erat ei ardor finem malis imponere, ut mallet ultima ex-
periri, quam regni calamitatem ulterius protendi. Opus chronicorum, ed. Riley (Rerr. Brit. med. ævi S.S. 1866), p. 10, a newly
published record, also written at St. Albans, which was used in
both versions of the continuation of Matth. Paris going under
Rishanger's name.

given glorious proof in Gascony. First of all he commended the event to Heaven, spending the night in
prayer, as was his father's habit, and as his unforgotten
friends and spiritual counsellors would have enjoined.
The good Bishop Walter of Worcester, steadfast and
like-minded, went from tent to tent along the ranks
receiving confessions, pronouncing absolution, and dispensing the sacrament. The white cross worn by each
man on breast and shoulder was the symbol of a holy
conflict. The enterprises against unbelievers in distant
lands, in which the general had once taken part, were
not yet discontinued. Like their fathers in 1215, the
English gathered together as an " army of the Lord "
against the same oppressors.

With the first grey of morning, on Wednesday, the
14th of May, the Earl rose and drew up his host on the
edge of the woody height overlooking the castle, town,
and priory of Lewes, and the noble river. In the
centre stood a chariot once used by Simon on account
of the bone fracture, from which he had still scarcely
recovered. According to the usage of the time it now
carried the great standard, and chained within it were
those four London burgesses who, in the previous
November, had designed to deliver up Simon to the
King at Southwark. All around, under a strong guard,
was a rampart formed of various kinds of carriages, and
the hosts destined for the onslaught stood closely
massed on the two wings. Just as the sun
rose out of the ocean, Simon bent his knee and
offered the last prayer, the whole army following his

L 2

example. The Earl dubbed Gilbert of Gloucester
knight, with two other youths, Robert de Vere, Earl of
Oxford, and John de Burgh; then with faces turned
eastward, they marched in steadfast order out of the
wood and down the valley towards Lewes.*

The royalists who had spent the night merrily, after
the fashion of cavaliers, in wine and song, and even, in
spite of their clerical quarters, in the arms of women,†
were taken wholly by surprise when the announcement
of their sentinels called them from their beds to battle.
The attack was received almost under the walls of the
town by a foraging party who had put to horse early in
the morning. But arms and armour were rapidly
donned, and the men ranged themselves in rank and
file under the escutcheons of their leaders. As soon as
the ancient standard of the Kings of England, the
British dragon, fluttered high in the air, the army, full
of chivalrous courage, advanced to the assault in three

---

* The principal authority is the description of the battle,
doubtless derived from an eye-witness, in Rishanger, ed. Halliwell, p. 31 et seq.; also information from the manuscript chronicle
of Rochester, ibid. p. 130, and Rishanger, ed. Riley, p. 25-26.

† Generally Thos. Wykes, p. 150. At illi stupefacti perpro-
pere surgentes . . . exeuntes in occursum multitudinis tam pro-
fanæ. According to the popular description of the time, Political
Songs, p. 80 :

Qui carnis luxuria fœda sorduerunt.
Factis lupanaribus robur minuerunt.
Unde militaribus indigni fuerunt.

Likewise Chronicon de Mailros, ed. Stevenson, p. 193, noctem
illam coreis et cantilenis occupans, potacionibus et scortacionibus
insistebat : adding, protestante mihi uno nobili qui ibi fuerat.

divisions, commanded severally by Prince Edward, the King of the Romans, and Henry himself. The Earl of Leicester had barely time to take up another position which his keen eye saw to be necessary from the nature of the ground. Three valiant young noblemen, Hastings, Segrave, and Borham, were commissioned to lead the scarcely disciplined London bands, and force the way from the north straight to the castle walls; the second division was commanded by Gilbert of Gloucester, and the third, at his right, by the two young Montfort's, Henry and Guy. Their father remained in the rear guard and directed the whole.

Full of wild impetuosity and bitter anger, Edward dashed forward to attack the citizens who had insulted his mother, chased them into the water on the right and up the hill to the left, and himself reached the spot where the standard was raised, slaying the guard, together with the four unfortunate prisoners. He kept up the pursuit and slaughter for hours, and believed that he had already defeated the flower of the enemy's army and their commander himself, whilst, in fact, Leicester, without paying great heed to the citizens, was causing his better equipped divisions to advance against the two kings. After a long resistance their ranks were completely broken. Those who were not slain in the fight sought to save their lives as best they might, some in the sanctuary of the Priory, others by surrendering on the battle-field to the victors· Warenne, Valence, Guy of Lusignan, Hugh Bigod, and three hundred horsemen, fought their way through to

Pevensey, and then set sail for the French coast. King Henry, whose horse had been killed under him, delivered up his sword to the Earl of Gloucester; even his brother Richard, after seeking refuge in a mill which had served as a post of observation and support during the fight, descended as a prisoner amid scorn and derision.* Many nobles were obliged to surrender, as the Earls of Hereford and Arundel, Philip Basset, Henry Percy, and the Barons of the Scotch lowlands, Bruce, Baliol, and Comyn. Only two noblemen of rank were slain on each side, and altogether about 5000 servants and soldiers. It was evening when the Prince and his cousin Henry returned, weary and unsuspecting, after they had, in the intoxication of victory, pursued the scattered citizens far into the country. In his first consternation on learning the events of the day, Edward proposed to throw himself into the castle, where the garrison still held out. They capitulated on the following day, and the Prince then resolved to share the fate of his house, and surrendered to the conqueror.†

* Motus est exercitus baronum versus quoddam molendinum circa Lewes. MS. Mus. Brit. Add. 5444, fol. 68ᵇ. For full details, Chron. de Mailros, 196, and the English ballad:

> The Kyng of Alemaigne wende do ful wel,
> He saisede the mulne for a castel,
> With hare sharpe swerdes he grounde the stel,
> He wende that the sailes were mangonel
> To helpe Wyndesore.

† The sources of information upon the battle of Lewes, to a great extent supplementing and corroborating one another are, in order of importance: Thos. Wykes, 149,-152; the two records

England had never yet seen such a conflict between the King and his subjects, between the nearest kindred, and people of one tongue and and one faith. A sacred although joyous thankfulness spread far and wide through the land, for the people, believing that one decisive event had freed them from insupportable oppression, hoped to reap a happy harvest from the seed of native blood. With a smaller force Simon had defeated the better equipped army of the enemy, and his enthusiastic national adherents celebrated his praise in almost Puritan spirit as a Moses who had rescued the people of Israel from Egyptian tribulation, as a Gideon or Matathias. Next to God they gave glory to him and his valiant sons; he was called the corner stone of English freedom.*

The ordeal of battle had decided against the King, who had persisted in governing by his own absolute authority, or in dependence upon unconstitutional favourites.† Now, he and his family and adherents

attributed to Rishanger: the Ann. Waverleienses, p. 356, 357, of the new edition; the Chronicon de Mailros, 392 *et seq.* ed. Stevenson. derived from the report of a Scot who was present. The greatest number of topographical and genealogical details are given by Blaauw in a work which is extremely serviceable, in spite of critical deficiencies, The Barons' War, including the Battles of Lewes and Evesham, 1844, p. 143–189.

        * Fides et fidelitas Symonis solius

          Fit pacis integritas Angliæ totius.

Wright, Political Songs, p. 85, the longest and most significant of these songs, composed in the same year.

   † The following official note to a decree, having reference to the

were in the power of men to whom, after a series of
fruitless experiments, no other resource remained than
to use force in dealing with him. The idea of abolish-
ing royalty in this State, once founded by the strong
hand of a King, did not occur to them. But when the
Sovereign accepted, under compulsion, a constitution
drawn up by his vassals, did he retain more than a
shadow of that dignity which had once bound together
State and people in one whole ? Could this new constitutional and parliamentary régime be attained by no
other means than by harshness and injury to the one,
under whose oppression the many had so long groaned ?

Montfort had scarcely put an end to the excesses
which followed the victory, when the more arduous
work of the statesman and ruler commenced. His
first steps were altogether sagacious and well-con-
sidered. Several Franciscans and monks of the priory
went busily to and fro between friends and enemies,
in order to prevent further blood-shedding. The King's
first proclamation commanded the garrison to lay down
their arms, because peace was concluded between him
and the Barons,* and a preliminary compromise, the
Misa of Lewes, was meanwhile negotiated. The docu-

French subsidies, and dated from Lewes on the 14th of May, the
day of the battle, is a convincing proof that all regular government was at an end : Et sciendum quod magister Arnulphus,
cancellarius regis Alemanniæ, dictavit et scripsit manibus propriis litteram supradictam, sine consilio et assensu alicujus clerici
de cancellaria ; et consignata fuit coram consilio Domini Regis
apud Lewes die supradicto. Rymer, i. 440.

*Rot. Lit. Pat. 48 Henr. III. membr. 13 : quia pax inter
regem et barones formata est.

ment, in seven articles, was afterwards suppressed,
like many more of that unquiet time ; but statements
of its contents are not entirely wanting. It breathed
a spirit of moderation, not holding the King account-
able, but aiming to make him compliant, and even
submissive. It showed that a desire still existed for
a higher court of arbitration, to be composed, since
King Louis's efforts had proved abortive, of French
and English bishops and peers, with the addition or
the new Papal Legate. The Provisions of Oxford
were regarded as the public law of the land ; they
might indeed be altered, but only after general discussion.* On the other hand, the exclusion of
foreigners from domestic offices and the King's
council, and strict frugality in the finances of the
royal household, were demands from which no abate-
ment could be made. The terms included a mutual
amnesty and exchange of prisoners ; those of Northampton in return for those of Lewes ; ransoms were
forbidden as inadmissible in a war between fellow-
countrymen. Until the terms were fulfilled, the Princes
Edward and Henry were to be retained as hostages,
as well as the castle of Dover, which was committed
to Henry de Montfort. King Richard and his younger
son Edmund were forbidden ·to leave Richard's estate
of Wallingford.

In London, the King's residences of the Tower and

* Ita ut cum deliberatione tractaretur, quæ provisionum et
statutorum essent pro utilitate regni tenenda et quæ delenda.
Rishanger, ed. Riley. p. 28. Also Halliwell, p. 37 ; Wykes, 152 ;
Lib. de Antiq. Leg. 63. Cf. Stubbs' Const. Hist. ii. 90.

Westminster were found unfit for his reception; he, therefore, took up his abode with the Bishop on the 28th. On the road to the capital, new measures were resolved upon for calming the excited people, who, in many places, were suffering bitter want. The occupants of castles on both sides must discontinue their hostilities; every man must lay down his arms, and release his prisoners; further breaches of the peace were threatened with death, offences against ecclesiastical property and the life and goods of the Jews receiving special mention. As the appointment of sheriffs had repeatedly been the principal occasion of renewed strife, it was a happy expedient to nominate provisional guardians of the peace (custodes pacis) in twenty-nine counties.* The Chancellor and scholars of Oxford were not forgotten; on the 30th of May they were invited to return to the university town.†

By far the most important measure, was the proclamation of a parliament at London for the 23rd of June, to include, not only Prelates and Barons, but also other liege subjects; four prudent and competent Knights from each shire were expressly invited to attend.‡ The highest ranks here co-operated with representatives of the Commons, so far as they pre-

---

* The proclamations of the 17th, 25th, and 28th of May, of the 2nd, 4th, and 11th of June. Rymer, i. 411–413. Compare Rishanger, ed. Riley, 29.

† Rot. Lit. Pat. 48 Henr. III. membr. 12. Compare A. Wood. Hist. et Antiq. Oxon, p. 113.

‡ Quatuor de legalioribus et discretioribus militibus dicti comitatus per assensum ejusdem comitatus ad hoc electos.

sented themselves, and an attempt at least was made
to carry out the new scheme of government proposed
at Lewes.//To promote the peace of the kingdom,
three persons were to be elected, with the King's
approbation, upon taking a solemn oath. They, in
turn, were to choose nine others, laymen and churchmen, who should conduct the business of government
at the seat of the court, either altogether or in alternate
groups of three. The King was to act by their advice
in making appointments, and in all other matters. If
they should disagree, or individuals among them appear
ill-qualified, the decision lay with the first three;
these could not lawfully be changed without consent of
parliament. The members of the council must be
Englishmen, like all sheriffs and custodians of castles;
for the rest, foreigners were permitted to pass freely
in and out of the kingdom, especially for purposes of
trade. All charters of liberty which had been granted
to the English people were of course brought to mind,
and assurances were given on behalf of the King, his
son, and their partisans, that they would cherish no
resentment on account of recent events. In accordance
with Magna Charta, the Church was left to regulate
its own affairs; but Archbishop Boniface made no
response to the invitation to return, and this might
be regarded as a first indication of mischief.*

Rymer, i. 442, June 4th. Stubbs, Select Charters, 411. The
Report on the Dignity of a Peer is hypercritical in doubting their
presence, because it is not mentioned in the documents, i. 154.

* Rymer, i. 443, 444. Stubbs, Select Charters, 413, 414. Const.
Hist. ii. 90, 91.

On the same 23rd of June, the Bishop of Chichester, Stephen Berksted, Earl Simon, and Gilbert of Gloucester, received authority from the King to elect the council of nine. The regent of the realm, the soul of the entire movement, the Protector, as his contemporaries already styled him, was necessarily included in this commission. In contrast to the baronial government, in which he had formerly taken part, his political sagacity now taught him to exclude large numbers from the chosen committee; partly for the sake of concord, chiefly in order to preserve his own personal power. Whilst he occupied the apex of the pyramid, the assembly of the Knights might serve as a broad and steadfast base.

The position to which a sense of duty and solicitude for the public weal, no less than actual lust of power, caused him to aspire, was altogether exceptional and outside the law. He reserved to himself, for his personal security, the right of bearing arms, though it was denied to all others.* For and against him and his work, keen and vehement opinions were formed by the two parties; opinions that could not be silenced, and found striking expression in words.

His opponents attributed to him the most selfish designs for his own aggrandisement, and that of his sons, whom he loved tenderly; they asserted that he had already assumed the wardship of King Richard's extensive English domains, and eighteen baronies be-

* Rymer, i. 445. July 16 : Præsertim cum ex hoc nulli de regno dampnum debeat vel periculum imminere.

louging to royalist peers; that he dragged his King about with him through the country like a prisoner; that he, an Earl, regarded himself as co-regent, and the equal of kingly majesty.* But the men who accused him of considering his own and his descendants' advantage alone, entirely overlooked his untiring and zealous devotion to public affairs since 1258, and shut their eyes to the disastrous abuses in which the country had been plunged more and more deeply by the former legitimate and absolute government. No one had struggled against them with greater energy than he, who was now reproached as a traitor and usurper.†

These contradictory opinions are set forth with remarkable dialectical acuteness in a contemporary poem, whose author was unquestionably clerical, probably a Franciscan friar, deeply religious, and at the same time patriotic and loyal. By a course of temperate reasoning, political and constitutional in its character, he shows free compromise to be the only way of escape from the strife. He celebrates the Earl of Leicester as wholly disinterested and self-sacrificing, as the

---

* Supra modum glorians in virtute sua sibi et filiis suis, quos tenerrime diligebat . . . regem suum regere non erubuit, a quo regi rectissime tenebatur. Thos. Wykes, 153. He wrote later, but in the same popular language which is peculiar to the age of the baronial war.

       † Seductorem nominant S. atque fallacem ;
       Facta sed examinant probantque veracem.

saviour and deliverer of the realm.* According to the
popular belief, Simon, sincerely devoted to the precepts
of the Catholic faith, and as a scholar conversant with
the canon law, adhered with immovable constancy to
the oath which he had sworn to reform the kingdom
by means of the Statutes of Oxford. Whilst so many
had grown faithless, no persecution had induced him
to waver; not even Prince Edward's menace of rope
and gallows. At length, the ordeal of Lewes had
determined the fate of the two Kings and their heirs,
who had once perjured themselves by rejecting a
righteous compact, and now, in deep humiliation,
reaped the fruit of their transgressions against divine
and human law. All English people owed thanks to
Almighty God for the victory without which their very
existence would have been annihilated.†

The poet avoids describing the King's character,
but he entertains a warm admiration for the valour of
his son, whom he compares to a lion; yet changeful as
the motley leopard's skin upon the escutcheon of the

---

* The poem, which has already been used, published very
indifferently by Wright, Political Songs, p. 72 *et seq.*

> Qui se Christo similis dat pro multis morti . . .
> Nec fraus nec fallacia Comitem promovit,
> Sed divina gratia, quæ quos juvet novit.
>
> Page 89.

† Hæc Angli de prælio legite Lewensi,
> Cujus patrocinio vivitis defensi ;
> Quia si victoria jam victis cessisset,
> Anglorum memoria victa viluisset.
>
> Page 92.

Plantagenets is young Edward's faith; for in his need, he made large promises, and broke them instantly when he was free. How can he ever be a King, without reverence for law? The doctrine that law and right are superior to the crown,* with all its splendour and all its absolute power, what may be called the Teutonic conception of royalty, as opposed to Roman imperialism, had penetrated to the very marrow of this insular race. Upon this pivot all the other arguments of the singular poem revolve. As the root of the strife,† it indicated the monarch's determination to act according to his own pleasure, and, regarding the realm as his own domain, to dispose of Chancellor, Treasurer, Justiciary, and governors of castles and shires without taking counsel with the Barons. From the idea of an absolute self-dependent dignity, believing itself superior to law, it followed as a necessary consequence that nobles, knights, and freemen, who sought to acquire by peaceful means a control over, and a share in, the government of the State, must appear in the light of rebels.

The court is described in contrast, its corruption by flatterers, knavish impostors, and the avarice of aliens, with the ruin of the country arising thence. To reform all this was the object of the Barons, and it is

---

* Nam quid lege rectius qua cuncta reguntur,
  Et quid jure verius quo res discernuntur?

Page 94.

† En radicem tangimus perturbationis
  Regni, de quo scribimus.

Page 96.

proudly asked how it could have been so much as attempted without them.* Misled by others, or harbouring evil intentions himself, the King might rank his authority above the law, but then the Barons were legally and morally bound to remove the evil by a reform involving no harmful consequences.† The objection that the King, the image of the majesty of God, would thus be robbed of his freedom, is met by a reference to human sinfulness, and by the brief and clearly conceived formula that every restraint is not injurious to liberty, but, on the contrary, the sovereign would add splendour and amplitude to his royal dignity when guarded from evil influences and able only to do good.‡ It behoved the King to remember that he also is a servant of God, for he can only claim obedience and love from his subjects when he himself practises them. It follows, indeed, as an inexorable con-.

---

* Non sine baronibus tunc reformaretur.

Page 99.

† Cur melioratio non admitteretur.
  Cui vitiatio nulla commiscetur?

Page 102.

‡ Non omnis arctatio privat libertatem.
  Nec omnis districtio tollit potestatem.
  Ad quid vult libera lex reges arctari?
  Ne possint adultera lege maculari.
  Et haec coarctatio non est servitutis,
  Sed est ampliatio regiæ virtutis.

  Ergo regi libeat omne quod est bonum,
  Sed malum non audeat: hoc est Dei donum.

Pages 105, 106.

sequence, that when he errs and persists in error his subjects may call him to account.* Every sovereign who really possesses truth, wisdom, knowledge, and grace from God, and does not merely assume that he excels all other men therein, will without difficulty convince his people of his virtues. On the other hand, human weakness and all the toils of government can find no better support than trustful co-operation with the commons of the realm, with free fellow-countrymen, to whom the principles of those universal rights inherited from their forefathers are better known than to men who are foreign to the kingdom.† The poet has confidence that this constitutionalism would not degenerate, for then freedom would be turning against itself. He recalls the mighty events which had recently disproved the maxim : "The King's will is law,"‡ and points out that a prince must not live for

* Si princeps erraverit, debet revocari
  Ab hiis quos gravaverit injuste negari,
  Nisi velit corrigi.
                                              Page 109.

† Igitur communitas regni consulatur,
  Et quid universitas sentiat, sciatur,
  Cui leges propriæ maxime sunt notæ.
  Nec cuncti provinciæ sic sunt idiotæ,
  Quin sciant plus cæteris regni sui mores,
  Quos relinquunt posteris hii qui sunt priores.
                                              Page 111.

‡ Dicitur vulgariter : "ut rex vult, lex vadit ; "
  Veritas vult aliter, nam lex stat, rex cadit.
                                              Page 116.

M

himself but for his sublime task and the honour of his realm. He concludes with a reference to the example of our Lord and his disciples, and with the injunction : a King should above all make known his resolutions to those from whom, according to usage, he solicits help.*

The whole course of argument indicates a marvellous ripeness of political intelligence which may have lain dormant in the germ of the English communal system, but was first called into life when Simon came forward. His mind had been impregnated by popular influences, and fertilised the nation in return. At that age the idea of a combination between constitutional monarchy and parliamentary government, both overarched by the sacredness of law, had scarcely been so clearly and distinctly enunciated elsewhere. The nation had already resolved to realise the conception, but it soon became evident that many conditions indispensable to this form of government were either entirely lacking or very imperfectly developed. Though it is in its nature to attain rapid maturity and clearness as an idea, and to find easy expression in words, its realisation is essentially difficult, and can only be accomplished at the price of a perfection of self-control to which men are seldom equal.

---

* Cur sua consilia non communicabit,
A quibus auxilia supplex postulabit?

Page 119.

CHAPTER V.

SIMON'S GREATEST POWER AND HIS FALL.

HOSTILE MEASURES ABROAD—THE LEGATE, WHO IS RE-
FUSED ADMISSION INTO THE COUNTRY, EXCOMMUNI-
CATES THE REBELS—SIMON SUMMONS THE NOBILITY,
CLERGY, KNIGHTS, AND CITIZENS TO PARLIAMENT,
JANUARY 20TH, 1265—NEGOTIATIONS FOR THE RE-
LEASE OF PRINCE EDWARD—MEASURES FOR CONSOLI-
DATING SIMON'S POWER—DESERTION OF THE EARL OF
GLOUCESTER—RETURN OF THE EXILES, AND ESCAPE
OF THE PRINCE—OUTBREAK OF HOSTILITIES ON THE
WELSH BORDER—THE YOUNGER SIMON GOES TO
KENILWORTH—DEATH OF THE EARL AT EVESHAM,
AUGUST 4TH—REVERED AS NATIONAL MARTYR.

THE Earl of Leicester had scarcely assumed arbitrary
power, firmly resolved to use it with all possible
moderation;* he had scarcely set himself to encounter

* Modeste agere conatus est, se nihil magis cavere quam ne
vel parvo detrimento vinceret magnates quos ad sacramentum
jusjurandi servandum flectere non posset : satis habebat in officio
continere, ut qui nusquam acquiescere vellent, minus nocerent,
are the words of the Opus Chronicorum of St. Albans, ed. Riley,
p. 12.   M 2

peace-breakers of every kind with unparalleled energy,
for the sake of the public weal, when he was immediately reminded from abroad that this power was
itself an intolerable anomaly in the eyes of his contemporaries.

Henry III. had been obliged to send early intelligence of the terms concluded at Lewes to his brother-
in-law of France, but, as he was a captive prince and
Louis now neither could nor would act as umpire, no
immediate reply had been vouchsafed.*   On the other
hand, active military preparations were permitted,
especially on the Flemish coast, where the nobles who
had escaped from the battle-field met with Queen
Eleanor.   She had remained on the continent since
January, and came in the company of her son Edmund,
and her uncles Boniface and Peter; the dispossessed
Bishop of Hereford and John Mansell were likewise
present.   Mercenaries of all nations, Germans, French,
Bretons, Gascons, and Spaniards, waited on the shore
of Damme for a favourable wind.   In repeated letters
to Louis, Henry vainly represented that these proceedings involved serious peril to his son and nephew, who
were retained as hostages.   Simon even caused the
King to appeal to the law of nations,† whilst he him-

* De quo turbati sumus et non mediocriter anxiati; Henry
to Louis, July 10th. Shirley, ii. 258.

† De jure gentium prædictis obsidibus supremum periculum
et status sui subversio. Shirley, l. c. All the property of the
Queen was given in custody on the 28th of July. Rot. Lit. Pat.
48 Henr. III. membr. 7. Compare Ranke, Englische Geschichte,
vi. 3.

self made vigorous preparations for defence. In the southern counties, Kent, Essex, Suffolk, and Norfolk, barons, lay and clerical, knights and common people, were called under arms, and the inhabitants from village to village commanded to equip themselves, each as well as he was able. The ships of the Cinque Ports and of the towns on the east coast, which were distinguished by their patriotism, carefully watched the open sea.* In August the King was brought to the camp on Canterbury heath. But very soon afterwards the hostile army on the opposite coast dispersed of itself, for the pay was exhausted, and then the sea-voyage appeared quite too formidable.

At the same time the revolutionary government were unwearied in their efforts to bring about an agreement by diplomatic means, still hoping to obtain a verdict which they could accept, not now from the French King but from a mixed commission. After Louis IX. had himself consented to put no obstacle in the way of a conference at Boulogne, the Earls of Leicester and Gloucester were empowered in the last days of July to

---

* Summons for Kent, July 8th, Rymer, i. 444; for Essex, July 7th, Lib. de Antiq. Leg. 67; for the Ports, August 16th; Rot. Lit. Claus. 48 Henr. III. membr. 4. The barons of the north and of the Scotch border were cited repeatedly, but in vain, July 18th, August 5th; Shirley, ii. 259, 269. The safety of the English merchants commended to the Countess Margareta of Flanders; ibid. 273, 279.

arrange the affair.* The Englishmen nominated were
the Bishop of London and the Great Justiciary Despenser; the Frenchmen, the Abbot of Bec and Charles,
Count of Anjou, who as candidate for the Sicilian
crown already passed for the Earl of Leicester's friend.†
As umpire, in case the four could not agree upon their
sentence, Archbishop Odo II. of Rouen was selected,
a Minorite, with whom, according to the surest testimony, Simon had had hospitable intercourse.‡ It is
plain that Simon sought, as far as. might be, to place
men upon the commission who were favourable to his
cause, but at the same time his desire for a peaceful
solution of the difficulty was so strong that he further
determined upon another noteworthy step. On the
4th of September King Richard's son, commonly
known as Henry the German, was provisionally
released from his confinement at Dover, upon the

* Henry to Louis : Celsitudini vestræ quantas possumus gra-
tiarum referimus actiones ; July 27th. To the two Earls together,
July 30th and 31st. The King entreats for delay on account of
the danger of war, August 2nd. Shirley, ii. 261–265.

† Rymer, i. 446, in September, the Thursday after the Nativity
of the Virgin. Attamen inclitus comes ille Andegavie Karolus
parti com. Leyc. favebat. Chron. Roff. MS. Cott. Nero D. ii.
fol. 175. To him and to many bishops and royal counsellors in
France Henry addressed entreaties that the military preparations
on French soil might be checked. Shirley, ii. 265–269, Aug. 2, 4.

‡ Utinam inclytus comes Leycestriæ vestræ sublimitati, sicut
veracitur comperi, in Christo devotissimus, pium sanctæ fami-
liaritatis contubernium apud vos invenerit, Adam of Marsh had
once written to him. Brewer, Mon. Francisc. 86.

surety of nine English bishops and three French
envoys, that he might go in person to the French
court and further the negotiations for peace.* But it
may be imagined how slight, in spite of all this, was
the prospect of frank and dispassionate discussion in
any quarter, and how bitter the temper of the two
nations, from the fact that when Henry and his suite
landed at Boulogne a fight with the inhabitants immediately ensued, and nine Englishmen were slain.†
But from the beginning one chief and insuperable
difficulty hindered all these well-intended efforts.

The Pope had a word to interpose, but after their
victory on the battle-field the Barons steadily refused
to grant admission into the kingdom to his Legate,
Guido, who had arrived in France some time before.
No man understood better than Simon de Montfort
how closely the universal supremacy of the hierarchy
was interwoven with the power of national monarchs;
he knew that when he, a vassal, sought to appeal to
the law as an equal against his liege lord, he ran
directly counter to the public opinion of Europe. A
captive King was incapable of entering upon any
binding treaty. Leicester could never rely upon a
general recognition of the exceptional and unparalleled
power to which he had risen, least of all could he
expect it from the Holy Father, the sole administrator
of international law. But to set the King free was
obviously equivalent to an immediate rekindling of the

---

* Rymer, i. 446.   † Chron. Roff. l. c.

baronial war. The confinement of Henry III. was an
ill-fated, although an unavoidable error, and necessarily
avenged itself; the dilemma into which it brought
Simon could scarcely have been more serious, for he
found himself compelled to maintain his illegitimate
authority against the mightiest opponents.

One more commission, composed of the Bishops of
Worcester and Winchester and Peter de Montfort,*
had been sent out to obtain from King Louis and the
Papal Legate a recognition of the compromise of Lewes.
Apart from the expulsion of aliens, who had, however,
become indispensable instruments in carrying out the
Papal system of the time, the commissioners were empowered to make conciliatory proposals upon all points
for the sake of re-establishing order in Church and
State. To the Pope's representative there was a distinct expression of deference;† the great majority of the
English clergy eagerly desired a friendly adjustment
of the questions at issue, if merely on account of the
tithes imposed by Rome, now collected by the new
government, and characteristically refused to it in the
province of York alone.‡ Some other prelates, as
those of London and Chichester, voluntarily crossed
the Channel that they might, as true peace-makers,

* Veritatis, pacis et tranquillitatis zelator, as he is called in
his safe-conduct. Rymer, i. 447.

† Subiciendo nos jurisdictioni et cohercioni prædicti legati, ut
ipse per sententiam excommunicationis et omne genus censuræ
ecclesiasticæ nos compellere possit ad observationem præmissorum.
Rymer, i. 446.

‡ Rymer, i. 445.

encourage conciliatory advances. All was to no purpose. Cardinal Guido declined to enter into serious
negotiations with them. Wrathful at his exclusion
from the kingdom, he held the thunders of excommunication ready to be launched against the present English
government and all its supporters, and, when the bishops
re-embarked in October after fruitless discussions, he
even sent the anathemas with them for proclamation
in their dioceses. It is narrated that when detained
by a cruiser from the Cinque Ports and searched at the
Dover custom-house, they willingly gave up the parch-
ments, and looked on as they were torn in pieces and
thrown into the water before their eyes. Immediately
afterwards, on the 23rd, the convocation of the English
clergy appealed from the Legate to the Holy See.*
The bull of excommunication, published on the 20th,
in the priory of Hédin, and directed for execution to the
archdiocese of Rheims, touched but cursorily upon the
conciliation vainly attempted in the conferences at Boulogne and Gravelines. It denounced in violent terms
the crime committed against the Legate, and excommunicated by name the Earls of Leicester, Gloucester,
and Norfolk and their whole party, with special mention of the town of London and the Cinque Ports.†
But a severer blow meanwhile awaited them, for Pope
Urban had died on the 2nd of October; the Cardinal
shortly departed for Rome, and he himself, the crafty

* Thos. Wykes, 156, 157. Rishanger, ed. Halliwell, 38, 39
Ann. de Dunst. 234. Matth. Westmonast. 385.
† Rymer, i. 447.

Provençal jurist, mounted the Papal throne on the 5th of February as Clement IV.

During the interregnum at Rome the attempts to shake the Earl of Leicester's rule were not discontinued. On the 18th of November King Henry was obliged to write to Louis, as well as to his own consort and Count Peter of Savoy, desiring them to resist the designs of certain persons to alienate the fiefs of his crown on French soil, with all rights and prerogatives appertaining to them.* Eleanor was gravely suspected of attempting to provide herself with money by such means. In England itself, especially on the Welsh marches, many daring and adventurous nobles, some of whom had escaped from the battle of Lewes, fiercely kept up their feud with Prince Llewellyn of Wales, the ally of the Earl of Leicester, and sought by craft to liberate the young Princes, who were held as hostages and at present confined at Wallingford. It was probably for this reason that the strong castle of Kenilworth was assigned to Prince Edward as a residence. There he spent Christmas at the brilliant court of Simon and Eleanor,† and was permitted to receive and confer with some of those zealous royalists, Mortimer, Clifford, and Leiburne,‡ who had at length bound themselves

* Rymer, i. 448.

† Green, Princesses, ii. 125.

‡ The King's mandate dated from Worcester, whither he had been obliged to follow the Earl, Dec. 15. Rymer, i. 449. Safe-conduct for the three nobles, Dec. 14th. Rot. Lit. Pat. 49 Henr. III. membr. 27. Eundo apud Kenylworth cum propria familia sua secum existente ad loquendum cum Edwardo filio suo primogenito. Compare Lib. de Antiq. Leg. 70 ; Thos. Wykes, 159.

to self-banishment in Ireland for a term of three years. These meetings prove that he was not harshly treated and that the head of the government did not oppose reasonable terms for his release, at that time a subject of frequent discussion. Even John Mansell, who had been so deeply compromised, was permitted to return home and reside upon his benefice.*

Though we find only single and scattered notices of these measures, they illustrate the policy of the statesman whose resources never failed under enormous difficulties, when France and the Pope, repelled all his overtures, resolved to make no terms except with the independent and legitimate King. He hoped now by a policy of reconciliation towards his domestic enemies to attach more firmly the various classes of the nation who were already amicably disposed towards him. Foremost among these was the Church, no longer the parochial priests and mendicant friars only, but likewise the majority of the bishops upon whom more and more of Grosseteste's enlightened wisdom seemed to descend, and who looked up with growing confidence to Simon de Montfort as he who was raising a barrier against the whole system of Papal Provisions, accomplishing what the King had neglected for more than a generation. The clergy did not willingly give up their home property to be the spoil of foreign avarice, and they met the champions of nationality with patriotic sympathy, so far as they had courage to declare it. Next were the knights, whom

* Dec. 14 ; Rot. Lit. Pat. l. c.

the crown had avoided consulting except in the rarest
cases of necessity upon single questions connected with
public affairs, and the towns, who had been assessed
at pleasure from time immemorial, whilst commerce,
the element of their life, had never rejoiced in the
monarch's fostering favour. Leicester resolved to
employ them with the Barons in the great council of
the realm as never before, and for this purpose he
summoned a Parliament to meet in London on the
20th of January, 1265, a stroke of daring genius which
was to immortalize his memory more than all else.

In the first writ from Worcester on the 14th of
December, " after the agitation was calmed, for salutary consultation upon the security, peace, and other
affairs of his realm," the King invited the Archbishop of York, twelve Bishops and twenty-four Abbots,
Priors, and Deans, and on the 24th of the month, from
Woodstock, eighty-three other Abbots and Priors,
amongst them the Masters of the Knights of St. John
and the Templars ; likewise five Earls, Leicester, Gloucester, Norfolk, Oxford, and Derby, and eighteen
Barons. Lastly, the sheriffs were charged to send two
Knights for each shire, the towns York, Lincoln, and
the other boroughs (burgi), each two burgesses, the
Cinque Ports each four men.* The comprehensive
number of ecclesiastical representatives, prelates and

* Rymer, i. 449 : duos de legalioribus et discretioribus militibus singulorum comitatuum . . . duos de discretioribus
et legalioribus et probioribus tam civibus quam burgensibus suis.
Summons of the Cinque Ports in the Report on the Dignity of a

heads of chapters, indicated the importance attached by
Simon to the clerical order, and the sympathy with his
movement that prevailed in it.

On the other hand only twenty-three lay Barons
received writs, probably all who at that time could be
reckoned of his party, whilst at least an equal number
were passed over, and this restriction showed no less
plainly the weakness of his position in regard to this
highest order of vassals, and the reason why he ventured to introduce knights and burgesses among them.
Subsequently, on the 17th of January, ten northern
Barons, including Bruce and Baliol, received safe-
conducts for the coming Parliament.* It is impossible that the city of London was omitted, the greatest
and most devoted community in the country, although
there is a singular absence of any intimation that an
election writ was issued to it. Moreover, no contemporary has indicated in what manner this most significant measure was received by the nation. But he who
reposed such confidence in the masses of the people in
town and country and who was realizing their ardent
aspiration, long clearly expressed by word and by pen,
to see the laws administered by native Englishmen, to
whom they were most familiar,† instead of by inca-

Peer, Appendix, i. 35: quatuor de legalioribus et discretioribus
portus viri. Cf. Stubbs, Select Charters. 115. Const. Hist. ii. 92. 93.
    * Rymer, i. 450.
        † Nec cuncti provinciæ sic sunt idiotæ,
            Quin sciant plus cæteris regni sui mores.
Political Songs, p. 110. Compare Ranke, Englische Geschichte,
i. 81, 82.

pable foreigners, he surely could rely with certainty
upon wide popular sympathy. Though the novel and
revolutionary character of the measure could not be
denied, it had been brought to maturity by the
necessities of the political situation. It was a bold
experiment in Montfort's hand, but it originated in a
profound knowledge of English communal life, where
the principle of representation had long been applied to
local affairs, and it contained the fruitful germ of a conception by means of which the contest of a century for
the right of taxation was to be adjusted in future days.

No picture is now obtainable of the proceedings of
that memorable Parliament, so entirely new in its
composition. It had been stated in the writs that the
liberation of Prince Edward was to be taken into
consideration, and on the 16th of February the King
reminded the Earls of Leicester and Gloucester by
letter that the date at which this important affair must
be concluded was fixed for the 19th. As they and
many of their partisans were notoriously about to ride
to a tournament at Dunstable, he warned them with
the utmost stringency not to cause delay in the business
by their absence. This royal writ was countersigned
by the Justiciary, the Bishop of London, and Master
Thomas de Cantilupe, nephew of the venerable Bishop
of Worcester.* He was one of the many pious

* The two writs of the 16th of February, Rymer, i. 450. The
nomination of Cantilupe, Rot. Lit. Pat. 49 Henr. III. membr.
22, February 25th. According to an official note, the King
folded the document with his own hands, and caused it to be
sealed in his presence.

churchmen entirely devoted to the national cause ; a few days later he was raised to the chancellorship.

Some progress was made hereupon in the business of this protracted session, especially burdensome to the representatives of shires and boroughs on account of its cost. In a spirit of mutual concession it was believed that the wisest expedient had been found when, on the 10th of March, the Princes Edward and Henry were released from their present confinement and delivered to the King.* Guarantees indispensable for the security of the State were drawn up in a comprehensive Act of Parliament, passed on the 31st. The King and Prince promised the Barons and commonalty of the land† to pledge themselves by public writs to preserve inviolate the decrees of the Parliament held the preceding June, or the Misa of Lewes, as incorporated in Latin in the French instrument. After recapitulating the amnesty for Leicester and Gloucester, the citizens of London and the Cinque Ports, the King and his son swore, with a reference to Magna Charta, never more to enter into friendly relations with their defeated partisans, and to execute the sentence of outlawry upon all who ventured to resist the convention. On the other hand, they

---

* Patent, Rymer, i. 452. The King notified Louis IX. and his consort of the liberation of his son, March 14th : ad commodum et honorem nostrum auctore Domino liberatus est. Shirley, ii. 280.

† Requere as haux homes e au comun de la tere par lur lettres overtes.

accepted a fresh oath of homage from all those liegemen with regard to whom they had renounced the
feudal bond at Lewes, the victors reserving the right
of release if the crown should repeat the renounce-
ment. The custody of castles was to be entrusted to
unsuspected persons ; no aliens might be brought into
the kingdom without consent of the council; the Prince's
suite must thenceforth be composed entirely of trustworthy natives, and he was prohibited from leaving
England during the three following years on pain of
losing all his possessions and dignities. Five of his
fortresses had been already occupied, the year before ;
and whilst these remained as pledges in the hands of
the government, and Bristol was added as a sixth,
Simon further required from him a personal security
which coincided with the necessary military defence of
the country. He transferred to the Prince a fief of his
own of corresponding value in exchange for the castle
and county of Chester and the castles of the Peak and
Newcastle in the north, the most important posts for
overawing Wales and Scotland. An appeal to the
Pope for intervention was expressly instanced as a
breach of faith. Lastly, all peers and subjects of the
realm, not only in England but also in Ireland and
Gascony, and even the King of Scotland, were made
acquainted with the terms of the agreement by a
public proclamation. It was signed and sealed by the
King, the Princes Edward and Henry, ten bishops
who with burning taper threatened with excommunication all who should act counter to it, the Prior of the

Knights of St. John, the Master of the Temple, and the Mayor and Corporation of London. Perhaps even ambassadors of the French King were present, for passports had been made out for them on the 15th, a noteworthy evidence that the feudal bond and even the international aspects of the case which had been of influence in the earlier direct negotiations, were not disregarded on this occasion.*

The court party naturally found no pleasure in this form of coercion, and only submitted with silent resentment in expectation of a reaction. They desired that even in duress the King should appeal to the inalienable right conferred by coronation and anointing; they noted every change of expression in the Earl of Leicester's face, and found instead of care and heaviness only firm and joyful resolution reflected there.† But the royalist and foreign party had now no other point of agreement than the offence against legitimacy, hence the innumerable bitter accusations

* The Act of Parliament, Edward's oath on the 10th, the King's charter of the 11th, safe conduct for the French ambassadors of the 15th, transfer of the five castles on the 17th, and the county of Chester on the 20th of March; all in Rymer, i. 451–454. Among the histories, the Lib. de Antiq. Leg. 71–73 alone contains authentic information, and shows the active part taken by the city of London in the conclusion of the treaty. Cf. Stubbs, Const. Hist. ii. 91.

† Nemo comitem Leycestriæ vel infractum mente, seu etiam tristem vultu vidit. Ita conscientiam altæ nobilitatis inspirabat Spiritus Sanctus et roborabat. Opus Chronicorum, ed. Riley, p. 17.

against the Earl of Leicester personally, the rapacity of his house, and his whole course of political action. That he had aimed directly at the crown could not be even distantly asserted, much less proved. The statement of one solitary royalist chronicler that Simon had appropriated eighteen baronies, corresponds with the truth only inasmuch as he had undertaken the administration of numerous estates of exiles, solely for public purposes. Whilst the circumstances were what they were, it was impossible to permit them to be enjoyed by the opposite party. During the sequestration of the wide domains belonging to the King of the Romans and held as security for his good faith, all his stewards and bailiffs were expressly retained in office.* On the 8th of May, Simon caused the promised equivalent for Chester and the Peak to be transferred to Prince Edward by the chancery.† His partisans, many of whom had taken the vow of absolute poverty, denied in words equally decided and enthusiastic that he had ever designed to enrich himself. They held his disinterested devotion to the public weal to be irreproachable,‡ and soon the confiscation of his own fiefs and possessions was to confirm their judgment. He was known to friend and foe as an affectionate father,

* Rymer, i. 448 ; December 13th, 1264.
† Rot. Lit. Pat. 49 Henr. III. membr. 17.
‡ Commodum si proprium comitem movisset,
    Nec haberet alium zelum, nec quæsisset
    Toto suo studio reformationi
    Regni, sed intentio dominationi.
               Political Songs, p. 88.

and it is possible that he connived at the arrogance and violence of his sons; but the accusation that one of them, Henry, the Warden of Dover, laid an embargo for his own benefit upon the bales of wool belonging to French and English merchants,* is unsupported and extremely doubtful. The sole example of a favour bestowed on personal grounds is the grant of a hospice in Westminster to his faithful comrade and cousin, Peter de Montfort.† Lastly, the stagnation of trade was not in the first instance the work of the Regent, though caused by the civil war and dissensions with foreign powers; the Legate when he published his bull of excommunication had exhorted the nations of the Continent to break off all intercourse with the heretical island. Great was the lamentation of the commercial classes on both sides of the water when the nimble guard-ships of the Cinque Ports began to search foreign vessels for goods of all kinds, as well as for Papal mandates and contraband of war. Many necessaries already deemed indispensable, articles of luxury and spices, rose enormously in price. If the Earl of Leicester really said that English productions would suffice for English people‡ without foreign imports, the sentiment does small credit to his economic sagacity, but it accords with the exclusively national atti-

---

* Suis usibus, Wykes, 159.

† Rymer, i. 453 ; March 14th. 1265.

‡ Quod sine commeatu extraneorum possunt indigenæ bonis propriis sustentari. Thos. Wykes, 158. Compare Gescht. v. England, iii. 785.

tude in political, ecclesiastical, and even material
concerns which, in reliance upon her insular position,
England assumed under his rule towards foreign
countries. The white cloth worn instead of that dyed
in Flanders may be accounted for with equal probabi-
lity by the fashion of a warlike age, possessed by
crusading ideas. All these influences were of a kind
to excite discontent, but they would not have been
sufficient to undermine the power of the prudent
statesman, who in moral greatness towered far above
his contemporaries. To effect this, disaffection must
gain ground once more among his associates, and his
own adherents make common cause with the exiles
who had long been lying in wait.   ,

During this Parliament the power he had grounded
upon wisdom and energy reached its climax. As if
seeking for it a designation which should in some
measure justify it, he assumed the title of Count
Justiciary* in addition to his hereditary dignity of
Seneschal of England,† although Hugh Despenser continued to hold the post of Great Justiciary. Is it
possible that after the impulse of a great popular movement and his own powers had made him the foremost
man in the nation, the model of Aragon presented

* Comes Justiciarius first in a document of January 7th ; Foss,
Judges of England, ii. 155. Comes Leicestriæ Justiciarius, proclamations of May 20th and June 7th, 8th, and 28th. Rymer, i.
155–457.

† Comes Leicestriæ et senescallus Angliæ, for the first time
again May 20th. Rymer, i. 454.

itself to him, where a guardian of national privileges
bearing a similar name and holding like authority
always confronted the King and permanently limited
his power ?

The parliamentary business proper came to an end
in March, and Simon went from London to Odiham
Castle in Hampshire, where his wife had held her
court for some weeks. Their son Henry accompanied
the Princes Edward and Henry thither on the 17th of
March; the Earl himself arrived on the 19th with a
retinue of 160 horsemen. He remained till the 2nd of
April, and very probably saw Eleanor and his household no more after this meeting.* It was not only
from the French coast or the Welsh border that the
enemy threatened him. Friends and adherents who
would not acquiesce in measures of right and justice
caused his gravest anxiety. Robert de Ferrers, the
wild and unruly Earl of Derby, who had joined the
friends of reform chiefly from motives of rapacity, was
convicted in the winter of a public breach of the peace
and sentenced by his peers in Parliament to imprisonment
in the Tower.† A most fruitful source of discord was the
avarice of many who had taken prisoners at the battle

* Rot. Hospic. Comitissæ Leicestriæ in Hudson Turner,
Manners and Household Expences of the XIII. Century (Roxburgh Club) p. 13–15 ; Green, Princesses, ii. 127.

† Ann. de Dunst. 235. According to Wykes, 160, he was
sacrificed to an intrigue of Simon's. According to Ann. Waverl.
358, the King was the complainant and Simon appeared as the
protector of a friend.

of Lewes and demanded ransoms or indemnification
out of their estates. Amongst them was John Gifford,
a knight of Leicester's household, second to none in
valour, and probity.* As his requests were repeatedly denied, he deserted and joined Gilbert of Gloucester, who, like his father before him, had been altogether unwilling to submit to Simon's supremacy.

This avaricious noble also thought only of rich
ransoms, the custody of extensive estates of exiles, and
redemption money from the King of the Romans,
whom he claimed as exclusively his captive. The opposition he encountered, and Simon's superior statesmanship, reminded the young and ambitious man more
and more forcibly of the traditional rivalry between the
two houses. Whilst he believed that he was in danger
of sharing the Earl of Derby's fate, royalist marchers
such as Mortimer and Leiburne, frequented his estates in
the west unhindered. The prohibition of the tournament announced between him and Henry de Montfort
at Dunstable had reopened the breach between the
two rival factions. The Earl of Leicester personally
provided for the preservation of the public peace.†
Gloucester avenged himself by a violent attack in Parliament upon the foreigner who assumed dominion over
the kingdom,‡ who kept the monarch a prisoner and

* Strenuitate militæ et animi probitate nulli secundus. Wykes,
l. c.

† Rishanger, ed. Halliwell, 42.

‡ Quod hic alienigena præsumebat sibi totius regni dominium
subjugare. Rishanger, ed. Riley, 32.

conferred posts and offices upon his bishops, whilst he deprived others of their portion. The Bishop of Worcester and Hugh Despenser vainly sought to bring about a reconciliation. It would almost appear that Gloucester, already conspiring with the emigrants, was able to acquire the greater influence over the King. The great Statute was confirmed on the 31st of March, and Henry set out from London on the 2nd of April; Simon and his suite had left the capital previously.*

His sons had now given notice of another tournament at Northampton on the 19th of April, and the Earl of Gloucester was bidden among others, but he, suspecting that some snare was laid for him, had withdrawn towards the Welsh border, where the symptoms of revolt were becoming more and more evident. After his departure from Odiham, Simon again kept the King and Princes with him. He had gone first to Northampton, probably in order to prevent the tournament and the danger it threatened to the public peace, and then turned westward by Gloucester and Hereford. Meanwhile, in the first days of May, John Warenne, Earl of Surrey, and William of Valence, the King's step-brother, landed in Pembroke with 120 armed men. The title of Earl of Pembroke had been once conferred upon William of Valence, but never recognised by the Barons. The two nobles were among those who escaped from Lewes to France, and by advice of the

* Juncta sibi militum turma non modica spreto parliamento secessit ad partes occiduas. Thos. Wykes, 161.

sheriff of Sussex they had been cited on the 19th of
March, with Peter of Savoy and Hugo Bigod, to the
Parliament on the 1st of June, there to be judged
and receive justice.* They had chosen rather to enter
into alliance with Mortimer and Gloucester, and acted
upon a distinctly preconcerated plan, having for
its object the liberation of the heir to the throne.
When the tidings of their arrival reached him, Leicester by royal proclamation on the 10th of May commanded the sheriffs everywhere to arrest all disturbers
of the peace. At the same time, in accordance with
the last decrees of Parliament, they were ordered
solemnly to proclaim the ancient charters and the
articles recently drawn up for the regulation of the existing government.† Against the revolt which would
restore the former hopeless condition of the country, he
appealed courageously to the public laws established
by an act of political contract.

He still did not relinquish the hope of preserving
peace to his country. To that end a pressing
message was despatched on the 18th of May to
the King of France, with whom intercourse had never
been broken off during the interval. As envoy the

* Rymer, i. 449.

† Antiquas cartas communium libertatum . . . ordina-
tionem super nostro et regni nostri statu nuper Londoniæ factam
nec non et quosdam articulos de nostro et magnatum terræ nostræ communi assensu de quibusdam constitutionibus dudum
provisis. Shirley, ii. 282. Also on the Patent Roll, 49 Henr. III.
membr. 10.

Earl again sagaciously chose Henry, Richard's son, who from the beginning had had intercourse with both parties. The King had to command him to depart with speed and to remain as long as his commission required.* The Earl of Gloucester, Gifford, and their confederates, had taken up a threatening position in Dean Forest north of the estuary of the Severn. With them also negotiations were opened, as they always asserted their intention of remaining faithful to the Provisions of Oxford. The Bishop of Worcester and four other mediators were indefatigable in their efforts, and in order to tranquillize the mind of the nation, it was announced on the 20th of May that the concord between the two Earls had never been disturbed.† Even the banished nobles, Clifford and Leiburne, were again admitted to the presence of their favourite, Prince Edward, as he sojourned at Hereford whilst following the progress of the court. Warenne and Valence, who had requested restitution of their estates from the King, were bidden to appear in person. But all these well meant measures only served to enable them to strike their blow with greater effect. Not in open and honourable encounter, but stealthily and craftily, they dealt the thrust, the consequences of which were destined to ruin the hated ruler.

Since the last Parliament Prince Edward had been

* Rex prorogavit ei terminum suæ reversionis usque ad terminum ab ipso petitum. Official note to the patent of May 18th. Rymer, i. 455.

† Rymer, i. 455.

permitted to move about upon parole with compara-
tive freedom in the society of Henry de Montfort,
Robert de Ros, and Thomas de Clare, a brother of
the Earl of Gloucester and the Prince's closest friend.*
The Earl of Leicester had a special affection for this
youth, and showed an unaccountable absence of
suspicion by retaining him in such a position of trust,
even after the recent rupture. On the evening of the
28th of May the young men were testing their
horses before the gates of Hereford. After the
Prince had tired out several horses, he mounted
afresh and suddenly galloped away, followed by
Clare, another knight, and four squires, towards a
thicket where Roger Mortimer lay concealed with
a few troops.† The Prince soon found himself free, ✗
and commander of Wigmore, his liberator's castle.
The alarm at court was enormous, for it was now
scarcely possible to prevent a combination on the part
of the fugitives with Gloucester, the marchers, and
other royalists who were advancing from Pembroke.
Two days later the whole feudal militia was summoned to meet forthwith at Worcester, with the excep-

* Tanquam familiaris et cubicularius. Thomas Wykes, 162.

† Die Jovis in ebdomade Pentecostes, circa horam vespertinam,
a militum comitiva, quos secum ad spatiandum extra Hereford
duxerat, cum duobus militibus et quatuor scutiferis, propositi sui
consciis. The official report in the royal proclamation of the
30th of May. Rymer, i. 455. The account given by Wykes,
163, corresponds therewith, and mentions Clare by name. Rishanger, ed. Riley, 33 ; ed. Halliwell, 43 ; Chron. de Mailros, 198.

tion of such as had declared for Gloucester. Whoever dared to aid the insurgents should himself be treated as a rebel, especially after the Earl of Gloucester had now publicly broken his oath and written word, for in the language of the official proclamation the conflict appeared as a feud between him and Leicester.* In these days Simon acted as Justiciary for the King, Peter de Montfort, Giles of Argenton, and Robert of St. John as counsellors; on the 8th of June Henry signed a mandate directing the Bishop of London and the other Bishops of the province to excommunicate all who had misled the Prince and induced him to break his oath,† especially the knights of the border. He lamented the hazardous exploit of which his son had been guilty, regardless of the solemn promise given as lately as the preceding March. He informed the citizens of London of the recent events in a letter of considerable length, perhaps even then with the design of winning their sympathy. Two days later, on the 10th, when dealing with the same subjects, in writing to the Archbishop of Dublin and the Irish estates concerning the Prince's confinement and those marchers who were originally banished to Ireland, Henry already described the battle of Lewes as detestable.‡ Even now the Protector no longer held the

---

* Rymer, i. 456; June 7th.

† Quem proh dolor! ad credendum levem et ad circumvenien-dum facilem invenerunt . . . qui cum eisdem se nobis con-tumacem, et rebellionis filium exhibet in præsenti. Rymer, l.c.

‡ Post illud detestabile bellum de Lewes. Rot. Lit. Pat. 49 Henr. III. membr. 13.

the puppet whom he kept near him with a firm grasp.

A few days after his flight Edward met Gilbert of Gloucester at Ludlow Castle and swore to him to preserve the ancient institutions of the realm, and never to employ foreign ministers. A junction with Warenne and Valence was effected; in the south and in the north of the marches the insurrection blazed unhindered. Simon's command to the garrison of Bristol Castle to hold it for the King alone, arrived too late.* The county palatine of Chester, the border fief which had been withdrawn from the Prince, espoused his cause with alacrity. Shrewsbury, Bridgenorth, Worcester, where the bridge was destroyed, and lastly, on the 29th, the town and castle of Gloucester, the entire line of the Severn, declared for Prince Edward, who now sought by means of this position to shut up the Earl of Leicester in Hereford, with the King, his involuntary companion. All fords and bridges were destroyed or occupied, and the ships were removed from the stream. In his despair Simon turned to Prince Llewellyn of Wales, the hereditary enemy of the English monarch. He had been for some years a welcome guest at Kenilworth, and served as an inglorious support to Montfort's policy with its national aspirations. Now, because of their immediate neighbourhood, his mountaineers were the only accessible allies, and in order to make sure of them, considerable districts,

* Rymer, i. 457 ; June 9th.

which had been seized by the English crown and nobility, were restored to Llewellyn. In return he was
to pay 30,000 marks and to swear fealty not to the King
only but also to the decrees of the last Parliament,
even in case the King should be unfaithful to them.*
Being in this locality and in such exigencies the champion of the constitution did not hesitate to admit a
semi-barbarous chieftain into the parliamentary system,
whilst the royalist knights in the conquest of the
Cymri adhered to the allotted task of their race. It
is possible that Earl Simon, as a Frenchman by birth,
was less inspired by hatred toward the Celts; it is
certain that conquest generally formed no part of his
programme.

From Hereford he now marched with the King to
Monmouth, where they remained several days. An
attempt to rescue the town of Gloucester failed, for
Prince Edward and Warenne were on the spot before
them.† They would have crossed the Channel from
Newport, but the enemy's ships barred the passage,
and the troops came to blows in the streets of the
town. They were compelled to march back to Hereford through forests and inhospitable regions where the

* Two written pledges of Llewellyn's, dated June 19th;
Shirley, ii. 283–287. The King's ratification of June 22nd;
Rymer, i. 457. The London Alderman says indignantly: per
iniquum consilium; Lib. de Antiq. Leg. 73.

† In Monmouth, on the 25th and 28th; Rot. Lit. Pat. 49 Henr.
III. membr. 12, and Rymer, l. c. Further information concern-
ing the movements on both sides in the fragment of a letter from
G. de Morley to H. de Manley; Shirley, ii. 288.

English soldiers pined for bread among people who subsisted upon milk and goats' flesh.*

Whilst at Monmouth, on the 28th of June, Leicester had summoned his son Simon and the guardians of the peace for Dorset, Devon, and Somerset to come to his assistance, and young Montfort had meanwhile raised the siege of Pevensey Castle, on the coast of Sussex, still held by the opposite party, in order that he might force a way of escape for his father in the north-west. But he wasted precious time by a series of incomprehensible movements. First he turned towards London, where the popular Mayor, Thomas Fitz-Thomas, who had been re-elected from year to year, already had difficulties in repressing the growing party of the aldermen by coercive measures.† Then, at the head of sixteen knights bannerets, and a troop of London infantry, he hastily returned southward to Winchester. The royalist citizens kept their gates closed, but he forced an entrance on the 16th of July, and Jews and Christians did heavy penance for their resistance. After marching hither and thither by Oxford and Northampton, evidently for the purpose of everywhere collecting troops, he finally reached Kenilworth, but, instead of taking up his quarters within the walls of the familiar castle, he imprudently occupied the farms and hamlets. Here, in the night of the 31st of July, he was suddenly surprised by Prince Edward,

* Wykes, 164–168. Ann. Waverl. 362, 363.

† Lib. de Antiq. Leg. 114, 115. The writer, Arnold Thedmar, a German by descent, was amongst those threatened.

Valence, and Warenne, who having exact information
of his movements from their spies, had hastily advanced
from Worcester. The Barons, the Earl of Oxford
among them, were taken without weapon or armour
and made prisoners; the young Montfort escaped in
his shirt, with a few companions over the lake into the
castle.* The Earl of Leicester had reckoned upon
successfully breaking through the line of the Severn
as his son advanced, and Prince Edward, fearing that
this bold counter-march to Kenilworth might give the
skilful strategist an opportunity of discovering a weak a
point, hurried back to his post as soon as he had
secured his booty and prisoners at Gloucester.

Without a suspicion of the fate of those who should
have succoured him, the Earl had started from Hereford
on Sunday, the 2nd of August, and crossed the Severn
at Kempsey, an estate belonging to Bishop Walter,
four miles south of Worcester. It was not till the
following evening that they proceeded unchecked to
the Abbey of Evesham, where the monks prepared a
friendly reception. Here they heard mass on the
following morning; the King desired to breakfast
before starting,† and whilst they tarried, mounted

---

* Wykes, 169, 170. Rishanger, ed. Halliwell, 44. The attack
especially described in the Chron. de Mailros, 199. The statement in the Waverley Annals, 363, 364, that the young Simon
had already lain six days in Kenilworth, and, confident of victory,
had accepted a formal challenge from Prince Edward, stands
alone.

† Wykes, 171: devenit Eveshamiam tertio die mensis supra-
dicti, feria secunda. Ann. Waverl. 364, die Martis . . . .

squadrons were perceived approaching from the north-
east. As they carried Montfort's banner, Simon joyfully believed that he was already saluting his son.
Prince Edward's leopards were first recognised from
the belfry; he had craftily taken the northern road
the day before, as if aiming at Shrewsbury or Stafford,
and, with the same design of deceiving the enemy, he
caused the trophies of Kenilworth to be borne before
him. Mortimer and Gloucester, who at first had been
hidden by a ridge, now appeared in rear and flank;
all the men of the assailing army were distinguished
by red crosses, so that the full gravity of the situation
became plain to Simon's troops, who were surrounded
on all sides. As he surveyed from an eminence the
admirable dispositions of the enemy, and observed
nothing of the mad impetuosity which had been so
disastrous to the Prince at Lewes the year before, he
exclaimed with a feeling akin to pride : "By the arm
of St. James, they have not learnt that from themselves, but from me. Commend your souls to God, for
our bodies are theirs."* The hoary headed Bishop of
Worcester had scarcely time to receive confession and
pronounce absolution.

Although the numbers were something like two
against seven,† each man scorned to desert singly and

mane versus Ewesham iter arripuit . . . . dominus rex
cum suis voluit jentaculari, quod et factum est. Noluit autem
dominus Symon de Monteforti ibidem aliquid cibi capere.

* Rishanger, ed. Halliwell 45 ; ed. Riley, 37 ; Chron. de
Lanercost, 76.

† Chron. de Mailros, 200.

trust to chance; all were as ready as their gallant
leader to sacrifice their lives in a cause which they
deemed sacred. The first onslaught, led by Edward
with blare of trumpets, pressed Simon and his army
into one closely entangled mass; it was a case, not for
strategic skill, but simply for courage to the death.
No other glory remained to them but, in closest conflict, hand to hand and shield to shield, to sell their
lives as dearly as they might. Not one man could or
would surrender. Henry de Montfort was hewn down
before his father's eyes; the cousin Peter, Hugh
Despenser, and Ralph Basset, faithful to their cause to
the end, fell at the side of the old warrior. He, after
his horse was killed under him, grasped his sword in
both hands and dealt vigorous blows to right and left,
until he received a mortal stroke from behind and died
a hero's death for the national liberties of his country.
Soon the youthful flower of many a noble house lay
dead, a Mandeville, a Beauchamp, one hundred and
sixty knights in all. The young Guy de Montfort,
two sons of Peter, the young Humphrey de Bohun,
and others, were dragged but half living from under
heaps of slain and made prisoners. Some thousands
of Welshmen early sought to make their escape as
best they might. Thus an instantaneous revolution in
the fate of the kingdom was effected, not by a battle,
for the victor had no noticeable loss to deplore, but by
a fearful slaughter that came to a decisive end between
six and nine o'clock in the morning. A brilliant
comet had long awakened among the people appre-

o

hensions of extraordinary events. On the 4th of
August a frightful storm devastated many districts.*

The old King narrowly escaped injury in the tumult,
for he was unrecognised by the victors until he cried :
" Hold, I am Harry of Winchester." They then led
him back in triumph to the Abbey, and there many of
the noble dead found honourable interment, amongst
them Henry de Montfort, Prince Edward's companion
in age, to whom, as the first-born of his brother-in-law,
the King had stood godfather. The basest vengeance
was wreaked only upon the body of Simon, of him who
had died a martyr's death for a deep and powerful
conviction. The soldiers, infected by the burning
hatred of their leaders, hacked the body in pieces.
The arms and legs were publicly exposed in certain
prescribed places as the limbs of a traitor ; the head,
with its ghastly decoration is said to have been
delivered to the bloodthirsty consort of Roger Mortimer
at Wigmore.† Such of the remains as the monks of
Evesham could collect, they interred quietly and
reverently in the chancel of their Abbey church.

* Upon the battle of Evesham it is well to compare Wykes,
172–175, with the numerous authorities who lament the Earl's
fall. A revision produced nothing essentially new to Blaauw,
The Barons' War, p. 242 *et seq.*, and Gesch. v. England, iii. 791
et. seq.

† Testiculi abscisi fuerunt et appensi ex utraque parte nasi, et
ita missum fuit caput, etc. Lib. de Antiq. Leg. 75, 76. Wykes
agrees with the other chroniclers in censuring the brutalities
which were committed. A miniature picture from MS. Cotton.
Nero D. ii. fol. 176 ; in Blaauw, p. 254.

They acted entirely in harmony with the universal veneration which beheld in the departed nobleman, not a rebel, but a disinterested benefactor of the people. Because of its bloody and tragic form, the heavy national loss which clergy and laity mourned in common, became in their eyes a glorious martyrdom suffered for the peace of the country, and the welfare of Church and State.* His death again brought the rare image in its completeness before the minds of his contemporaries. His courage and his loftiness of temper, seeking not its own, but aiming ever to protect the poor man from oppression and establish righteousness and justice in the State, became articles of belief to which Heaven itself had set the seal of truth. He had been an ally of the clergy at all times, and they now, high and low, priests and monks, celebrated his profound knowledge of the Scriptures no less than his reverent and constant devotion. Himself, sure and steadfast as his word, he trusted implicitly in their mediation and vied with them in fasting and watching. His intimate connection with the ever memorable Bishop of Lincoln was a household word under innumerable roofs. The people would have it that Grosseteste had once charged his friend, as penance for his sins, to devote himself till death to the cause

---

* Rishauger, ed. Halliwell, p. 48 : Præcipue religiosi, qui partibus illis favebant vel favere credebant. Ann. Waverl. 365 : Martyrium pro pace terræ et regni reparatione et matris ecclesiæ, ut credimus, consummavit gloriosum. The chronicle of these Cistercians is contemporaneous till 1266 ; Luard, p. xxxvi.

for which he fought, because the peace of the English Church could not now be secured without the instrumentality of the sword of iron.* He was second to no man in the nation in genuine piety, and the crown of saintship was the guerdon of his undying merit; enthusiastic followers had predicted it, and it was conferred by the people themselves, not by the Pope at the King's request. From the miracle said to be performed by the dissevered hands when they were taken to Wigmore, there grew a catalogue of two hundred and twelve, chiefly benevolent acts of healing upon men and beasts. The pious and superstitious gratitude passed ere long into a fully developed cult. A liturgy, in prose and verse, used in the adoration of this political saint is still extant, but some enemy's hand has carefully cut out two pages containing the biographical sketch customary even for church services.†

It cannot be without reason that, with a few remarkable exceptions, all contemporary records, the annals

---

* Asserens pacem ecclesiæ Anglicanæ sine gladio materiali non posse firmari, et constanter affirmans, omnes pro ea morientes martyrio coronari. So in St. Albans, Rishanger, ed. Riley, p. 36.

† MS. Cotton, Vespasian A. vi. fol. 189 :

　　　　　Salve Symon Montis Fortis,
　　　　　　Totius flos militiæ
　　　　　Duras pœnas passus mortis,
　　　　　　Protector gentis Angliæ, etc.

Ora pro nobis, beate Symon ! ut digni efficiamur promissionibus Christi. Halliwell, Rishanger, p. 67 *et seq.* Wright, Political Songs, 124. Chronicon de Mailros, 201–216.

of monastic houses, whether old or new, give to Earl
Simon the most enthusiastic reverence, as the defender
of ecclesiastical and national freedom. The higher
ranks also, the baronage and knighthood, so far as they
had adhered to him, entertained like sentiments. A
French ballad sings, not unworthily, the last heroic
struggle of the Earl, the 'Flower of martial glory,'
and his faithful comrades. Strangely enough, and
with little appropriateness so far as Pope and King are
concerned, it places him side by side with the solitary
national saint, the universally venerated St. Thomas
of Canterbury.* It was rumoured that the monk's
hair-shirt was found after death upon Simon's body as
on his. All people were exhorted therefore to cry to
Heaven for Simon's mediation, as well as Becket's,
with the Holy Virgin's Son, that the faith and its loyal
servants in the Church might be delivered at a time
when many had become unfaithful.

Neither Simon's piety nor his military genius was

---

* The third verse runs :—

> Mès par sa mort, le cuens Montfort
> Conquist la victorie,
> Come ly martyr de Canterbyr
> Finist sa vie ;
> Ne voleit pas li bon Thomas
> Qe perist seinte Eglise,
> Ly cuens auxi se combati
> E morust sauntz feyntise.
> Or est ocys la flur de pris, que taunt savoit de guere,
> Ly cuens Montfort, sa dure mort molt enplorra la terre.

Ritson, Ancient Songs, i. 15 ; Wright, Political Songs, 125.

the sole reason of his enduring fame. It was due no less to his championship of the oppressed classes, in which he had at that time no rival, and to the great political experiment of convoking classes of the people hitherto unrepresented. But no man could yet foresee that through it the way would actually be prepared one generation later for deliverance from the conflict of a century, and the English government advanced by contract and stipulation to the form best befitting it. Simon himself probably died without the assurance that he had earned immortality by this means.* It first became clear to the nation when the conqueror of Evesham, the great King upon his throne, found himself compelled to readopt that creative idea, and introduced representatives of the commons in the name of the crown into the political system, for the purpose of sharing in the right of taxation. But at that time men overlooked the many impure motives that had influenced the course of conduct pursued by the Earl, and the disasters he might have brought upon the State. His foreign birth, the personal quarrel with the King, his violence of temper and lust of power, the fatal necessity of always exercising illegal coercion after he had conquered, all these circumstances combined to form a chain in which he himself became ever more closely bound. True, only he among the rival parties

* As Sir James Mackintosh well puts it, History of England, i. 238 : " He died unconscious of the imperishable name which he acquired by an act which he probably considered as of very small importance."

displayed constructive genius and a warm zeal for justice. But did he and the nation really understand
each other, though the English celebrated him as a
martyr and a hero of romance? Morever, it would
have been impossible for England to tolerate in the
thirteenth century any approach to the republican form
of government under an illegitimate Protector which
proved impossible when it was atttempted in the
seventeenth. The monarchy upon which the State
had been grounded could not be uprooted, even from
the hearts of those early friends of constitutional
government. For the sake of the public weal it must
be restored to its rights. The papacy, whose doctrine
no one in this land of ancient orthodoxy yet ventured
seriously to question, possessed claims of which it
could not suffer itself to be deprived, least of all by
revolutionary means. Both combined proved event-
ually stronger than the popular movement.* Only
when they were again disunited, a new epoch dawned
of change, concessions, and reforms.

* See the excellent characters of Simon and Edward I., drawn
by Stubbs, Const. Hist. ii. 99, 100, 298.

CHAPTER VI.

END OF THE CIVIL WAR AND OF THE HOUSE OF MONTFORT.

RESTORATION AND REACTION — AGREEMENT OF KENIL-
WORTH, 1266—REVOLT OF THE EARL OF GLOUCES-
TER AND THE CITY OF LONDON—PEACE THROUGH
THE MEDIATION OF THE LEGATE, 1267—FATE OF
THE COUNTESS OF LEICESTER AND HER CHILDREN—
ELEANOR IN FRANCE—THE MURDER AT VITERBO,
MARCH 13, 1271—DEATH OF THE BROTHERS SIMON
AND GUY—AMAURY, AND ELEANOR, THE LAST PRIN-
CESS OF WALES.

THE elaborate political structure, which an architect
of genius had sought to raise from the provisions of
the mad Oxford Parliament, fell to pieces on the day
of Evesham. The King was once more his own master,
and immediately laid claim to the full authority of his
office. He announced by public proclamations that
he would now rule by his own independent power, as
in former times, and he revoked the mandates extorted
from him and issued by the Earl of Leicester, who

had made an unwarrantable use of the great seal.*
The King's sheriffs were immediately appointed to all
the counties. After Simon the younger, who had
vainly sought to bring assistance to his father from
Kenilworth on the 4th of August, had thrown himself
behind the strong walls of the castle, he at least liberated his prisoners, King Richard with his younger son
Edmund. The widow of Despenser capitulated in the
Tower. Although warlike and energetic as no other,
Edward nevertheless advised an immediate treaty with
the hostile garrisons, and fair terms to the inhabitants
of the Cinque Ports if they would desist from their
marine expeditions, and freely return to their obedience
to the King.†

As soon as the gates of the kingdom were again at
the disposal of the conquerors, a Parliament was convoked at Winchester. All the Bishops were invited,
except the four specially compromised, London, Lincoln,
Worcester, and Chichester, and among the higher nobility all who had either remained faithful to the crown,

* Præfatus comes literas sigillo nostro, quo non nos, sed comes
ipse pro suo utebatur arbitrio formari fecit. Rymer, i. 458;
Worcester, August 7. Literas sigillo nostro, quo pro suo libito
voluntatis utebatur, signari fecit ; to Archbishop Boniface. Rot.
Lit. Pat. 49 Henr. III. membr. 9, August 24th. Wykes says,
p. 168, of the conclusion of the treaty with Llewellyn : Eamque
sigillo regio consignavit, quod duobus laicis deportandum com-
miserat, viz., Domino Petro de Monteforti et Domino R. de
Sandwych militibus, quod a seculo fuerat inauditum.

† Dum tamen voluntati domini nostri se submittant. August
24th, Shirley, ii. 289.

or, after suspicion of disloyalty, came forward now to
make their peace.   Even the widows of royalist gentlemen slain in the civil war were represented.   With the
vengeance and precipitancy inevitable in all reactions,
every act of government since the battle of Lewes was
here declared null and void, all the rebels were outlawed who had borne arms at Kenilworth or Evesham,
their estates confiscated, and the greed of the victors
satiated from the enormous mass of property thus left
without owners.   Gloucester, Valence, Roger Mortimer,
and Philip Basset, as well as the Princes Edward and
Henry, took care to be recompensed for their services.
The spiritual and temporal Barons were solicited for
advances of money to assist in discharging the enormously swollen debts of the King of the Romans.   Edmund, once King designate of the Sicilies, was consoled
with the whole fief of the late Earl of Leicester, the
office of Lord High Steward of the realm, the earldom
of Derby, and other estates of rebels.   Even loyal
partisans shook their heads at a revolution so extrava-
gant.*   Property changed hands much more rapidly
and extensively than in the previous year, when the
Regent had sought to suppress with a firm hand the
most self-seeking of his partisans, and to put the
property of his adversaries under the guardianship of
the State.   The country swarmed with outlawed
patriots, who began to collect together in scattered

---

* Wykes, 183 : Rex et sui complices non sicut decuerat cautiores
effecti, sed potius stultiores.   Further, Gesch. von England, iii.
797, *et seq.*, and Catalogue of Transfers, Blaauw, 267, 268.

groups in remote and inaccessible regions, especially in the low lying marshes around Ely and Cambridge, precisely in those districts where the last Anglo-Saxons had defied the iron rule of the conqueror. The fate of the City of London was peculiarly hard when it was compelled to surrender at discretion in October, and its plenipotentiaries were confined at Windsor in spite of safe-conducts ; not only did it atone for the demo-cratic government of recent years, but also it was compelled, by the banishment and plunder of many citizens and the payment of 20,000 marks sterling from the City treasury, to make expiation for offences against Henry and his consort, King Richard and Prince Edward. The ancient charter conferring the right of self-government was nullified so long as the Constable ruled unrestrained in the Tower as King's Seneschal, and a number of citizens were held as host-ages for the obedience of the restless populace* even after the pardon granted on the 10th of January, 1266.

The sharpness of the antagonism, defiance on one side and imprudent revolution on the other, prevented the pacification of the kingdom for more than a year. At first, moreover, the Pope's movements indicated an intention to inflict chastisement. Clement IV., who when Legate had vigorously opposed this revolt, dan-gerous alike to throne and altar,† had, before he heard

* Lib. de Antiq. Leg. 77-82. Rymer, i. 464, October 6. Re-port of Earl Humphrey of Hereford ; October 6th, Shirley. ii. 293.

† Clement IV. to Louis IX. Reynaldi, xxii. 179, 1265 : Quid putas, fili charissime, in iis agi? quid per talia machinamenta

of Simon's fall, despatched Ottoboni, the Cardinal Deacon of St. Adrian, to England, with instructions to warn the Barons and the Prince against all fellowship with him.* After the news of victory he came to the King's assistance with a grant of tithes for one year, absolved the Earl of Gloucester, and congratulated the Prince and his father upon their liberation.† When, at the end of October, the Cardinal Legate crossed the Channel with the Queen who had remained two years in France, his journey to London took the form of a triumphal progress of the victorious ecclesiastical power. The Pope advised conciliatory measures, since severity, though it subdued individuals, would only irritate the great body of the nation,‡ but both parties were still too warmly excited to listen to the voice of reason. Prelates who had been so deeply implicated as the Bishops of London, Chichester, Winchester, and Worcester, were necessarily called to account; it was enough that in the previous year they had not executed the sentence of excommunication entrusted to them

quæri? ad quid per tales eorundem baronum insidias anhelari. nisi ut de regno illo regium nomen aboleatur omnino et extincto ibi semine regio ipsi regnent? nisi ut Christianus populus a devotione matris ecclesiæ et observantia fidei orthodoxæ avertatur. Compare Ranke, Englische Geschichte, i. 82.

* Two bulls of the 13th of September ; Rymer, i. 460, 461.

† Læta nobis et tristia nunciasti to Ottoboni XIII. Kal. Oct. in MS. Add. Mus. Brit. 15, 362, fol. 83, and five bulls in Rymer. i. 462–465.

‡ Clement IV. to Henry III., October 4th : Cum fervor vindictæ paucorum odium reprimat, multorum irritet.

against the Earl of Leicester and his party. The
Legate suspended them from their office in solemn
session, and the three first were further condemned to
a penitential pilgrimage to Rome. The aged Walter
of Cantelupe, immovably loyal to his convictions, was
rescued by death from the evil days in store for him,
as even an adversary expresses it;* he died on the
12th of February, 1266. It was universally believed
that the glory of saintship would have been his if he
had not thrown in his lot with Leicester.

To exercise grace and mercy towards those who
persisted in keeping up a finale to the drama of the
civil war was still more difficult, for the garrison of
Kenilworth held out with the heroism of despair, and
the strong bands of outlaws in the midland and eastern
parts of the island repeatedly extended to them a
helping hand. It was not till the summer of 1266
that a regular siege of the fortress could be formed,
and even this gave no promise of speedy success. In
September the Pope renewed his sentence against the
rebels with added severity ; at most the Legate might
only absolve from excommunication upon the bed of
death.† But the obstinate resistance which they still

---

* Qui tanta sanctitatis eminentia cæteris præpollebat episcopis,
quod nisi contra juramentum quod Domino regi de fidelitate
[fecerat] imo etiam contra inhibitionem sedis Apostolicæ Comiti
Leycestriæ tam familiariter et fortiter adhæsisset, in catalogo
Sanctorum non immerito fuerat ascribendus. Wykes, 180.
Compare Rishanger, ed. Riley, 47.

† Rymer, i. 469 ; September 15th.

encountered, gradually forced the government to consider their own position. In the higher and lower
ranks alike, those who had either remained faithful to
the crown, or ultimately submitted, began afresh to
murmur against the endless military and financial exactions. So it came to pass that at a Parliament held
on the 24th of August, in sight of Kenilworth Castle,
the King and his counsellors nominated three Bishops
and three Barons, with whom an equal number of deputies from the estates were permitted to co-operate.
Under the guidance of the Legate and Prince Henry,
these twelve drew up the sentence (Dictum) of Kenilworth, an earnest attempt to restore peace to the
kingdom and to make fair terms with the dispossessed
nobles.*   On the 31st of October this decision received
legal sanction in the national assembly, then transferred to Northampton. The Legate himself confirmed
the Great Charter, though only in the form used at all
ratifications since 1225. The tithes were granted to
the King for three years at the Pope's suggestion, and
but little to the satisfaction of the clergy. The outlaws, with the sole exception of the descendants of
Leicester and Robert Ferrers, the wild Earl of Derby,
were to receive back their estates from those to whom
they had been transferred, upon condition of giving
up the revenues for one, two, three, four, or five years,
according to the measure of guilt in each case. All
legislation developed from the Provisions of Oxford

* Annales Waverl. 371 *et seq.* For the particulars, Stubbs.
Const. Hist. ii. 96.

was once more solemnly annulled.* There was no lack of dissension during this and the next following reign, but these concessions, inspired by the prudent advice of Rome, first wrought a substantial improvement in the condition of the country, after it had steadily deteriorated since the beginning of the century.

The courageous defenders of Kenilworth still persevered in their resistance, perhaps because from them alone seven years income of their confiscated estates was required as ransom.† They did not capitulate till all means of sustenance were consumed, and all prospect of help had vanished. And still the public peace was not established, for the rebels were so strong in the eastern counties that they even obtained possession of such towns as Lynn, Cambridge, and Norwich, and at the same moment the most dreaded peer in the country rose in arms once more, because the new securities for the national privileges now by no means satisfied him. Like many contemporaries of the same rank, Gilbert de Clare, Earl of Gloucester, had fought both for and against constitutional rights ; in the committee of twelve he had zealously supported the agreement of Kenilworth, but encountered violent opposition from the ultras of Roger Mortimer's faction, who would not hear of restoring the estates forfeited by high treason. Thus he was placed in the same position as

* Dictum de Kenilworth. Statutes of the Realm, i. 12 ; Select Charters, 419.

† Ann. de Dunst. 243.

that to which he himself had once helped to bring
Montfort. Apprehensions of an attack from the Barons
of the border compelled him to consider means for securing the safety of his person and his neighbouring
domain, and, as a mediation attempted by Warenne
and Valence failed, and he did not venture to appear
himself with the army when, in February, 1267, the
King lay encamped near Bury St. Edmunds, he suddenly appealed once more to the Provisions of Oxford.
He referred to the oath sworn to him by Edward
immediately after his liberation, that foreigners should
thenceforth be excluded from possessions and influence.
And did not Valence claim the earldom of Pembroke ?
Was not the King about to transfer Norfolk from the
haughty Roger Bigod, who had likewise been implicated in the popular movement, to his own son-in-law,
the son of the Duke of Brittany ? Taking his stand
upon the Dictum, Gloucester further demanded that
the outlaws should receive an amnesty, instead of being
subjugated by force. He expressly asserted that he
took up arms solely against Mortimer and his confederates, not against the King and his son.* When
the Legate summoned the insurgents in the fens
of Ely and Axholme to return to their obedience to
Church and Crown, they replied defiantly in the phrase-
ology which had meant so much under Simon de

* Wykes, 198–202, Ann. de Dunst. 215. Rishanger, ed.
Halliwell, 60 ; ed. Riley, 47. See on the checkered policy of the
two Earls of Gloucester, father and son, Stubbs, Const. Hist. ii.
297. 298.

Montfort, calling themselves loyal sons of the Church and truest patriots; then, that the defenders of the nation's liberties might not be utterly overpowered, Gloucester rose, and in April marched rapidly upon London. There, attempts to suppress the democratic party had produced so little effect that very recently, in spite of confiscations and the expulsion of their most energetic comrades, the citizens had tumultuously demanded the reinstatement of their long idolised Mayor, Fitz-Thomas. Cardinal Ottoboni, who resided in the Tower, could not, or, rather, would not, hinder the Earl's march across the town to Southwark on the 8th day of the month. Gloucester even had an interview with the Legate, who, with Italian adroitness, was probably playing a deep-laid game for the purpose of duly intimidating the court and inducing it at last to desist from its obstinacy.* Very soon John d'Eyville, one of the boldest partisans in the eastern districts, joined the Earl with his troop of horsemen; they took possession of the bridge and all the gates; again the popular party was supreme in the City, and the Legate sat near by in the Tower.

The King, terrified by the threatening attitude of London,† found himself compelled to relinquish his enterprise in the east and to summon the Prince from the the north. But it was not till the beginning of May that

---

* Unde manifestum est quod comes habuit introitum civitatis per consilium et assensum legati. Lib. de Antiq. Leg. 90.

† Audito quod civitatum Angliæ principissa per infidos indigenas in dolo fuerat occupata Wykes, 200.

P

they were able to approach cautiously from Essex, whilst Gloucester commanded all the western roads. The Legate repaired to the royal head-quarters, freely and unimpeded according to some accounts, rescued from the distresses of a siege according to others. As he, King Richard, his son Henry, and others, urgently advised a reconciliation, terms were at last concluded in the middle of June. The interdict upon London was only nominally renewed. Upon condition of admitting the royal bailiffs and their own aldermen, the citizens now received complete pardon, and the Earl of Gloucester, who had helped them to obtain it, procured the same for himself and for Eyville's followers. The confederates on their side must consent to make compensation and give bail.* The outlaws around Ely now raised no material difficulty. After their leader, Nicolas of Segrave, one of Leicester's most faithful adherents, had come to an understanding with Prince Edward, they capitulated on the 11th of July, all the advantages of the Dictum of Kenilworth being still preserved to them. Lastly, with Cardinal Ottoboni's help, the Welsh Prince Llewellyn made his peace at Montgomery on the 29th of September, and thus the last convulsions of the civil war were presently stilled.

Rome had recognised that she must not continue to encroach recklessly, as hitherto, upon the independence of the English church, claiming its riches as her own, and obtruding her protectorate over the kingdom in

* The charters for the Earl and for the City, both of the 16th of June. Rymer, i. 472, and Lib. de Antiq. Leg. 93, *et seq.*

face of the growing sentiment of nationality. The crown at last desisted from the practice of conferring fiefs and offices upon foreign kinsmen and favourites. Even the franchises now raised to the rank of national law were applied in a manner well adapted to restore the long disturbed harmony between government and people. In the Parliament summoned to Marlborough in November, 1267, besides the great Barons and experienced administrators (discreti), such as chancellor and judges, some men of lower rank were also admitted.* It re-enacted the Provisions of 1259, thenceforth to be accepted as part of the legislation of the realm, inducing thereby the people, both high and low, to yield dutiful obedience to law. It is not improbable that the shires were represented by their chosen Knights. They and the Barons were courteously consulted, but no definite right of participation in State affairs, especially in questions of taxation, was conferred upon them. Except the demand for the appointment of the ministers and the election of sheriffs, almost everything was conceded that had been asked for at Oxford ten years before. Born of the bitterest experience, a spirit of frugality at last prevailed in the treasury, and justice in the tribunals which spoke in the King's name. After King and Barons in conflict with one another had appointed great justiciaries,

---

* Convocatis discretioribus regni tam ex majoribus quam minoribus. Statute of Marlebridge ; Statutes of the Realm, i. 19. Compare Report on the Dignity of a Peer, i. 159. Cf. Stubbs, Const. Hist. ii. 97.

endowed with a high political authority which could
never be advantageous to the development of the
monarchy, this office now entirely disappeared, giving
place to supreme judges who presided over the several
courts and were irremovable so long as they discharged
their functions with integrity.*

Thus the revolution and the breach with the court
of Rome came to an end; a disturbance of many years
standing was settled, and bore some good fruit as well
as much that was evil. Now all who were called by
the name of Montfort appeared to be driven away under
outlawry and ban. What was the end of the race
which, as if smitten by a curse, rapidly died out in the
branch transplanted to England?

When Prince Edward escaped from his guardians on
the 28th of May, 1265, the Countess Eleanor with her
brilliant household was still at Odiham Castle in
Hampshire. Upon hearing of the occurrence she first
went to Porchester, where she had an interview with
her son Simon; on the 15th of June she arrived at
Dover and took up her residence in the castle, the
custody of which was in the hands of her eldest son.
It was fully intended to defend the castles upon the
coast in order to command the straits of Dover as long
as possible. French ambassadors, who kept up constant intercourse with the court, now shut up at
Hereford, were hospitably entertained,† and numerous

* Foss, The Judges of England. ii. 155, 221.

† Rot. Hospitii Comitissæ Leicestriæ, ed. Hudson Turner, p.
51, where, from the 19th of February till the 1st of October,

messengers despatched in various directions; the last
was sent directly to the Earl as late as the 1st of
August. Then came intelligence of the cruel blow at
Evesham that decided the greatest venture of Eleanor's
life, and robbed her at once of her husband and her
eldest son. All the proud hopes of this aspiring woman,
who for years had declined to follow the paths appointed her, were crushed in a moment. Bowed down
to the very earth, she laid aside her purple and put on
the widow's weeds she had worn long before in her
early youth.* She shaped her life thenceforth after
the pattern of a cloister, fasting and dispensing alms.
At various times, on the 19th of August and the 3rd of
September, masses were said for the soul of her
departed husband.† She only gradually relinquished
the idea of offering resistance at Dover, as her son
Simon did at Kenilworth. But when she recognised
the full force of the reaction, meaning for her not
princely and fraternal grace but outlawry and banishment, then she hoped by giving up the castle to win a
gleam of pity. So the garrison was discharged, and
all made ready for a journey. With motherly affection
she had caused her younger sons, Richard and Amaury,

1265, every date is recorded, every change of residence, and
every trifling expenditure.

 * Habitum vidualem, quem voto castitatis temere violato per
carnis petulantiam indiscrete reliquerat, reassumens. Wykes.
179.

 † Rot. Hospitii, 68 : twelve shillings and nine pence for the
mass. Many details from the same document collected in Green's
Princesses, ii. 145, *et seq.*

to join her as quickly as possible, and on the 18th of
September she sent them across the Channel to Gravelines.* Amaury already held a canonry at York, which
was now forfeited. They took with them the considerable sum of 11,000 marks; this the King sought
to recover some weeks later in a letter to Louis IX.,
but apparently in vain.† On the 1st of October she
closed her account with the messengers for the last
despatch to Kenilworth.‡

Now there was immediate need that she herself should
seek refuge for the last time in France, for on the 28th
of September a royal order charged the Barons of
the Cinque Ports on no account to suffer her to depart
with her treasures.§ She knew her brother's malice
and cold-heartedness, but she had consolation in the
generosity of her nephew Edward, whom she had
entertained as a hostage at Kenilworth and Odiham,
and who in her need gratefully requited the kindness
and consideration with which she had constantly
treated him. Whilst the King henceforth dropped
the designation " our sister " in all his proclamations,
the heir had still a courteous word for her. On the
16th of August she had received a letter from the

---

* Rot. Hospitii, 74.

† Rot. Lit. Claus. 49 Henr. III. membr. 2, dorso; October 10th.

‡ Rot. Hospitii, 75. The manuscript once belonged to the
nunnery of the Montforts at Montargis. It was saved from the
destruction of the French revolution, and placed in the British
Museum. MS. Add. 8877.

§ Green, ii. 454. and Shirley, ii. 292.

young conqueror, perhaps giving fuller details of
Simon's tragic end. The Prince was already the soul
of a judicious system of restitution, and on the 26th
of October, after Eleanor had escaped across the
Channel, he presented to the Chancellor, Bishop
Walter of Bath, a considerable list of noblemen who
had belonged to his dear aunt's court, and whom at
her request he commended to mercy and the restoration of their landed estate.* To this was added, three
days latter, a special intercession for John de la Haye,
who had always been one of Leicester's most faithful
servants and partisans.† Her brother, the King of
the Romans, had also expressed, privately at least,
unalterable affection for her and her children, and
promised to assert their rights as far as he was able.
The appearance of the first of the sureties whom he
brought was a moving incident; it was no other than
the venerable Bishop of Worcester.‡

When the Countess arrived in France, accompanied
by her daughter and namesake Eleanor, the King gave

---

* Ad instantiam carissimae amitae nostrae, dominae comitissae
Leycestriae, Dover, October 26th. Green, ii. 454; Shirley, ii. 291.

† Edward to the Chancellor, November 5th. Shirley, ii. 296.
Spelling the name as de la Hare must be erroneous according to
Adam Marsh; Brewer, Mon. Franc. 268, 298.

‡ This remarkable document from the French archives is
printed by Blaauw, The Barons' War, appendix, p. 2: Richard
par la grace de Deu Rey des Romeins tot jors cressaunt . . .
Donne en la priorie de Kenilwerthe le Dimeinche prochein avant
la feste de la Nativite nostre Dame l'an du rengne le Rey quarante
nevime (September, 1265).

her the same respectful reception that had always been
accorded there in so striking a manner to the house of
Montfort. Louis was still ready at all times to interpose a word on behalf of the unfortunate family. He
induced the English King soon to lay aside his cruel
and relentless mood, and at least to entertain the
idea of an accommodation with his sister. The revenues
of her widow's dower, her personal possessions, were to
be reserved to her.* But one serious difficulty remained in the spirited resistance of the younger
Simon at Kenilworth. For months the garrison
spread terror and dismay† through the midland districts of the island by their devastating sallies, until the
blockade of the place could at last begin in June, 1266.
But meanwhile the young Simon had departed secretly
in order to profit by the good will shown to his
mother in France, perhaps to obtain direct aid for himself. He could not be ignorant that Louis IX. was
urgently interceding on their behalf.‡ But the inclination chivalrously to adventure his life was stronger
than the resolution to obedient submission. So he

* Rot. Lit. Pat. 49 Henr. III. membr. 29, November 18th ; see
Green, ii. 151.

† Cum . . . quendam de nuntiis nostris nuper per partes illas
transeuntem ceperint et ei manum truncaverint, etc. Henry to
the Sheriff of York, March 15th, 1266. Shirley, ii. 300. Compare Rishanger, ed. Riley, 43.

‡ Ad procurandam pacem et amicitiam liberorum S. quondam
comitis Leycestriæ, nepotum vestrorum, ac comitissæ genitricis
eorum, vestræ sororis, etc. Louis IX. to Henry III., May 5th,
1266. Shirley, ii. 304.

stole back, defying a warrant for his arrest,* and joined
the insurgents in the fens of Ely instead of returning to Kenilworth. His was the blame, therefore, that
the Dictum of October excluded the members of his
family from its benefits and referred their fate at best to
French arbitration.† It is true that he is reported
to have recommended the garrison of Kenilworth to
surrender the castle upon fair conditions. But, under
the command of the valiant knight, Henry Hastings,
they are known to have held out some months longer,
protesting that the castle had been entrusted to them
by its mistress, the Countess, not by her son.‡ This
bulwark of the power of the Montforts in England
did not fall till the 21st of December, 1266.

Meanwhile the Countess had retired to Montargis,
the Dominican nunnery founded by her husband's
sister Amicia; § though full of grief and sorrow she
was still indefatigable in her efforts to save some fragments from the shipwreck of their fortune for herself and her children. Through the mediation of her
sister-in-law, Queen Eleanor, she obtained for herself an

---

* Rot. Lit. Pat. 50 Henr. III. membr. 18, dorso.

† Statutes of the Realm, i. 17.

‡ Dicentes se nullam a Simone suscepisse castri custodiam,
sed a Comitissa, paulo ante a regno expulsa ; nec ulli viventi de
resignatione proposuerunt, nisi ipsimet Comitissæ et in sua
præsentia respondere. Rishanger, ed. Riley, 43.

§ In domo Sororum de ordine Prædicatorum apud Mountargys,
a sorore viri sui fundata, morabatur. Rishanger, ed. Riley, 87.
Compare Gallia Christiana, xii. 256.

annual pension of £500 from her former possessions,* but with this she could not rest content because she had the fate of her sons equally at heart. Simon had fortunately escaped across the sea when his last comrades in the eastern counties at length made their peace in the summer of 1267. He was followed a little later by his brother Guy, who had been confined by the victors since the battle of Evesham and effected his escape from Dover by bribing his guard.†

At the same time Louis had also interceded on behalf of the sons. Whether he were led to renew his application by personal esteem for the mother, with whom he had so often had intercourse, or by a deeper political calculation, it is certain that at the moment when the humiliation of the house of Montfort was most complete, he persuaded the King of England to listen to him more willingly than before. In response to a formal embassy, a decree was issued on the 24th of June, 1267, to the effect that Simon the younger should receive an equivalent for his father's former possessions, as estimated by his own agent and the King's. The King of the Romans was named as umpire. But again hard conditions and qualifying clauses made the whole of little value. In the first intoxication of the reaction, Leicester's estates had been already transferred to Prince Edmund, and Henry reserved to himself the right of assuming possession

* Rot. Lit. Pat. 51 Henr. III. membr. 20, dorso.

† Custos Guidonis de Monte Forti in castro Doveriæ corruptus ipsum dimisit liberum. Rishanger, ed. Riley, 47.

of them at any moment, after a valuation which was
entrusted to the French King. It was expressly
stipulated that the losses suffered by the crown from
the Montforts should then be deducted.* Simon
and his brothers must further renounce every hostile
alliance or design against the English King and the
Plantagenet dynasty. All were forbidden to set foot
on English ground without permission. It is no
matter for surprise that these conditions, scarcely
honest in intention, were not accepted by the other
side. A few months made it evident that all the
efforts of the mediator were fruitless. On the 6th of
September Henry III. wrote to the French King that
he was prepared to receive the Countess or her son at
any moment, and to afford them justice so far as
the laws of the realm permitted. He must, however,
adhere to the former conditions which, if not now
accepted, would afterwards become void.† It is noteworthy that at this time the litigious Countess made
serious attempts to obtain from the French tribunals,
for the support of her family, a fragment of the inheritance of her mother, who had married the Count

---

* Precium vero speramus esse taxandum. si vestræ serenitatis
circumspectio diligenter advertat turbationes et damna innu-
merabilia quæ sustinuimus hactenus et adhuc etiam sustinemus,
occasione seditionis per patrem suum, etc. Henry III. to Louis
IX., Stratford, June 24th, shortly after the conclusion of terms
with London. Green, ii. 155.

† Quod si ad præsens admittere recusaverit, ad hoc alias re-
gressum si voluerit non habebit. Shirley, ii. 315.

of Marche and Angoulême as her second husband.* She may have had reason to despair of a reconciliation between her brother and her children. The attitude of the sons, at least, indicated no desire to facilitate it.

Simon fully realized his position as the heir of his race, and the songs which sang his father's death, centred the hopes of the party upon him.† The lingering connection with the patriots was not entirely severed, even after the defeats of 1267. Guy had soon left the French asylum in search of adventure, and joined Charles of Anjou and his army in the conquest of Naples and Sicily.‡ The elder brother appears to have followed him into Italy somewhat later, but not until he had carried out a singular adventure in England. Towards the end of the summer of 1270, Prince Edward entered upon his crusade to Palestine, and a great part of the English nobility joined him, amongst them, Gilbert of Gloucester. The young Montfort took advantage of the quiet and emptiness of the kingdom to make a clandestine visit; he prayed at the tomb of his father and brother at

---

* Green, Princesses, ii. 155.

† Priez touz, mes amîs douz, le fitz Seinte Marie,
  Qe l'enfant, her puissant, meigne en bone vie.
                                    Wright, Political Songs, 127.

‡ Concerning his relation to the King, Guil. de Nangis, Recueil, xx. 438. Charles made him his deputy in Tuscany, G. Villani. Muratori Rer. Ital. S.S. xiii. 261.

Evesham,* and then fled beyond the Alps, carrying thoughts of vengeance with him.

After the death of Pope Clement IV. on the 29th of November, 1268, the cardinals had failed to agree upon the choice of a successor, and a long interregnum ensued. When Edward put to sea from Palermo in February, 1271, he despatched his cousin Henry, son of King Richard, to England; he, probably provided with secret commissions to the conclave, met his uncle, Charles of Anjou, and King Philip III. of France in Rome, and on the 9th of March the three Princes repaired to Viterbo, where it was hoped that the papal election would at last take place.

Here, as finale to the English Civil War, an unparalleled crime was committed, of a type even then rare in the north, and more consonant with the usages of the hot-blooded south. Simon and Guy of Montfort were also at Viterbo in the company of Count Aldobrandini, Rosso dell'Anguillara, who held estates in Tuscany, and whose daughter Margaret had been married to Guy some time before. According to the statement of a Papal partisan, Henry the German was charged, with Charles of Anjou's assistance, to persuade his unfortunate cousins to a reconciliation with Prince Edward.† The miserable men were either

* The remarkable statement in Bartholom. Cotton. ed. Luard, p. 146, a. 1271 (Rer. Brit. med ævi SS).

† Processus Gregorii X. Papæ contra Guidonem, Rymer, i. 501: ad quos restituendos ad carissimi in Christo filii nostri E. Regis Angliæ illustris gratiam.

ignorant of this, or, regardless of the bonds of kindred,
they forgot how much affection and esteem they had
once interchanged with him. When Simon was taken
prisoner at Northampton in the spring of 1264, King
Richard had rescued him from shameful death. Subsequently, after the decisive day of Evesham, Simon
entertained Richard and his son at Kenilworth, until
he voluntarily set them free. Had the Montfort
brothers no other ground for ill-will towards their
kinsman than that, after joining the patriot cause,
he had abandoned their father at a critical moment?
Or were they incited by their Italian connèctions to
a treacherous crime? Suffice it that on the 13th of
March, as the sovereigns of France and Sicily were
performing their Lenten devotions among the Franciscans, Simon and Guy appeared suddenly with an
armed band in a church opposite Henry's dwelling,
where he was attending mass.* With the cry : "Now
thou escapest not, traitor!" they fell upon him with
sword and dagger as he knelt in prayer, suspecting
nothing. Guy, more audacious than the rest, tore the
expiring man from the altar, dragged him by the hair
through the throng and through the portal, and com-
pleted the ghastly murder without the church. They
then sprang upon their horses to seek a refuge with

---

* Philip III. to King Richard, March 13th, 1271, in Lib. de
Antiq. Leg. 134. Wykes, 241, calls the church St. Blasius,
Rishanger, ed. Riley, 67, and Guil. de Nangis, Recueil, xx. 484,
St. Laurentius, Annal. de Wintonia, 110, St. Silvester. The
Pope : in quodam parochiali ecclesia ejusdem civitatis. Rymer,
i. 501.

their patron, Count Anguillara.* The King of Naples immediately took measures for seizing the murderers,† but in that lawless country their safety had meanwhile been more effectually provided for. Simon died a natural death in the course of the same year at Siena, or, according to another statement, in France.‡ It was not till March, 1273, that the church interposed against the murderers,§ after a new pontiff, Gregory X. had ascended the Papal throne, and when Edward, now by his father's death King of England, was leisurely returning through Italy from Ptolemais. This Pope pardoned the Bishops of London and Chichester,‖ who had been suspended ever since the time of the civil war, and it almost appeared as if he sought a pretext for delay in this affair, but Edward I. was urgent, even suspecting the Kings of France and Naples of concealing the crime. Thus Guy and his father-in-law at least were called to account. The former had the audacity to make an appeal through his brother Amaury of Montfort, who was an ordained priest, and according to one report had been cognizant

---

* Andonne salvo e sano in Maremma nelle terre del Conte Rosso suo suocero. G. Villani. Muratori, xiii. 262.

† Charles of Anjou to Edward, Viterbo, March 13th. Rymer i. 488.

‡ Matth. Westmonast. 401. Ann. de Dunst., 259. Simone fatali sorte rebus humanis exempto : the trial in Rymer, l. c.

§ The citation in Rymer, i. 499, March 1st.

‖ May 31st and November 26th, 1272. Copies in MS. Add. Mus. Brit. 15,363, fol. 24, 87.

of the conspiracy.* In three letters to Gregory still
extant, Guy entirely denied his own complicity.† The
Count of Anguillara alone succeeded in exculpating
himself; Guy was declared an outlaw by the sentence
of the Church, but in the autumn, as the Pope passed
through Florence, he threw himself at his feet, bare-
foot and wearing a cord round his neck, "so that the
door of mercy was opened to him."‡ Ten years he did
penance in a solitary cell, until Martin IV. released him,
employed him as his condottiere in the Romagna, and
permitted him to lay claim to his wife's inheritance.§
During his confinement in the monastery the King of
Naples had sought to obtain favour for him from the
King of England, but Edward refused to listen to any
proposal short of the blood-stained man's eternal
banishment beyond the Alps.|| In 1288 Guy fought
again for the Neapolitans at sea, but he was captured
with the Prince of Salerno and thrown into a Sicilian
dungeon; there he ended his life, for all attempts to

* Non sine assensu, ut credi poterit Emmerici fratris eorundem.
Wykes, 241.

† The three letters copied in MS. Add. l. c. fol. 52, 55, 61.

‡ Rymer, i. 501, April 1st, 507; November 29, uxoris suæ
præsentia.

§ Rishanger, ed. Riley, 105, a. 1283.

|| Edward I., April 11th, 1279; Rymer, i. 568. Pene novit
totus orbis, qualiter ille Simon, pater suus, et idem Guydo
cæterique fratres et complices sui, olim sanguinem nostrum
sitientis, domino H. regi patri nostro et nobis mortales insidias
præparaverunt. Two letters of the Prince of Salerno, p. 584,
586.

purchase his release failed.* The bloody deed per-
petrated upon the son of the King of the Romans lived
long in the memory of Europe. It was painted upon
the walls of the sacred spot where it occurred, and
Dante placed this son and grandson of the two great
Simons among the murderers in the bloody pit of Hell.†

It was a sign of nobleness in Edward I.'s character
that he, at least, did not visit the trangressions of
the sons upon the unhappy mother. As he returned
through France he confirmed to her, upon the application of Philip III., the payment of her widow's
dower, and, so long as she should cherish no hostile
designs, the recognition of all her rights. He paid
debts for her out of his treasury, and caused certain
still outstanding claims of her first husband to be
collected for her benefit. On the ground of St.
Louis' will, she made application for 1500 marks from
the English deposits placed at the time of the civil
war in the house of the Templars at Paris, but these
she could not recover, in spite of the French King's
advocacy.‡ After Eleanor had at length made her

* Ptolemæus Lucensis, Muratori, xi. 1164. Girard de Fran-
cheto. Recueil, xxi. 9. Compare Rymer, i. 695.

† Viterbienses vero in memoriam interfecti modum interfec-
tionis in pariete depinxerunt. Rishanger, ed. Riley, 67.

  Mostrocci un' ombra dall' un canto sola,
  Dicendo: colui fesse in grembo a Dio
  Lo cor che in sul Tamigi ancor si cola.
        Inferno, Canto xii.

‡ Edward, Melun, August 10th, 1273. Dum tamen bene et
fideliter versus nos et fideles nostros se habeat. Philip to Edward,

Q

last will in January, 1275, and commended it and her
surviving children to the dowager Queen Margaret, she
died in the spring of the year, probably at Montargis,
where she was interred with the strictest privacy.*
At Margaret's request her executors were admitted
without delay before the English tribunals.† If
Eleanor had been capable of greater self-control, and
if, instead of goading and inciting Simon's powerful
nature, she had won a softening influence over him, she,
as a daughter and sister of kings, and with her talents,
would have been pre-eminently fitted to promote
concord in the royal family and peace in the realm.

Of the other children, Richard disappeared, probably
before the mother's death, and left no trace.‡ By her
death-bed stood Amaury and the only daughter,
Eleanor, Simon's youngest child, born twenty-two
years earlier whilst he was absent in Gascony. An
attachment to the young lady on the part of the stately
and beautiful Prince Llewellyn of Wales dated as far
back as the intercourse at Kenilworth in 1265, and the
betrothal was ratified by the dying mother in memory
of the political alliance of that time. We do not know
what secret communications with Wales were carried
on in France. It appears, however, that Amaury was

October 10th, 1273. Green, ii. 456, 457. Compare p. 158, 159.
Champollion Figeac, Lettres, i. 159.

* Ann. de Dunst. 259, 265.

† Margaret to Edward : la Contesse de Leycestre nous pria et
requist a sa fin, etc. Green, ii. 457. Rot. Lit. Claus. 3 Edw. I.
membr. 13.

‡ According to Annal. de Dunst. l. c.

again permitted to come to England, where he was
received and protected by the Bishop of Chester in
the capacity of chaplain.* In the spring of 1276,
after those differences had already begun which
resulted a few years later in the violent subjugation
of the mountain country by Edward I., the younger
Eleanor went to Wales by sea, under the escort of her
brother Amaury, two French knights, and two mendicant friars. Notwithstanding every precaution, they
were carried off near the Scilly Isles by four ships from
Bristol, unquestionably by the King's command, since
he afterwards caused a reward of 200 marks to be
paid for the capture.† Amaury was confined, first in
Corfe Castle, afterwards at Sherburne; his sister, the
plighted bride of an enemy of the country, was conveyed to Windsor. Llewellyn's fierce demands, his
vehement complaints to the Pope, were of no avail.‡
The mighty King did not condescend to be gracious
until Llewellyn had madly rushed into war, and conducted it with such ill fortune during the next year,
that he lost the whole of his country, except the isle
of Anglesey and some districts around Snowdon;
then, after he had taken away his independence,
Edward gave his bride into his hands. The marriage

* Cepit in societatem suam Emericum de Monte Forti ad con-
ducendum et veniendum secum in Angliam. Lib. de Antiq. Leg.
159, a. 1273.

† Rishanger, ed. Riley, 87. Wykes, 104. Bartholom. Cotton,
153. Compare Green, Princesses, ii. 163.

‡ MS. Add. Mus. Brit. 15,363; John XXI. to Edward,
January 30th, 1277. Q 2

was celebrated at Worcester in the presence of the English court on the 13th of October, 1278.*

Thus a tragic and romantic fate had made the daughter of the great Simon de Montfort "Princess of Wales and Lady of Snowdon." As such she reminded Edward I. of her mother's still unexecuted will, in order that at least her share of the inheritance might be delivered over to her.† It was probably owing to her husband's attitude, and the English King's design of completely crushing Cymric liberty, that the business was delayed. Amaury was not set free until 1281, when Archbishop Peckham of Canterbury became surety for him.‡ He himself thanked the King for his grace in a letter written at Arras, and begged for support in his necessitous condition.§ Subsequently, he also went to Italy, where he threw off his clerical garb and caused himself to be knighted, about the time of his brother Guy's imprisonment by the Aragonese: his death followed soon after.‖ He was the last of the branch who bore the name of Montfort, for Guy left only daughters, and it is doubtful whether Simon or Richard ever had children.

The Princess of Wales still addressed herself to

---

* Rishanger, ed. Riley, 92. Annal. Waverl. 389. Compare Green, ii. 163, and Geschichte von England, iv. 23.

† Her letter of October 9th, 1279. Rymer, i. 576.

‡ Rymer, i. 602, 603, 605.

§ Champollion Figeac, Lettres, i. 301, May 22nd, 1282.

‖ MS. Roff. in Cotton. Nero D. ii. fol. 182, an. 1287. Emericus frater eius clericus eminentis litterature qui ultimus fuit de progenie Guenelonis factus est miles abjecto habitu clericali.

Edward at various times in the friendly tone of a
relative, although it soon appeared that her mother
had left only debts, and even bills for her Lucchese
banker which were drawn upon Edward. She interceded for her husband and her brother, and at the
beginning of 1281 she spent some time as a guest at
the court in Windsor.* But she was not able to avert
the storm from the Celtic land which she, the granddaughter of an English king, had chosen for her
home. In the spring of 1282 her brother-in-law David,
and then Llewellyn himself, roused their rough mountain tribes to a war of independence, and soon afterwards, on the 21st of June, Eleanor died in childbed.
She knew nothing of the subjection of the entire
principality to the English crown, and she died before
her husband's head was planted upon the battlements
of the Tower of London. The little daughter whom
she bore was christened Guenciliana by the conqueror,
and spent her life in the convent at Sempringham.
The King of England provided graciously for her main-
tenance, yet he was careful that she should remain a
nun until her death on the 7th of June, 1337.†

It was indeed, a strange mingling of blood, the
granddaughter of Simon of Montfort being the only
child of the last native sovereign of Wales. That was
reason enough to seclude her for half a century as
a person dangerous to the crown.

* Rymer, i. 587. Compare Green, Princesses, ii. 166–168.
† Continuatio Florent. Wigorn. ii. 226 (Engl. Hist. Soc.).
Many grants in the Rot. Lit. Pat. and Rot. Lit. Claus.; Edward
III. from 1327 to 1337.

EPILOGUE.

Jurists and historians, especially in England, are wont to compare with pride and pleasure the early political development of this country with that of Aragon.* And it is true that, at the first glance, a remarkable correspondence is perceived, not only in time but also in the elements forming the two constitutions. In the Pyrenean peninsula, also, the seclusion of a narrowly bounded kingdom materially assisted the combination of West-Gothic customs, and the ancient popular liberty of the Teutonic race, with feudal institutions. As early as the twelfth century we find knights and citizens admitted to the Cortes side by side with the higher nobility and the clergy. Here, as in England, the term honor is applied to the fief of highest rank, with the same double conception of a greater possession and a loftier dignity. The Commons call themselves *brazo de universidades,* the term used by Matthew Paris and in the popular verses of the English friars. Finally, Aragon had the celebrated office of the Justicia, who may well be compared with the great justiciaries as they appear in the British island from Henry II. to Henry III.

* In lieu of many others, we quote only Hallam, View of the State of Europe during the Middle Ages, ii. 43, ed. 1855: " Perhaps in no European monarchy except our own was the form of government more interesting than in Aragon."

But among these points of analogy it is important to keep in view the great and essential divergencies which from the first necessitated a totally different development. Under what Aragonese king before Pedro IV. (1348) was the authority of the crown comparable to that of the Normans and Plantagenets in England? Though there were conflicts between the sovereign and nobility of Aragon in the years 1264 and 1265, forcibly reminding the student of contemporary events in England, nothing corresponds in any measure to Magna Charta until the *Privilegium generale Aragonum*, granted at the Cortes of Zaragoza in 1283. The knights, infanzones and hidalgos do not appear in great numbers, neither have they the county as basis for uninterrupted communal and self-governing administration. For them, therefore, the representation of the district could not be introduced as a higher and further stage of progressive develop-ment. Moreover, only a few royal towns anciently sent deputies to the national assembly, but the number for each was considerable, Zaragoza alone sending from eight to ten. Even the sixty-first article of Magna Charta did not aim at a permanent right of armed resistance to the absolute power of the crown, such as was customary in the Spanish kingdom.* And finally, with regard to the Justicia Major, his

* The power of the estates was expressly limited : donec fuerit emendatum secundum arbitrium eorum. Cf. Gneist. Geschichte und heutige Gestalt der Aemter und des Verwaltungsrechts in England, i. 288, second edition.

appointment was for a long time as much in the King's
hands as in England the nomination of Ranulph de
Glanville, Hubert de Burgh, and others, to their
supreme judicial dignity. The office necessarily
disappeared in this country as soon as the courts of
justice and their commissions were more fully developed,
and gave judgment in the name of the crown as
institutions of the realm. It was only after 1348,
when the kingly power gained greater strength in
Aragon, that the Justicia acquired his life-long and
wholly exceptional position. It might be called
the perpetuation of authorized opposition, whilst in
England, Simon de Montfort, the last great Justiciary,
grasped in passing at the dignity solely in order to
obtain for his unconstitutional authority the legal
prestige of an office that had once rendered the most
substantial services to the crown.

It can scarcely be questioned that the Earl of
Leicester was acquainted with the Aragonese constitution, especially with the place it assigned to
knights and towns in the Cortes.* Whether these
institutions pressed themselves upon him as models
for his projects of reform in England is, on the other
hand, extremely doubtful. His father had certainly
known the system as it had existed in southern France,
furnishing one proof of the direct connection of
the district with the country and people south of

* Ranke's Englische Geschichte, i. 81 : "Und leicht konnte
Simon Montfort hiervon wissen, da sein Vater in so mannig-
faltiger Berührung mit Aragon gestanden."

the Pyrenees, and the marked contrast between the political life prevailing there and that north of the Loire. But, stern and uncompromising as in other things, he, as conqueror, had immediately introduced the system of northern France in opposition to it. In 1212, when at the climax of his power, he summoned a Parliament to Pamiers to enact new statutes through the instrumentality of a committee of twelve—four churchmen, four French nobles, and four natives, of whom two were burgesses,—and the Coutumes of Paris were then expressly made the basis of the new laws of inheritance.* Beginning with one of the most important departments of life, the firmer discipline of the north was to take the place of southern license. Thus the elder Simon also vainly staked his life for a reform. And did the son differ essentially from the father in sympathy for political institutions on the slopes of the Pyrenees? He was scarcely ten years old when his father died; he spent his youth in northern France and then went to England. He was never again brought in contact with the south for any length of time, except during his government of Gascony, and then he appears occasion-

* Tant entre les Barons et Cheualiers, que Bourgeois et Ru-
reaux, les heretiers succederont à leurs heritages, selon la cous-
tume et vsage de France pres Paris. Vic et Vaissette, Histoire
Générale de Languedoc, v. Additions et Notes, p. 54. The
editors add the remark, p. 51 : La malheureuse idée d'introduire
en Languedoc, dans ce pays de franchises et de libertés, les
coutumes de Paris, n'eut qu'un succès passager.

ally as a refuge for the oppressed, but chiefly as the
restorer of royal power in conflict with a haughty
nobility and town communities who were equally
refractory. His experiences there and the state of
Béarn or Jaca cannot have encouraged him to make
his English experiment. On the contrary, it arose
entirely out of national conditions already existing,*
and perhaps precisely because it was not bound to
follow any foreign analogy, it succeeded only one
generation later.

In England, the aspiration of the lower classes to
express their will in the great Council of the realm, as
well as in the town and county, is closely connected
with the origin, it might be called the discovery, of
representation for carrying out this purpose. The
entire thirteenth century works more and more con-
sciously towards this double goal.

The right of judgment by peers, and a share in police
and penal regulations, had been retained from Anglo-
Saxon times by the tenants in chief and the independent freeholders of the county. Under the Norman
sheriff these customs had acquired only more distinct
form and fuller life at periodical sessions, as in the
grand jury. Here the practice of election and representation of the freeholders for judicial and fiscal
purposes had long been established by usage. The

* But the presence of such influences, however fully admitted,
does not make it the less true that it is from an English root
that the House of Commons sprung, and that root no other than
the English county court. Shirley, ii. p. xxiii.

twelfth article of the Magna Charta of 1215, providing
also that the entire body of lesser crown vassals should
in two prescribed cases be convoked through the sheriffs
to the great Council of the realm, was never put into
execution in this form, but it remained as a suggestion
for the future.

We frequently hear of summonses to individual
knights from the counties, though they did not appear
in a regular Parliament. John certainly followed some
more ancient precedent in 1213, when he summoned
four *discreti milites* from each shire to Oxford in order
to confer with them upon imperial business, to wit, a
proclamation of war against France. Again in 1226,
four knights were admitted from eight several counties for another still less general purpose, namely, to
present accusations against the sheriffs who acted
counter to Magna Charta; it was here expressly
ordered that they should be elected by their peers.*
The, case of the 11th of February, 1254, namely, the
summoning of two knights to appear at Westminster
in the stead of each and all in their county, was therefore a remarkable event,† at least inasmuch as the

* Rot. Lit. Claus. 10 Henr. III. membr. 13 : Dicas militibus et
probis hominibus baillie tue, quod quatuor de legalioribus et
discrecioribus militibus ex se ipsis eligant.

† Rot. Lit. Claus. 38 Henr. III. membr. 13, dorso : Vice
omnium et singulorum eorundem comitatuum. The significance
of this Writ is admitted in the Report on the Dignity of a Peer
i. p. 96 : " The election of two knights for each county might be
considered as a substitution for the general summons provided
by the charter of John."

P

first attempt was thus made to consult the representatives of communities in the same manner as the great barons, if not to introduce them to the national council. The clergy met at the same time, and for the same cause. There is no indication of joint deliberation with the nobility, or of the presence of town members; the purpose of the citation was the same as in 1213, the need of an extraordinary military aid, and those bidden presented themselves as influential representative men, not as formal deputies. No vestige remains of writs to the "mad" Parliament at Oxford in 1258, but knights and smaller tenants-in-chief must have been among the crowd who arrived there with the nobles. It is evident that knights as well as barons were elected on several of the commissions.

The keen eye of the Earl of Leicester had long watched the germination and growth of this new element. It must not be forgotten with regard to him that, as a Frenchman, he had much more of the culture of a gentleman and a man of the world than his contemporaries among the English barons, who were uniformly of a rougher type. What he had still lacked of familiarity with the old English county life was soon supplied by daily experience as a Lord of the Manor, and by the intercommunication between the gentry and the towns which was then beginning. His ideas were doubtless matured by intercourse with such men as the Bishops of Lincoln and Worcester, who, through the influence of the Franciscans, were followed by a great part of the nation. We remarked his first step in this direction when he, Worcester, and Gloucester, who had all three been members of the governing committee in 1258, and were now in open opposition, summoned three knights from each shire to meet at St. Albans on the 21st of September, 1261, and the King commanded the same men to appear before him at Windsor. The project, which, if carried out, must have resulted in a supreme assembly, was thus dexterously defeated once more.* Nothing was yet established in these matters either by law or custom, but revolutionary attempts to effect a radical change were constantly renewed.

It may excite surprise that Simon did not take immediate advantage of the victory of Lewes and the defeat of the King to pass a legislative measure of this character. But the times demanded that first the stipulations of the Misa, that is, of the peace, should be passed into statutes with all possible promptitude. The Parliament summoned to meet in London for this purpose at Midsummer, 1264, was essentially an assemblage of Barons, for the four lieges, fideles, therefore men likewise holding fiefs immediately of the crown, who were bidden from twenty-nine counties only, were admitted simply in order to assist in establishing public peace, although the principal statute was issued in the name of the whole community of the realm. The Mayor and Corporation of London alone are found among the guarantors of one charter.

* Shirley, ii. 179 : Henry III. to all the Sheriffs on this side of the Trent, September 11th, 1261. Compare Report on the Dignity of a Peer, i. 133.

It was not till later in the year that the Earl's constitutional plans ripened, and led, as we know, to the
Parliament of the 20th of January, 1265, the composition of which has made it so famous. (Now for the
first time two representatives were expressly summoned
for each shire, representatives not of the smaller crown
vassals alone but of the county itself, that is, of the
entire body of feudal tenants and freeholders.) A number of towns were invited to send deputies in like
manner. Their advice was not asked merely upon a
single question of peace or war, but upon the affairs of
the realm in general.* So the model for the future
was complete, even to the allowances of the deputies,
though soon a reaction in favour of the restored kingly
power set in, and no law pronounced till long after
that the presence of representatives of towns and shires
was constitutional and indispensable in the discussion
of statutes and the granting of subsidies.† Nevertheless, the birthday of the Commons was in that memorable year.

* Report on the Dignity of a Peer, i. 154. Hallam, View of
the State of Europe During the Middle Ages, iii. 15. Gneist i.
310: "Die kleinere Vasallenschaft und das Freisassenthum
hatten zum ersten Mal einen formirten Körper erhalten und das
Bewusstsein, dass ihnen unter Umständen eine mitentscheidende
Stimme im Rath des Königs gebühre." Compare the remarks in
Stubbs' Const. Hist. ii. 222.

† Duobus militibus . . . racionabiles expensas suas in veniendo
ad dictum parliamentum ibidem morando et inde ad partes suas
redeundo provideri et eas de eadem communitate levari facias.
To the Sheriff of York ; Report on the Dignity of a Peer,
Appendix, i. 35.

The children of that generation were to grow to man's estate before Edward I., the Conqueror of Evesham, equally great as warrior and ruler, ratified at Ghent with a heavy heart on the 5th of November, 1297, that famous confirmation of the Charters whereby he pledged himself to raise no more taxes except by common consent of clergy, nobility, and commons, and for the public weal*. He was then reduced to sore straits by the simultaneous conflicts with Scotland and France and with the Papal see; but, fortunately, he had already called upon the commons at various times to assist in bearing the public burdens; and in 1295, in order to obtain large subsidies, he had even summoned two knights from each shire and two burgesses from 115 towns. This great monarch never thought of giving up his prerogative when he pledged his word; among other points he expressly avoided a renunciation of the right to amerce the towns at pleasure. Yet their aids constantly approached more nearly to those of the feudal tenants, as knights and burgesses during the two following reigns became gradually united in the Lower House, which, in this form, far surpassed the boldest anticipations of the first creator of a deliberative and governing assembly of Commons.

---

* Que mes pur nule busoigne tien manere des aydes mises ne prises de nostre Roiaume ne prendrums fors ke par commun assent de tout le Roiaume e a commun profist de meismes le Roiaume, sauve les aunciencs aydes e prises dues e accoustumees. Charters and Liberties, p. 37 in Statutes of the Realm, vol. i. Stubbs, Select Charters, 495.

PRINTED BY TAYLOR AND CO.,
LITTLE QUEEN STREET, LINCOLN'S INN FIELDS.